The man was trespassing

He had his back to her as he held a wide-mouth glass tube of dirt...her dirt...up to the sun. Liz moved in closer and leveled her shotgun at him.

"Put it down and turn around."

The man raised his arms and turned to face her.

Liz gasped. "Gabe Barzonni?"

Gabe chuckled. "Hi, Liz."

She glared at him. "Spill. Why are you stealing my soil?"

"I wasn't stealing. Exactly." He started to smile, but catching Liz's suspicious scowl, he obviously thought better of it. "I followed some tourists out to the vineyard. Your *chef de cave* told us we were free to walk around."

"Sure you are. Among the Cabernet grapes. Not over here."

"I didn't know," he said. "Liz, can you please put the shotgun away? It makes me nervous."

"Good," she said. "I want you to be nervous. Maybe you'll start telling me the truth."

Dear Reader,

I hope by the time you've picked up *A Fine Year for Love* you are as enthralled with the characters in Indian Lake as I am. I realize that as the author I am supposed to love my people, but with each new romance I am finding some very strong-willed, dedicated and loyal folks who are fascinating enough to keep me up at night telling me their story.

You may remember that I introduced Liz Crenshaw in *Love Shadows* and explained that she and her grandfather owned a vineyard north of Indian Lake. In my fairy-tale life, I have romanticized a world in which I was a vintner. I adore vineyards. I love the precise rows of thriving vines that undulate up and down hills and soak up the sun. If I ever did own a vineyard, I would be so obsessed and possessive, I'd probably be ostracized by all my friends for being obnoxious about my life's calling. Therefore, I nailed those flaws to my heroine's heels.

When love does finally come to Liz's doorstep, she holds Gabe Barzonni at gunpoint. Little does Liz realize she is right to be suspicious of Gabe, whose secret desire is to become a vintner and leave his father's lucrative farm. From their first encounter, when Gabe is trying to steal a sample of Liz's soil, sparks fly left and right. Through revelations of decades-old family secrets to the heartbreaking awareness of Sam Crenshaw's dementia, to a life-and-death crisis, Liz and Gabe must finally come to terms with what truly makes life precious to them.

I would love to hear from you and your thoughts about our friends in Indian Lake. You can find me on Facebook, Twitter, LinkedIn and Pinterest. My website is catherinelanigan.com or you can email me at cathlanigan1@gmail.com.

Then join me in a few short months for more heartwarming romance in the fourth book in the Shores of Indian Lake series.

Catherine Lanigan

HEARTWARMING

A Fine Year for Love

Catherine Lanigan

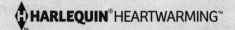

Recycling programs
for this product may
not exist in your area.

ISBN-13: 978-0-373-36709-2

A Fine Year for Love

Copyright © 2015 by Catherine Lanigan

HARLEQUIN®
www.Harlequin.com

Printed in U.S.A.

Catherine Lanigan knew she was born to storytelling at a very young age when she told stories to her younger brothers and sister to entertain them. After years of encouragement from family and high school teachers, Catherine was shocked and brokenhearted when her freshman college creative-writing professor told her that she had "no writing talent whatsoever" and that she would "never earn a dime as a writer." He promised her that he would be her crutches and get her through his demanding class with a B grade so as not to destroy her high grade point average too much, *if* Catherine would promise never to write again. Catherine assumed he was the voice of authority and gave in to the bargain.

For fourteen years she did not write until she was encouraged by a television journalist to give her dream a shot. She wrote a 600-page historical romantic spy-thriller set against World War I. The journalist sent the manuscript to his agent who then garnered bids from two publishers. That was nearly forty published novels, nonfiction books and anthologies ago.

Books by Catherine Lanigan

HARLEQUIN HEARTWARMING
Heart's Desire
Love Shadows

MIRA
Dangerous Love
Elusive Love
Tender Malice
In Love's Shadow
Legend Makers
California Moon

SILHOUETTE DESIRE
The Texan
Montana Bride

Visit the Author Profile page
at Harlequin.com for more titles

This book is dedicated to my son, Ryan Pieszchala.
I love you deeply.

I've said it before and I will keep saying it. I am so
very blessed with extraordinary editorial expertise.
Each time I begin to stray, Claire, you bring me
back and I can't thank you enough. Any accolades I
receive—they belong to us.

And to all the editors and staff at Harlequin
Heartwarming. You are truly a most unique group
of creative and visionary people. I am honored to
work with you all. Most especially I want to thank
Victoria Curran for bringing me into this very
supportive and caring new family at Heartwarming.
And as always, deep gratitude and affection to
Dianne Moggy. A very big hug to you all.

CHAPTER ONE

DRAPED LIKE GLITTERING prisms of rubies from a princess's neck, pinot noir, French burgundy and cabernet grape clusters danced in the summer breeze at the Crenshaw Vineyard. In precise rows, the vines ran down the hills and stopped just shy of the valley. Lolling lazily in the warmth of the sun, the grapes were ripening and stretching to perfection.

Liz Crenshaw wore cutoff blue jeans and a white shirt she'd tied around her narrow waist. She drove her ATV, its attached utility trailer filled with compost, among the rows of vines. Long ago, her grandfather had banned tractors or trucks from the fields because their hard rubber tires compacted the earth and kept the rainwater from seeping properly into the roots. Liz made the compost herself. It was organic, like everything grown on Crenshaw land. They didn't use fungicides or pesticides on the grapes, fruit trees or berry bushes.

Liz liked the idea that she and her grandfather were vestiges of a simpler time and way of life. For so long, it had been just the two of them against the world. Sam often joked they were not just related, but joined at the hip and the brain, like Siamese twins. Sam's pet name for Liz had been *petite chérie* ever since she had been a little girl.

Liz had no problem with that.

She had been born on this land, in the same farmhouse in which her father had been born. Liz had always felt she was a child of the earth. Her grandfather, though seventy-seven years old, was her hero.

Liz rode the ATV to the top of the hill and looked down on the rows of vines. They ran from north to south—the morning sun would strike one side of the grapes, high noon would bathe the tops in light and the afternoon warmth would finish the task on the clusters' horizon-facing side.

Liz inspected each vine with a sharp eye. Her vines were her life, and though sometimes her friends voiced concern that she was extremely single-minded, Liz didn't care.

She lived a life of bliss with her grapes, her loving grandfather and their ever-expanding business.

As she crossed a line of cherry trees that

helped to shelter her prized pinot noir grapes from the sometimes brutal western wind off Indian Lake, she noted the plants this year were balanced with the right amount of green leaves. The strong vines and clusters were not too fat, nor too withered from the summer heat. Years ago, Sam had made the mistake of thinking the very rich soil in the valley would produce perfect grapes. He'd learned, sometimes the hard way, that many other factors affected the productivity of the vines. Often the buds froze early in the spring, and if they lived through that, the abundant summer rains that swooped off Lake Michigan could gorge the grapes, the wine from which would be uninteresting and unmarketable. Allowing the grapes to remain on the vines even two weeks past the normal growing season meant both a superior grape and, eventually, high-quality wine similar to that which Liz had tasted in France.

Liz wanted her wines to be the epitome of excellence, to have a taste so rare in America that other vintners would recognize how special her little plot of earth truly was. Knowing she shared that dream with every vintner on the planet did not diminish her enthusiasm—it only heightened her ambitions.

Liz took out her cell phone and snapped

some pictures of the vines to show her grandfather, who didn't walk the hills or even ride
them any longer. Despite his age, Sam was
healthy and just as obstinate as he'd always
been, but he was slowing down. Now that construction on his tasting room was complete, he
preferred to work there.

The tasting room had elevated the Crenshaw
Vineyard into the upper echelon of vineyards
in Michigan and northern Indiana. Many of
the surrounding vineyards outsourced the re-
tail side of their business, selling bottles and
cases to tasting rooms in Saugatuck, Douglas,
Buchanan, St. Joseph and other coastal resort
towns. The problem, Liz knew, was each vintner could never be sure what the "sommelier"
behind the counter was trying to sell that day.
The person pouring the wine was just as likely
to be a college student who would be happy at
any summer job. Liz wanted each of her employees to be at least as much of a wine snob
as she was.

Liz was the first to admit she was the ultimate
control freak. It was a real handicap in life, but
she had long ago accepted this fact about herself. She toiled workaholic hours because she
believed she knew best how each and every task
should be completed. In her mind, only she could

do the accounting properly. Only she knew when her pinot noir and burgundy wines had reached their peak age. Only she knew which French chardonnay grapes from which terroir should be used for their champagne. Most important for Liz, only she knew how to talk to the vines and encourage them into abundance.

Last year, when Liz hired her best friend, Sarah Jensen, and Sarah's boss, Charmaine Chalmers, to design the tasting room and sales office and oversee the construction, she'd nearly driven them both to nervous breakdowns over her many last-minute changes. It was a miracle the building was ever finished. To make up for her idiosyncrasies, Liz had given both women two cases of her best wines.

Liz stopped her ATV close to the top of the rise when she noticed several yellowing leaves. She pulled on a pair of lime-green gardening gloves and whisked a spade out of the back of her trailer. She spread her compost around the base of the vines and tilled it in with a hoe.

She took a long slug from her water bottle and glanced at the sky. The sun had moved its apex, and Liz knew she had missed lunch with her grandfather at the farmhouse—again. He hadn't called to remind her or to scold her. Grandpa understood her.

Liz stuck her gloves in a satchel next to the gun boot on the side of the ATV. When she was out in the fields, she toted a loaded shotgun to scare away the coyotes, deer and wild hogs that destroyed the vines. Through the winter she'd frightened off most of the harmful animals, and this spring she'd only seen one coyote. Still, she had to be prepared.

Shielding her eyes against the sun, Liz surveyed her glorious domain. From the rise, she could see across their twenty acres of planted vines and one hundred acres of unplanted, rugged terrain. Looking back to the south, Liz kept her eyes peeled for marauding animals and any sections of vine that might need fertilizer.

"What the…" Liz gasped as her gaze landed on the next rise, where her prized French chardonnay grapes were growing. "I don't believe this."

She hopped onto her ATV and switched on the ignition.

When she was still fifty or so yards from the top of the next rise, she cut the motor and let the vehicle roll silently across the valley. The ATV came to a stop and Liz dismounted it. She grabbed her shotgun from the boot and moved forward stealthily.

The movement Liz had seen from a distance was not, as she'd initially assumed, that of a deer or coyote. It was that of a man. He was too tall to be Aurelio, their hired hand.

There was the odd chance that it was Giovanni Fiorinni, an agronomist who split his time between Crenshaw Vineyards and several other wineries up in Michigan—but Giovanni had visited five or six days before. She didn't expect him back for weeks. Perhaps the man was a weekend tourist who had wandered over here by accident.

Liz quickly dismissed that idea. This area was fenced, gated and locked.

She had brought the chardonnay vines from France herself. It was in this precious section of the vineyard that she had placed her dreams of producing champagne—real champagne. The first in the Midwest.

No, there would be no cause for anyone other than her and her grandfather to be on this part of the property.

This man was trespassing.

He was well over six feet tall. His nearly black hair had been precision cut and styled, which told her he probably didn't employ a local barber at six bucks a pop. He wore clean and fitted jeans, expensive-looking black leather cowboy boots and a blue-and-white-striped Oxford shirt.

Was this guy a farmer?

The man dropped into a crouch. It was clear he hadn't heard her approach. Liz couldn't tell what he was doing, but he seemed intent on his work as he scooped up a handful of earth. Still moving forward, Liz noticed he was wearing plastic gloves. Next to his foot was a box filled with some sort of equipment.

This man had a purpose.

He had his back to her as he held a wide-mouthed glass tube of dirt—her dirt—up to the sun.

Liz lifted her gun, aimed it at him and stood her distance in case he made any quick moves.

"Put it down and turn around," she ordered harshly.

The man raised his arms and slowly turned to face her.

Liz gasped. "Gabe Barzonni! What are you doing here? You're trespassing."

Gabe guiltily looked at the soil in the test tube, then flashed Liz a charming smile.

She frowned and continued to glare at him down the barrel of her shotgun.

Gabe chuckled. "Hi, Liz."

She remained silent as she slowly lowered her gun. "Spill. What are you doing?"

"Actually, I came here to check out your tasting room. Very nice. I like the maple wood floors, by the way. Then your sommelier there—"

"Louisa," Liz interjected.

"She's very helpful. Said she's from the Champagne region…" Gabe smiled winningly.

"I know where she's from," Liz growled. "And you're beating around the bush. Why are you stealing my soil?"

"I wasn't stealing, exactly." He started to smile again, but catching Liz's suspicious glare, he obviously thought better of it. "I was very impressed with the wines I tasted. Very impressed. I followed some other tourists out to the vineyard. Louisa told us we were free to walk around."

"Sure you are. Among the cabernet grapes. Not over here."

"I didn't know," he said. "Liz, can you please put the shotgun away? It makes me nervous."

"Good," she said, though she put the butt end on the ground and held the gun, by the barrel, at her side. "I like you being nervous. Maybe you'll start telling me the truth."

"I am telling you the truth."

"Fine. Then dump the dirt."

Gabe lowered his hands slowly and looked at the tube as if it held gold dust. "I wanted to test it is all. It's a hobby of mine."

"Yeah? Since when?"

"Liz, you know me. We went to high school together."

She shook her head. "Hardly. I'm four years younger than you. I was a kid when your name was being plastered across the sports section of the newspaper for a touchdown or something."

He glared at her. "A lot of touchdowns. We went to state."

"You and I were never part of the same crowd. Okay?" She pointed at the vial. "Dump the dirt."

"Fine," Gabe replied. He reluctantly deposited the dirt on the ground.

"Now leave," she ordered.

"Don't be like that, Liz. Maybe we could go back to the tasting room and you could tell me more about these chardonnay grapes…"

"You don't hear so well, Gabe. I want you to leave."

Gabe threw his hands up in the air. "I'm leaving," he said angrily. He shoved his test tube into the metal box he'd brought with him.

"I'm thrilled," Liz said.

She watched as Gabe hoisted himself over

the whitewashed wooden fence as if he'd been training for a gymnastics team. He walked past the tasting room and over to the gravel parking lot, got into a black Porsche convertible and drove away.

Liz knew the Barzonni family, though not all that well. She was most familiar with Gabe's brother Nate, a cardiac surgeon, because he was engaged to one of her closest friends, Maddie Strong. Gabriel Barzonni was the eldest of the four Barzonni boys. As far as Liz could remember, none of the Barzonnis had ever come to visit her or her grandfather.

She couldn't even remember the Barzonnis coming to her parents' funeral. But then, she'd only been six years old, and she hadn't really known the family at all. As far as Liz was concerned, she didn't have a history with Gabe.

His trespassing was more than a little bit suspicious.

Clearly he wanted something. But what? The Barzonnis were hugely successful and owned a great deal of farmland. What could Gabe possibly want that Liz had?

The more she thought about him, the more her stomach churned and her nerves fired with alarm. She felt as if she'd just come upon an intruder during a home invasion. Yet this was a person she knew. Sort of.

She bent down and grabbed the handful of soil that had fallen out of Gabe's test tube. His actions made no sense at all. He didn't come from a family of thieves, and if he wanted to run some kind of local soil experiment, why hadn't he just asked her permission to take samples? She would have been happy to help him out.

On the face of it, Liz had no real evidence against Gabe. She'd always had a highly suspicious nature, and her girlfriends often accused her of being paranoid. Maybe she'd developed the trait after the car accident that had killed her parents. Years of worrying about her aging grandfather and pushing herself to secure the future of the vineyard certainly hadn't made her a more trusting person.

Liz pursed her lips. Intuition told her Gabe was up to something.

She rubbed her arms, trying to push down the hairs that had pricked up as they always did when danger loomed nearby.

"Something tells me I should keep you in my sights, Gabriel."

CHAPTER TWO

LIZ RODE THE ATV to the utility barn and put the vehicle away. She pulled her Remington Spartan 310 out of the boot and walked over to the worktable her father had coarsely constructed over twenty years ago. She ejected the shell from the chamber and placed it on the table.

She picked up the shotgun and peered down the over/under barrels, remembering what Gabe had looked like at the end of her sight. Despite her trepidation about his motives for trespassing, Liz had to laugh to herself. He'd been caught red-handed doing whatever it was he had been doing, and he'd tried to get out of it with his charm.

Liz pushed the trigger blade forward to select the top barrel of the gun, rather than the default bottom barrel. Then she checked the tang behind the top lever to make certain the safety was on, even though she believed the gun was empty. Both her father and grandfather had taught her to be very careful when cleaning and using weapons. She had to admit her mind hadn't been set on safety when she'd threatened Gabe. She'd been reacting to her basest instinct: to protect herself and her land. Her suspicions were baseless, but every cell in her body told her Gabe Barzonni was a threat to everything she held sacred.

Remembering the moment she'd leveled her shotgun at him, she wondered if he'd actually felt he was in danger. Now that she thought back on the audacity it had taken for him to walk onto her property like a tourist and break into a clearly gated area to steal soil samples, she wondered if she'd be better off if she'd filled his backside with buckshot.

She oiled the gun and polished the walnut stock, then put the gun back in the boot, ready for her next encounter. The question was whether she would be facing beast or man.

Liz left the utility barn and walked across an open area next to the gravel parking lot. She noticed all the tourist cars were gone. If that were the case, then Louisa, her *chef de cave*, probably would not be in the tasting room, but would steal a few moments in the fermenting barn. Liz unlocked the door to the large natural wood building with green trim. The fermenting barn was where Liz stored barrique barrels and oak *botti* for the chardonnay and the cabernet sauvignon they made.

Two years ago, Liz had made a trip to the Château de la Marquetterie, which was located south of Épernay, France. She toured several of the smaller vineyards and inspected not just the vines, but the process of champagne-making, in the process finding her next obsession. Champagne. She knew still wine—making would never be enough for her challenge-driven psyche. Of all the difficult, time-consuming and nearly impossible ideas she'd ever had, an Indiana sparkling wine made from a hybrid of French chardonnay and pinot noir grapes was probably the most ambitious.

To execute the technically challenging process the way she had seen it done in France, Liz knew she'd need a *chef de cave* who believed in innovation as much as she did. She'd chosen twenty-four-year-old Louisa Bouchard. Louisa was smart and feisty, and was the seventh child and only daughter of a small champagne vintner in Éparnay who apparently was deaf, blind and dumb when it came to his headstrong daughter. When they met, Louisa had told Liz her father would only listen to her six older brothers. He always ignored her.

When Liz came to visit the Bouchard vineyards, Louisa was angry, frustrated and ready to break out.

Liz saw an opportunity and took it. She told Louisa she couldn't promise her anything except free rein to create the first sparkling wines in Indiana. It was a world away from France, but Louisa was ready.

Louisa had been with Liz for over a year now, living in the apartment attached to the tasting room and obviously thriving in her life at Crenshaw Vineyards. Knowing Louisa had no friends in America, Liz made certain to include her in as many activities with her own friends as she could.

Still, Louisa appeared happiest when making wine and strolling among the grapes.

Liz believed their hearts were so much alike, they could have been sisters.

Liz entered the barn and walked among the stainless steel tanks, which would be filled to capacity during the grape harvest.

"Louisa! Are you here?" Liz shouted.

"Oui," Louisa yelled from a distance, the hard heels of her leather boots thumping on the cement.

Louisa was of medium height, but her slight frame and taut muscles made her look like a couture model. She walked toward Liz with a practiced woman's gait, the soft cotton fabric of her spring dress billowing around the tops of her boots and creating an ethereal effect.

"How was the tasting room this afternoon?" Liz asked. "Busy?"

"Very. I only came over here to find you," Louisa said. "Where were you?"

"On the hill. You could have called if you needed me."

"I did. Your phone…it's not working."

"Sure it is," Liz replied, pulling it out of her pocket. "Oops. It was off."

Louisa frowned. "I was going to tell you about the man. He wants you."

"What man?"

"I don't know his name," Louisa replied, shaking her head. "He's too beautiful. I don't trust him."

"Gabriel."

"You know him?" Louisa asked, surprise illuminating her face.

"A little bit." She shook her head. "His brother is going to marry Maddie Strong."

"That was Nate's brother?" Louisa asked. "Why does he want you?"

Liz bristled involuntarily in response to Louisa's words. "If only I knew," she said with exasperation. She didn't realize she'd clenched her fists. Gabe didn't *want her* personally. But he absolutely wanted something. She just had to figure out what she had in common with the thing it was he wanted.

"Ah. He stirs your blood. Makes you angry," Louisa observed, peering with critical eyes at her boss.

"I just don't trust him," Liz replied uneasily.

Tires crunched on the gravel outside. "More tourists." Liz smiled broadly, glad to have the conversation diverted from Gabriel Barzonni. "This is shaping up to be a good day for us."

"Oui," Louisa said as they walked out of the barn and into the bright sunlight.

Three cars had driven up nearly at the same time. One was an SUV with an Illinois license plate and two couples inside. The couples had just entered the tasting room. A sports car with a handsome pair in their mid-sixties pulled up beside a black Porsche convertible.

Liz stared disbelievingly at the shiny black car that looked as if it had just been detailed and polished.

Starched and pressed. Just like the owner.

"Gabe—" Liz breathed out his name with an undercurrent of frustration.

"Looks like he's back," Louisa said with

a taunting grin, already walking away from Liz toward the tasting room. "I'm off to see to those guests. *À tout à l'heure!*"

"See you later," Liz said, gazing past Louisa at the cluster of tourists. Gabe wasn't among them.

Immediately suspecting him of going back to her vines, she spun around, her eyes tracking from one end of the vineyard to the other. He hadn't had enough time to go very far.

She hurried around the corner of the tasting room and glanced up at the big white farmhouse with its wraparound porch. Climbing the three front steps to the beveled glass Victorian door was Gabe, a bouquet of flowers in his right hand.

"I'm not up there," Liz shouted.

Gabe turned around as Liz marched forward.

"Hi," he said, not taking his eyes off her. "You're not armed this time, are you? Concealed .38? Maybe a poison dart in your clog?"

"Very funny," she growled, gesturing at the flowers. "Those for my compost pile?"

"Uh, sure. You can do whatever you want with them."

"Hmm." She eyed the flowers and the cellophane sleeve around them. It still had the price tag on it. "Get those at the grocery store, did you?"

"Actually, yes. That's where the closest florist was," he said weakly. He thrust the flowers at her. "Please accept my apology."

"Why don't you just tell me the truth, Gabe. I won't bite."

"Ha! You're just saying that because you aren't toting—at the moment."

"No, Gabe. I do want the truth," she replied earnestly, taking the bouquet.

"I did tell you the truth. I needed some soil samples from your vineyard. I heard you were going to try to make real champagne out here. I couldn't believe it. I didn't think we had the soil for that."

"How did you hear that?" she asked, trailing off as she realized the answer. "From Nate?"

"Yeah. Don't be mad at Maddie—she just let it slip. Nate swore me to secrecy. I haven't told a soul." He crossed his heart.

Liz shifted her weight and put her hand on her hip. "But that information intrigued you so much you snuck out here on a Saturday when you knew no one would be in the vineyard. And then you tried to take my dirt. Why?"

"I'm insatiably curious. I've studied pedology and agricultural soil science since college. I'm fascinated when a new pioneer hits the scene. Like you."

"A pioneer? Some would call me a fool." She snorted derisively.

"Not me. I think you may be the real genius."

Liz drew in a breath and paused. She stared at him for a long moment. Louisa was right. He was really handsome, and it was her bet those good looks had gotten him out of many tight spots. She frowned. "You're laying it on pretty thick, Gabe. I'm not buying it. There's more here than your curiosity over what could have been idle gossip."

"Not if you confirm what I heard. Are you making champagne out of vines you brought back from France?"

She knew she shouldn't confirm even one iota of a fact for him. But if she didn't, she might not ever learn the real reason for his trespassing.

"Yes. I am."

"No kidding?" A smile broke across his face and he slapped his thigh as he looked across at the rows of chardonnay vines. His smile dropped off his face in an instant. "How good is it?"

"I don't know yet. Last fall's harvest was

adequate. My *chef de cave*, Louisa, has riddled some bottles. They have to age another ten months or so before we try the first bottle."

Gabe seemed impressed, and Liz knew she'd gained his respect. "That's amazing."

"It's good business," she replied. "I've never been satisfied with the status quo. I want more. Much more."

"I get that." He nodded. "I really get that, actually." He glanced to the south, his gaze going past her land into the distance. He was silent for a long moment.

Whatever he was thinking obviously didn't please him. What was wrong with having ambition or challenging oneself? Liz wondered. She didn't care what he thought of her plans for her future. She had the right equipment, vines and people to ensure her success. She only had the unpredictable vagaries of the wind, rain and sun to contend with, just like any other farmer. Gabe ought to know that much.

He looked back at her. "You'll need a lot of luck, Liz. I wish you that," he said.

She chortled. "Luck? You don't think I'll make it. You don't know me very well, do you?"

"No, I don't," he admitted. "But I'd like to change that."

She felt surprise mingled with distrust. She leveled him with a glare hot enough to wither healthy vegetation. "Yeah, right."

"Well, I do owe you an apology. I want to make up for trying to steal your dirt."

"You know, Gabe, I would have given you a sample. Farmer to farmer."

This time, he was the one to be cynical. "No, you wouldn't, Liz," he retorted sharply. "You would have asked me a thousand questions, just like you're doing now, because you don't know me. You know *of* me. I'm Angelo Barzonni's oldest son. These days I run his business more than he does, truth be told. That's all people know. They don't want to know anything else."

Liz could almost taste his bitterness, though he spoke with the calm and detached observation of a journalist, as if he were only recording his life and not living it. Her empathy nearly went out to him, but then he flashed his charming smile. He had practiced this masquerade. He knew exactly what he was doing. He was reeling her in…but why?

"I'm going to ask you again, Gabe. Why are you really here?"

"I thought it was obvious. I want to pick your brain."

She stuck her left hand into the back pocket of her cutoffs and slapped the bouquet of flowers against her thigh as if she could beat down her rising anger. "And the only reason you would want to do that is because you're going into the wine business."

Silence.

Gabe kept his eyes on Liz.

"You must think I'm a fool, or that I'd fall for your good looks—"

"You think I'm good-looking?" he interjected.

"Don't change the subject."

"Look, I came here to taste that great chardonnay of yours. I wandered off to check out the grapes after a bunch of tourists left. I had a soil-gathering kit in my trunk and I went and got it. The gate was open."

"It's always locked," she countered with a glare.

"It was open, okay? I told you. I'm naturally curious. Just as I was collecting the soil, you came up."

"Caught you red-handed."

He rolled his eyes impatiently. "Can't you let it go? I'm sorry."

She ground her jaw and glanced away, wondering why he unnerved her this much. "You better leave. We have nothing more to say."

"Liz, come on."

She shot him a stinging look. He shut up. "You want me to get my gun?"

"No!" He put up his hands. "I'm going. Okay?"

He started past her and as he reached her side, he stopped and leaned in close to her ear. "We have a lot in common, Liz. I can see it. Why can't you?"

He walked away, got in his car and drove off.

Liz walked up the porch steps and stopped at the front door, noticing her grandfather was standing just inside. The door was opened just wide enough he could have easily heard their conversation.

"Hi, Grandpa," she said with a wave of the bouquet.

Sam Crenshaw was as tall as Gabe, about six-foot-four, with a thatch of white hair that had thinned over the years and which no pair of scissors could ever tame. Liz always said she inherited her wild curls from Sam. He stood straight-backed and square-shouldered, as he always did when he sensed confrontation. Liz smiled to herself, validated that her grandfather also sensed the presence of a foreign substance.

Gabe was like a sliver, Liz thought. Inconsequential at first, but the longer you took to deal with it, the more harm it could cause.

"So that's Gabriel, huh?"

"Yeah," she replied, glancing back as Gabe's convertible left a dusty rooster tail in his wake.

"Good-looking kid. Resembles his mother."

"I guess," she said, moving inside.

"He give you those flowers?"

"Yep. I'll throw them in the compost heap. It's all they're good for."

Sam nodded resolutely. "Very wise. I've never met a Barzonni who wasn't up to no good."

Liz was surprised by Sam's pointed comment. She'd never heard him mention anything in particular about the Barzonni family in the past, but judging from the way his jaw was set as if he'd just tasted something acrid, her curiosity was piqued.

Sam's eyes had narrowed to piercing blue slits. Liz knew he used these discerning eyes when he needed to ponder a situation. She also knew he didn't want to talk about Gabe, at least for the moment. Later, she might be able to coax an explanation out of him.

"I've got work to do." Sam plucked his straw

hat off the hall tree stand and stepped outside, leaving Liz alone.

Liz looked sadly at the summer bouquet.

It was the first time a man had given her flowers.

CHAPTER THREE

GABE SAT ACROSS the kitchen table from Sophie Mattuchi and her parents, Mario and Bianca. Mario was of medium height and fit build, much like Gabe's own father, Angelo. His black hair was veined with streaks of white, as if the man had been hit by lightning. His face was deeply lined and very tan from years of toiling in the sun.

However, Gabe quickly learned Mario had never been a farmer, as his appearance would suggest, but a car mechanic. Apparently, he was just as fascinated with Gabe's Porsche as he was with the purpose of Gabe's visit.

Bianca busied herself around the kitchen, bringing tall glasses of iced tea with lemon and homegrown mint to the table.

Sophie's ninety-year-old grandmother, Bella, sat silently in a rocking chair in the corner near an enormous brick hearth. Despite the heat, she wore a colorful shawl around her thin shoulders while she watched Gabe with guarded crystal-blue eyes.

"Mario, as you and I have discussed, I haven't told anyone about your condition," Gabe said with compassion.

"Thank you," Mario said, choking back emotion. "And thank you for taking me up on my offer."

"Mario, you're helping me make my own dream come true. I can't tell you how much I appreciate it. I'm happy I could make this work for both of us."

"I just never thought I would be in this position," Mario said, looking from Bianca to Sophie.

Sophie smiled at her father. "You're going to get well, Papa. And you'll have many more years on the farm. By that time, Gabe will be making all kinds of wonderful wines. Right, Gabe?"

"Sure will," Gabe replied, catching her upbeat tone. "So, Mario, I've had all the soil samples analyzed down at Purdue." Gabe opened his briefcase and took out a plot map of the Mattuchis' small farm and vineyard and placed it on the table. "This section here is the best." He pointed at a spot on the map and glanced over at Bella. "You should all take a look. This is very exciting." Sophie smiled at her grand-mother and urged her to join them, but Bella shook her head violently and refused to move. Gabe noticed the very tight purse to the old woman's lips and thanked his lucky stars he hadn't been negotiating with Bella.

Mario and Bianca leaned in. Mario pointed to the easternmost ridge on the map, where the land lay fallow. "This is what you wanted?"

"Yes." Gabe smiled widely. "This section here, next to the Crenshaw place. I have reason to believe I can grow pinot noir grapes up there. These slopes are perfect."

"We've never had anything grow there." Sophie had pity in her eyes. "Are you sure you should do this, Gabe?"

"Sophie, I'm sure you're the best darned cardiology nurse at the hospital, but I know about grapes and soil, and I'm telling you this section is worth the entire vineyard. I'm willing to buy the whole vineyard since Mario isn't all that interested in expanding his operation."

"Expanding?" Mario laughed. "Certainly not now, of course, but why would I want to compete with Sam Crenshaw? He's got the best land around these parts, and plenty of it. That granddaughter of his has made all kinds of improvements and talked him into hiring experts from France, for goodness' sake!" Mario gestured wildly.

Bianca handed an iced tea to her husband without saying a word. Mario took a long slug. The icy liquid appeared to have dampened his excitement.

Gabe nodded. "I have to agree. Winemaking these days isn't a hobby. It's big business. Very big business."

Bianca shrugged. "We were never serious about it. We made the wine for ourselves. Sophie would give some bottles to her girlfriends as gifts. That's all."

"Mama. We made good wine. Gabe thinks he can make it better," Sophie said.

"What I believe," Gabe continued, "is that this line of apple trees is your problem. They block the sun too much—they won't allow the grapes to ripen properly. Pinot noir grapes need morning, midday and afternoon sun. If I take these trees out…"

"You're going to cut them down?" Sophie asked in horror. "I climbed them when I was a child! I love those trees."

Gabe shook his head and reached over to pat her hand. "No, I'll move them to the southern end, where we'll plant the pinot gris. The apple flavor will enhance that of the grapes. I'll also plant some pear trees there. I won't get rid of anything on the property. My intention is to make everything better."

Sophie glanced down at her hand, which was covered by Gabe's larger one. She smiled.

Gabe caught her smile and took back his hand. He edged the map closer to Mario, but didn't miss Bianca throwing Sophie a quelling look.

Gabe was sure Bianca didn't want her daughter to blow the deal. Sophie had a reputation for going after guys and then tossing them in a heap after a few days.

Gossips around Indian Lake said the same kind of thing about Gabe because he'd never dated anyone seriously. He simply didn't have the time. Gabe had never told a woman he loved her. He'd never asked anyone to be his girlfriend or fiancée. He'd steered very clear of relationships that smacked of anything permanent.

Gabe liked to go to dance, but he preferred to leave alone.

He had his sights set on his future, and to attain the kind of international success he wanted for himself as a vintner, Gabe had to stay focused on his goal.

As he turned back to the map, Gabe felt his

heartbeat accelerate. This vineyard, and the possibility of seeing his own name on a wine label, filled him with euphoria. There wasn't a feeling on earth like it.

"In addition to restructuring the rows of vines and bringing in new varieties, I want us to do some high-density planting."

"How high?" Sophie asked, her eyes widening.

"Twenty-two hundred vines per acre."

Mario whistled.

Sophie bit her lower lip. "This is no hobby."

"Let me show you how serious I am," he said, pulling a manila folder out of his briefcase. He opened it, revealing engineering drawings, machinery blueprints and a second land survey. "This is the equipment we'll need by next year's harvest in order to maximize our winemaking. I'll keep the oak casks you have to age the wine, but we'll need these stainless steel tanks in order to ferment it. We'll build the barrel cellar along with the first fermentation barn. Since you've used your small barn for fermentation before, we'll connect the plumbing from there to the new barn. There will be a radiant cooling system in the cellar roof. With this design you see here—" Gabe slid a set of photos across the table "—we'll be one of the most modern wineries around. But we'll keep the rustic charm, too. You'll note the barn's wood frame still has traditional hand-joinery. It's done just as it was in the 1880s— probably when your first barn was built. Am I right?"

"Yes. It was built in 1882," Mario replied. "I love that old barn."

"We should capitalize on its charm."

"What about a tasting room like Liz has?" Mario asked.

"Too soon," Gabe said. "We're a long way from that. I may pool our wines with the tasting rooms up in Saugatuck. Right now, I'll be investing in fermentation barns, underground cellars and staff."

"Staff?" Sophie and Mario said in unison.

"Absolutely. I'll need help. I still have my father's business to help run. Rafe has his mind on racehorses, and Mica would rather be designing some new piece of machinery than running the farm. That leaves the bulk of the Barzonni business squarely on my and my dad's shoulders."

"Angelo is a good businessman," Mario said quietly as he studied the drawings and plans.

Gabe nodded. "He is. But he's slowing down a bit these days." He gave Mario a pointed and inquisitive look, but the older man quickly glanced away.

"Sophie told me Malbec wine is very popular with her friends," Mario said. "It's a big seller. Will you make Malbec?"

"I do want to give it a try. After all, vintners in the southwest of France and Argentina shouldn't have a monopoly on that market." Gabe gestured to the eastern side of the vineyard on the plot map. "These blackberries will enhance the wine. We'll also add some black pepper flavor to give it an open texture."

"Lovely," Bianca said, folding her hands in her lap.

Gabe could read body language well enough to know that Bianca, for one, was itching to get a hold of his cashier's check. He could only imagine the medical bills that had been piling up. Mario was on the mend after his surgery and was starting chemotherapy in a week. He would get well. They all had to believe that. Still, his treatments had put a strain on the family's finances. Gabe was surprised by the sense of pride he took in being able to help them.

"Mario, this set of drawings is for you and your family. I want you to continue to look them over. I know we've talked about what I hope to create out here, but I need to be sure you're happy with this deal. Do you still want to sell to me?"

Mario didn't hesitate. He stood immediately and thrust out his hand. "Yes, we do, Gabriel. I'm very pleased you are going to make my little vineyard into a modern operation."

As they shook hands, Gabe smiled so widely his cheeks hurt. This was more than a very exciting day in his life. And it felt very, very fine.

Gabe signed the papers, then handed them to Mario. "Congratulations to us."

While Mario countersigned them, Gabe took out the cashier's check and handed it to Bianca.

She smiled gratefully at him. "Thank you."

As soon as the paperwork was done, Gabe would own roughly twelve acres of vineyard, most of which contained the same soil that was on Liz Crenshaw's land.

This tiny parcel wasn't even a speck of lint on the hundreds of acres, both planted and fallow, that Liz and Sam Crenshaw owned, but it was a start.

Since his freshman year at UC Davis, when he'd taken his first classes in viticulture and enology, he'd known that the tomatoes, soybeans and corn his family grew would never hold the allure for him that grape-growing and winemaking would. He had not only excelled in his classes, but also seemed to know as much or more than his professors. He remembered everything he read about wine as if the information had been burned into his brain. He was obsessed with California—the weather, the soil, the rock, the grapes, the other fruit and the estates. Gabe was drunk on the knowledge that flowed into him. Like the casks of wine he someday intended to make, Gabe knew he had to bide his time. His dream had to be held in reserve. Aged and not rushed. He'd returned to Indian Lake that summer, forever changed.

Still, Gabe had always felt the strong sense of duty to his parents that often befalls first-born children. When Nate ran off to join the navy after high school, not telling any of his family where he'd gone, Angelo had exploded with rage. Gabe had assuaged his father's anger by promising to be his right-hand man on the farm after he graduated from Purdue. Gabe had been putting his dreams and passions on hold for nearly a decade now. This opportunity to buy this small patch of land from the Mattuchi family had been the key to unlocking his hidden desires.

Once the papers were signed, his life was never going to be the same. It was time for him to break free from his father's grasp, and this purchase was his first step.

He needed to learn as much as he could as fast as he could, because all his moves would be swift from this point forward. He intended never to look back.

Gabe's ultimate dream was that one day his vineyard's name, Château Gabriel, would grace a wine so rare and unique that it would be sold, revered, saved and even auctioned off around the world. He would be recognized among the world's great sommeliers and collectors. He would have left his mark.

When the time was right and his plans called for it, he intended to travel to Argentina, South Africa and France to buy exceptional varieties of grapes with which to create masterpieces.

"Thank you, my friend," Mario said as he handed the papers back to Gabe. He kept a copy for himself. "This makes me very happy."

"I'm glad I could help. And thank you, Sophie, for suggesting I buy your father's land."

Bianca and Mario led Gabe to the door.

Sophie squeezed between them. "I'll walk you to your car, Gabe," she said sweetly.

Too sweetly, he thought. "Thanks." He turned to Bella. "Good day to you, Mrs. Mattuchi," he said with a polite nod.

Bella only grunted at him, then folded her arms over her chest and stared at the wall.

"Don't mind her," Sophie whispered. "It's past her nap time."

Gabe nodded. "I'll be seeing you, Mario. I'll give you a call on Monday before Mica and I come out to get started on the construction. He wants to look the place over."

"Certainly," Mario replied with a wide grin. He put his arm around his wife's shoulders and pulled her close. "This is a wonderful day for us."

"I'm glad," Gabe said and ambled down the flower-bordered front walk toward his car.

Shielding his eyes, Gabe glanced over at Bella's sunflower acre. "That's really spectacular," he said.

"Grandma sells to three florists in town, and a wholesaler from Chicago drives in every other day during her harvest."

Gabe's jaw dropped. "My kind of entrepreneur."

"She can be a lot of fun," Sophie assured him with a dazzling smile. "We can all be fun," she said, leaning closer.

Gabe unlocked the car. "I'll remember that," he said.

She put her hands on the top of his door as

he slid into the seat. "I'll be seeing a lot of you this summer and fall, I guess."

Gabe caught Sophie's flirtatious undertone. Romance was the last thing on his mind. "Sophie, we should have an understanding. I'm looking forward to seeing you more this summer, but I'm doing a business deal with your father. We should keep things professional."

The seductive smile slid off her face. She gave him a sharp nod. "Got it. Can't blame a girl for trying. I'll see you around."

"See you around," he replied.

Gabe drove down the gravel drive to the country road that would lead to the highway. As he passed the Crenshaws' fenced-in vineyard, he began to slow down.

It wasn't possible, he supposed—not according to any meteorologist or climatologist he'd heard, anyway—but Gabe could swear the sun shone more brightly on the Crenshaws' grapes than it did on the Mattuchis'.

Just looking at the land brought back the vision of Liz standing tall and tan and beautiful, the summer wind blowing her long, honey curls around her shoulders as she pointed a shotgun at him.

Staring over at Liz's thriving vines, he realized she truly was a child of the earth. And she seemed to want nothing more than to wipe him off that particular planet. Now they were going to be neighbors. He wondered if she would ever come around to being neighborly toward him. And if she did...

Would she be willing to sell her fallow land to me?

Gabe rubbed his jaw thoughtfully. The Mattuchi acreage was no more than a starter garden in the grand scheme Gabe had painted for himself. He needed something exceptional, and Liz Crenshaw had just that. She was experimenting with several different wines, including an ice wine. But how far did her imagination and drive take her?

If he could combine Liz's harvest with imported Argentinian grapes, he would be able to create perfection.

This had been Gabe's plan all along. But until his recent exploration to the Crenshaw tasting room and onto the land itself, he'd had no idea how valuable the Crenshaw plot truly was.

Sitting on a protected pocket of land where the earth, sun, wind and humidity combined to create a vintner's paradise, Liz Crenshaw reigned over one of the most priceless slices of winegrowing land in the United States, outside of California.

Gabe nearly squirmed in his seat thinking about it.

He could just come right out and ask Liz if she would be willing to sell, but after their initial encounter, his best guess was she'd kick him off the land, shoot him, or both. No, he had to be careful with Liz. He had to take his time. He had to use some charm and plenty of wit. She was perceptive, bright and suspicious. A bad combination, if he was trying to swing a land deal.

He needed to win her trust first. He would make her a very fair offer—even more than fair. Both of them would come out on top.

If he were dealing with any other businessperson, the way he did at the farm and the corporate canneries, Gabe would have felt his usual confidence. But oddly, the thought of negotiating with Liz filled his gut with butterflies.

It was going to take a lot of convincing to win her over.

CHAPTER FOUR

LIZ LAY IN BED staring at Gabe's bouquet. She'd put them in her mother's favorite crystal vase. They would find their way to the compost heap soon enough, so she might as well enjoy them first. It wasn't the flowers' fault they were from Gabe.

She stared at the single salmon-pink rose in the middle of the arrangement. It might have been her first time receiving flowers from a man, but it was undoubtedly Gabe's hundredth time giving them to a woman. He must have been pretty sure of himself to come back to her vineyard so quickly, which meant he hadn't had to think very long to devise a plan to placate her. Showing up with a bouquet and an apology had obviously worked for him in the past.

Liz prided herself on not making snap judgments, on allowing people to prove themselves to her. She'd done it since high school with her employees. She had one of the best working crews around Lake Michigan, and she'd won their loyalty by dealing with them fairly.

With Gabe, she didn't have much to go on. Of course, she'd heard about him nearly all her life. But that was either gossip or hearsay. What people said about Gabe was that he'd had dozens of girlfriends, though no one was ever mentioned by name. He was dating the "new blonde," the "new redhead" or a woman vaguely identified by her profession.

Gabe's supposed popularity with women didn't surprise Liz. Most of her girlfriends thought he was the best-looking guy in Indian Lake, though none of them had ever dated him. None had even gone to a movie with him. Gabe had graduated from high school before any of her crowd had had a chance with him.

Gabe was nearly an icon by the time Liz had become a freshman. He had been Mr. Everything in high school. He was All-State quarterback and went to regionals for the five-hundred-yard dash. He was on the debate team and acted in several school plays. Some said he was better on stage than he was on the grid-iron. She was sure Gabe had made it nearly impossible for his three younger brothers to keep up. Gabe had achieved every goal he set. He'd always won.

Back then, even her grandfather had said Gabe was a "golden boy."

It stood to reason a person who had always been a winner would expect that kind of life to continue. Such an outlook would tend to make a person arrogant and bigheaded.

Pigheaded was more like it.

The more Liz thought about Gabriel Barzonni, the more intense the fire within her became. Apparently, his charms had always worked on women. Apparently, he'd lumped her into that group of easy-to-manipulate females, and apparently, he hadn't tried to get to know her in the least. He didn't have the slightest idea what it would take to impress her, and he obviously wasn't interested in finding out. To a man like Gabe, she was just an object, a problem to be either solved or forgotten.

"Well!" she exclaimed aloud. "We'll just see about that!"

She bounded out of her bed, tossing her grandmother's counterpane quilt aside, and walked barefoot across the honey-colored hardwood floor to the window.

It wasn't dawn yet.

Liz hadn't slept, which made her angrier with herself. It wasn't like her to dwell on inconsequential matters.

She combed her long hair with her fingers and then massaged her scalp. Something wasn't right. In fact, it was all wrong. There was no good reason for Gabe to be on her land. And he hadn't come clean about his real reason for trespassing. Then he'd sent her the flowers. But why?

She was beginning to hate that word.

There was only one smart thing for Liz to do.

I have to pretend he doesn't exist. I never saw him on my land. He never brought me flowers.

LIZ WORE A fire-engine red bathing suit with white spaghetti straps and white river shoes as she helped her friends carry their sculling boat from the boathouse at Captain Redbeard's Marina out onto Indian Lake.

The early dawn rays slid across the glasslike surface of the water, making it look like silver mercury. The sky was dotted with only a few clouds, now tinged in pink and lavender, a spectacle Liz knew would only last moments.

Placing the boat in the water, Liz went back for the oars and distributed them to Sarah, Maddie and Isabelle, and kept one for herself.

"Before we start," Maddie said with an impish smile, "I have something to ask Liz and Isabelle."

"Sure," Liz said, pulling on a pair of rowing gloves she'd bought at the marina's new gift shop. Sarah thought wearing gloves was cheating, but Liz didn't care. Her hands were a wreck from thinning the grape vines the past week. She needed to give them a chance to heal, not torture them further.

"Would you both be my bridesmaids?"

"Are you kidding?" Isabelle whooped and nearly knocked Maddie down with a hug. "I'd love to!"

Liz beamed from ear to ear. "I'm honored, Maddie. Wow." Then she looked at Sarah, who was smiling at them all. "What about Sarah? She's not going to be a bridesmaid?"

Maddie playfully shoved Liz's shoulder. "You goofball. She's my matron of honor."

Liz shook her head. "Of course! What was I thinking?"

"I've asked Olivia to be a bridesmaid, as well," Maddie said.

"So," Liz said, "you've set a date?"

Maddie waved her hands in the air. "Oh my gosh! I didn't tell you, did I? It's December twenty-eighth. It has to be after Christmas because I'll be catering for weeks and I won't get a wink of sleep. And Nate says the end of the year is booked solid with surgeries for him. It'll be an evening wedding. I thought that would be pretty. All the snow and Christmas lights. The reception will be at the Lodge. Then Nate and I will fly to Paris to spend New Year's Eve under the Eiffel Tower."

Liz nearly melted at the idea of New Year's Eve in Paris. "Perfect, Maddie. Just perfect. You'll love Paris."

"I can't wait. Then we'll fly to southern Italy and spend two weeks there. It's like a dream," Maddie said.

"You deserve it," Liz said. "You've worked so hard for so many years. You deserve a great guy and a wonderful trip…"

"Oh, yeah? You've worked just as hard as Maddie," Sarah quipped.

"Yes," Liz replied. "But I've already been to France."

"That's right!" Maddie said. "She's been to France, so she's a step ahead of all of us. Right, Liz?"

"Well, I wouldn't say that, but I would say going there with someone special should be wonderful."

They eased the boat off the shore, then climbed in and took their seats. Oars in place, in minutes they were synchronized and sluicing through the reflective water.

Sarah called out the strokes, as she always did. Liz concentrated on her muscles, the fit of the oar in her hands and the feel of the wind on her face.

Back straining, thighs tight in order to stay properly seated, the four friends worked as a team and became one.

As they rounded the north end of the lake, Maddie pointed to a heavily treed space. "See that, guys?"

"That's the old Hanson lot, isn't it?" Liz said, shielding her eyes. "I heard Mr. Hanson died back in May or June, wasn't it?"

"Right," Maddie said. "Nate and I bought the lot. We're going to start building next month."

Liz grabbed Maddie by the shoulders and shook her slightly. "You're really doing this. Jumping in with both feet. First, all the wedding plans. Then a trip to Europe for a honeymoon and now building a house together."

Isabelle laughed heartily. "They should be divorced by Valentine's Day."

"What?" Maddie screeched. "Don't say that!"

"Oh, don't listen to Isabelle," Sarah said. "I say go for it. Charmaine and I can work out some blueprints for the interior."

Maddie smiled wistfully. "I want it to look like a summer cottage—dark wood floors, rag rugs and lots of French doors overlooking the lake."

"Sounds perfect," Liz said as they rowed back toward the marina.

"So, do I get any vote on who will be my groomsman?" Isabelle asked from the back of the boat.

"You'll be with Mica. Scott Abbot will escort Olivia."

Suddenly, Liz felt her entire back break out in icy chills. She should have realized Nate would want his three brothers to be his groomsmen.

"Rafe is going to be the best man," Maddie continued. "He'll be escorting Sarah."

"That leaves Gabe to be my escort," Liz said, feeling her mouth go dry.

"Yeah," Maddie replied gleefully. "You two will look great together. You're both tall, and he's just so handsome."

"What Barzonni isn't handsome?" Sarah laughed. The boat came ashore and they got out.

As they took out their oars and lifted the boat onto their shoulders, the full impact of Liz's commitment to Maddie hit her. She would have to sit with Gabe at the rehearsal dinner for the pictures. At the wedding, he would walk her down the aisle and back out again. They would be seated next to each other at the reception. That was something she couldn't wangle her way out of. But it was just one dinner. One night. She could deal with it. It wasn't going to be so bad.

"Yeah," Maddie was saying. "Both Liz and Isabelle will have the awful burden of being around those handsome boys for my engagement party at the Barzonnis' house and the couples' shower at Mrs. Beabots's. Then there's a cocktail party being thrown by the hospital doctors, which is going to be a really big deal. Tuxedos and gowns and the whole thing. I'll love that. I figure that through the rest of the summer and fall, we'll all be doing something special together on the weekends. Doesn't that sound great?"

Liz was silent as they stored the boat and oars and locked the boathouse, a smile plastered on her face.

She'd just promised herself she would pretend Gabe Barzonni didn't exist. Now she was going to be thrown together with him for months. Then an idea hit her. She rushed up to Maddie's car just as Maddie was getting in.

"Hey, I just had a quick question," Liz said. "Was it you or Nate who decided on which groomsman would be with Isabelle and me?"

"Nate," Maddie assured her. "Funny you should ask, though."

"Why?" Liz cringed. That word again.

"Last night Nate told me he and Gabe had been having a beer at the Lodge and decided it would be cute to pair up Isabelle and Mica, even though Scott Abbot would be the obvious choice for her. She's always giving Scott a hard time. Maybe if she made Scott a bit jealous, he would make a real commitment to her instead of beating around the bush all the time. Isn't that the cutest idea? Do you think it would work?"

Ire rekindled its flame in Liz's belly and exploded inside her. She felt an acid burn all the way up to her throat and she could hardly get out her words. "Gabe."

"He's been such a help to Nate with the plans," Maddie said.

"A help."

"Nate's so busy with surgeries, so Gabe's just been great. Organizing the engagement party with their mom. He even got the Tom and Jason Big Band to play until midnight," Maddie said effusively.

"An orchestra." Liz swallowed. There would be dancing. Arms entwined. Her head nuzzled in the crook of his neck. Liz felt the heat inside her boil over. She hadn't trusted Gabe when she'd found him skulking around her vines. Now he was deliberately manipulating her social life.

"Isn't it great?" Maddie asked.

"Sure. Yeah," Liz said, trying to cover her shock and frustration. "I was just curious."

"You know, I didn't ask you, but have you ever met Gabe?"

"Uh. Only in passing."

"Well, I'd better get to the café. Chloe can only do so much without me. Call me later."

Liz watched her friend drive away, then went over to her pickup. She stared out the windshield at the lake.

Her grandfather believed all Barzonni men were up to no good.

Guess Grandpa's right.

CHAPTER FIVE

FOR THE NEXT several days, Liz was busy with a hundred tasks. Because she was the general manager, the winemaker, the sales manager and the office manager all rolled into one, her list of duties was like a black hole. She never got it all done. On summer days, she worked dawn to dusk at the vineyard, and though she relished every moment of the work, it was still exhausting.

On Thursday morning, a series of semi-trucks barreled up the country road that ran between the western edge of her property and the Mattuchi farm. Semis weren't unusual on that road, which led to the highway, but a constant stream of eighteen-wheelers was out of the ordinary. Trucks carrying large loads of lumber, pipes and building materials could only mean one thing. Someone up the country road was building a new house or barn.

Liz didn't have time to be curious or to gossip with neighbors. She had her eyes on the clouds gathering over Lake Michigan. She took out her cell phone and opened her weather radar app. Unfortunately, radar or not, the fickle westerly winds had a mind of their own once they reached the lake. The rain could easily pass her over and fall just north of her vineyard, showering her northern competition and jilting her vines. Again.

They were in desperate need of a good soaking. It had been nearly three weeks without rain, and this kind of summer heat would only do one thing—produce inferior grapes.

Liz lifted a cluster of Seyval blanc grapes she'd personally cluster-thinned three and a half weeks after fruit set. Though this grape produced the fresh and dry white wine they sold midseason in the tasting room, Louisa had suggested they experiment with it to produce a sparkling wine cuvée. Liz loved the idea—making something new out of a longtime standard grape in the vineyard.

As Liz slung her long leg over the seat of her ATV, she heard yet another truck downshift as it began its trek up the country road hill.

Natural curiosity urged Liz to ride over to the edge of her property to inspect the scene.

The semi was hauling a long flatbed trailer that held what looked like a mountain of lumber and three pallets of cement bags. She noticed there were piles of steel framing and insulated metal sheeting.

"Not a house," she said to herself. The materials on this truck were used for warehouse and commercial buildings. Because their area was primarily farmland, she assumed one of her neighbors up the road was upgrading his or her silos. She'd heard from her grandfather last summer that Gerald Finstermaker, who owned a large apple orchard, had opened up a fifty-acre area, though no one knew exactly what he intended to plant there. The joke in town was that Gerald, paranoid and intensely secretive, was the only person who could keep his crop a secret until after the harvest. Five years ago, Gerald had experimented with roses and raised them under enormous grow tents, not so much to increase the productivity and excellence of the roses as to keep prying eyes out. After that fiasco, few in Indian Lake paid much attention to what Gerald Finstermaker did or didn't do on his farm.

Liz was turning away from the fence to head back to the tasting room when she saw a second truck, also hauling a long trailer stacked with building materials. She laughed to herself and wished Gerald all the luck in the world with his new venture, whatever it was. She tossed the driver a friendly wave and then froze.

Following the last truck up the country road was a very familiar black Porsche. The top was down, and she could clearly see Gabe inside. He did not seem happy.

No doubt he was angry because the trucks were moving slowly up the grade and she'd already learned that Gabe liked to drive a bit on the fast side. But Gabe didn't honk or try to pass them. *He must not be in a hurry after all,* she thought.

As Liz drove her ATV back down the slope, the first drops of rain stung her bare arms. Then the dark storm clouds moved over her property and opened up with a vengeance... The next second, the drops were huge, pelting her with enough force she found it difficult to see.

She bumped her way across the vineyard and smiled to herself. If she was caught in the rain, so was Gabe. And that meant both he and the interior of his expensive car had been deluged. She couldn't help laughing a little. Served him right. Even if she hadn't had a chance to pay him back for trespassing and stealing from her, Mother Nature had taken restitution into her own hands.

By the time she got to the utility barn, Liz was completely soaked. Her white shirt looked like a second skin and her shoes squished as she walked across the gravel to the tasting room, where she always kept a fresh shirt and a long black apron to wear when serving the tourists.

Liz noticed with satisfaction the parking lot was full of cars. The tourists would be trapped inside to avoid the downpour. That could only mean one thing. Increased sales.

Opening the door, Liz found the place packed. Sam was engrossed in one of his sales pitches with a man dressed in a golf shirt and khakis. Louisa was at the bar, pouring a flight of white wines for a strikingly beautiful, auburn-haired woman who wore a business suit and designer shoes.

The woman was not a local, but she was buying a lot of wine, if the smile on Louisa's face and twinkle in her eye were any indication.

"I'll be right there," Liz told her *chef de cave*. Louisa nodded and continued talking to the customer.

Liz rushed into her office, shut the door and pulled out a clean white blouse from the closet. She towel-dried her hair and rolled it into a twist. She didn't have a smidge of makeup left after the rain pelting, but she didn't care. As she tied her apron on, she noticed the morning's mail. As usual, Louisa had left it on the old leather desk blotter.

Sitting on top of the stack was the familiar green paper envelope from the County Treasurer's office containing the yearly property tax bill. Always diligent about the vineyard's accounting, Liz reached for the envelope and opened it.

What met her eyes was a shock.

"Twenty-three thousand four hundred dollars…past due?" Liz read the numbers again. Twice.

This was impossible! They were not a year in arrears.

"I paid this bill," she groaned, sinking into the desk chair. She could remember purchasing the cashier's check from the bank to pay the taxes. "There has to be some mistake."

Liz called the Indian Lake County treasurer's office and spoke to one of the clerks. The woman assured Liz that although the Crenshaw taxes had always been paid promptly each year, there had been no payment in the past twelve months. Liz thanked the woman and hung up.

She dropped her face to her hands, feeling

as if the world had just crashed down upon her. There was no mistake. Liz now owed not only her taxes, but a penalty, as well. According to the bill, she had ninety days to pay in full.

How could I have forgotten to pay this? Liz berated herself. *I'm always so careful...*

She drew in a quick breath and clamped her hand over her mouth. "Sam."

Last year, the taxes had been due when Liz was in France. She had left the cashier's check with Sam for him to take to the treasurer's office. Amid the flurry of her decisions about Louisa, the champagne vines and the newly built tasting room, she hadn't given the taxes a second thought. And because she'd always paid the taxes with a cashier's check, she had no record of the check being cashed.

This was about the same time she'd begun to notice the first signs of Sam's forgetfulness, she realized with a lurch in her stomach. His slips were always minor, and she'd thought they were more of a nuisance than a real danger. But this...

Losing over twenty thousand dollars could ruin them.

Liz had already taken out two new mortgages to pay for the tasting room and all the improvements to the fermenting barn and the cellars. She doubted any bank in town would advance her any more money on her harvest. Liz had yet to prove herself and her wines' abilities to bring in big sales. Though they were doing well—even better than she'd hoped with the tourist trade—she still hadn't secured a large retailer. That was her plan for next year. Not this summer.

She had to find the check.

Panic overtook Liz as she scrambled through her desk drawers. Her search was in vain. She went to a small wall safe that Sam had installed behind a family portrait. In the safe, she found the deeds to the vineyard, copies of the mortgages, Sam's will, her father's will...but no cashier's check.

Where would he have put it? she asked herself as she scanned the room. Through the office window, she saw the rain was dissipating. Then she spotted her truck.

She left the office through the side door and rushed across the parking lot to her pickup. She took everything out of the glove box and examined the papers. No check. She crammed everything back inside, then looked under both visors and checked under and between the seats.

She raced up to the farmhouse and went to

the living room. She hoped she could find the check before she had to bring the incident to Sam's attention. Then she would simply pay the taxes and Sam would be spared any concern or embarrassment. She rifled through the drawer in the end table next to Sam's recliner. Suddenly she stopped. There was only one place he would have put the check for safekeeping.

His rolltop desk.

At the far end of the living room was a hundred-year-old burled walnut desk with a glassed-in upper library case that soared to the ceiling.

Liz pulled out every drawer and checked the contents. She went through old papers, newspaper clippings from her father's high school years, her parents' wedding announcement and their eulogies. She found old receipts and outdated warranties for appliances they'd long ago donated or thrown away. There were stacks of Christmas cards and sweet birthday cards her grandmother had given to Sam. But no check.

She took over half an hour to examine everything in the desk. Liz grew more concerned as she rifled through each drawer and cubbyhole with no results. At this point, Sam's humiliation was only one of her concerns. Liz now realized that unless Sam could remember where he'd put that check, they would be facing a grave situation.

Someone else could have found the check and cashed it. If it had been destroyed, the money would be unrecoverable.

Liz wanted to scream, cry and curse. She had to believe she would find the missing money. She had to stay positive, even if it felt as if the world had just gone black.

LIZ'S MIND WAS REELING with the consequences of losing the check as she walked back to the tasting room, where Louisa and Sam were expecting and needing her assistance with the tourists who were continuing to drive up to the vineyard. Liz opened the door and nearly ran into Maddie.

"Liz!" Maddie exclaimed. Her broad smile instantly fell away. "What's wrong?"

Liz tried to erase the worry and concern from her expression. "Huh?"

"You look terrible. Are you sick?"

"Sick? No. I just got caught in the rain is all. What are you doing here?"

"Ordering wine for the engagement party on Saturday."

Saturday? That soon? Liz felt her stomach

roil. On top of the new situation with the taxes, she'd have to see Gabe.

Maddie peered closely at Liz, disappointment filling her face. "You forgot."

Liz grinned sheepishly. "You told me next Saturday."

"This *is* next Saturday, you goof," Maddie said, giving her friend a hug and mushing Liz's still-wet hair. "You got caught in the rain, but I bet you're glad for this downpour."

"Love it." Liz glanced at Maddie's extensive list. She'd ordered two cases of chardonnay, two pinot grigio and two cabernet sauvignon. Hmm. Four white to two red. The preference for white was a trend Liz was noticing more and more. It further confirmed her decision to bring French chardonnay grapes to her vineyard. If this kind of market buying kept up, her Vignoles, Seyvals and Vidal blanc grapes would help her produce more white demi-sec and dry barrel fermented, and excellent ice wines. Liz smiled broadly. "Yes, the rain…" The vision of Gabe in his convertible shot across her mind. Something wasn't right. "So, tell me about the engagement party. It's still being held at Gabe…I mean, Nate's parents' house, right?"

"Yes, and Gina is like a field marshal with

a battle plan. Honestly, Liz, I didn't have to do much at all. She wanted Italian imported wines, and there's nothing wrong with that—"

"I love them," Liz interrupted.

"Yes, but I insisted on buying the wines because I wanted them to be yours. I love your wines and so does Nate—we wanted to show off your expertise. By the way, Nate has a lot of friends from Chicago who are going to spend the entire weekend in Indian Lake. We're going to show them around on Sunday, but I was hoping we could bring them out here then. They'll buy tons from you. You should see the orders they've been sending me for cupcakes."

"You're mailing them now?"

"Sure. I overnight them. It's amazing. My bottom line is getting very happy," Maddie gushed.

Liz knew her smile was a bit forced, but it was all she could manage. Maddie was one of her best friends, but she couldn't possibly come right out and say her future brother-in-law was a thief. "Thanks for networking and marketing for me."

"You already do the same for me," Maddie said, lifting one of her Cupcake and Cappuccino Café brochures off the counter. "My Chicago franchise opened well. My investor told me nearly a dozen people have walked in with this brochure in their hands. The only place they could get them was out here at your winery."

"True," Liz said, admiring the brochure she'd made for Maddie, which was similar to one she'd designed for the vineyard. Liz had laid it out herself, using photos she'd taken of the vineyard, tasting rooms, fermenting barn and, of course, photogenic Louisa and even Grandpa Sam. She was proud of the natural talent she had when it came to selling. She liked success, and even tiny victories added up to big ones over time. But with her love of success came her fear of failure.

She rubbed the back of her neck. She hoped she'd feel better after she had a chance to talk to Sam about the cashier's check. But still, she felt unsettled—as if some other secret was hanging in the air. Oddly, each time these feelings clutched at her, Gabe's face flashed in her mind's eye.

"You know what's crazy, Maddie? I thought I saw Gabe earlier today."

"Here?" Maddie asked, glancing around the tasting room. Her smile melted and was replaced with a serious expression.

"No. On the country road that runs along

my western property line." Liz scrutinized her friend's green eyes. Maddie was hiding something. "What is it, Maddie?"

Maddie turned her gaze to a group of tourists. The women, young and tan, were laughing together. Louisa had just gone to their table, and they'd ordered another bottle of wine and more cheese and crackers. Liz waited for Maddie to look back at her. "You're one of my very best friends..."

"Oh, this is going to be bad," Liz said. "Gabe is up to something. I can feel it in my bones."

"He just bought the Mattuchi vineyard."

Shock hit her like the thunder rolling outside. "What? That's impossible. First of all, the Mattuchis don't have a vineyard. They have a farm. They grow a few grapes every year and make grape jelly and some horrible wine that my grandfather says even Boone's Farm wouldn't buy."

"I know."

"So what is he thinking?"

"He told Nate it's good business," Maddie explained.

"The Mattuchis have owned that land forever. I can't believe Gabe would deprive them of their livelihood. This is just monstrous!" Liz exclaimed. "You know, if anything happened to me and my grandfather was left here all alone and some man-eating shark like Gabriel Barzonni came to steal his land away from him, I swear I would haunt these hills until the end of eternity to make sure the creep suffered the fires of—"

Maddie grabbed Liz's arm and squeezed it. "Liz, honey, don't you think you're getting a little carried away? I mean, Gabe just bought part of their farm. We don't know that he swindled them or hurt them."

Liz was practically hyperventilating. She could see Gabe's handsome, wicked eyes gloating at her.

"I'm just not believing this. The Barzonnis own enough land in this area to create a new state! They don't need more land. And poor Mr. Mattuchi. I've known him since I was born. He and his wife are hardworking people, but he's not a farmer. Never was. He's repaired my equipment here for years. Best mechanic I've ever seen. Grandpa really likes him. Oh, I just can't believe this!"

Maddie eyed her friend suspiciously and released her hand. "You know, Liz, I don't think I've ever seen you like this. What's really going on?"

"I'll tell you. I caught Gabe Barzonni two

weeks ago," Liz replied breathlessly. She felt flushed, and her heart was tripping inside her chest at a mile a minute.

"Doing what?" Maddie asked.

"He was stealing from me," Liz answered self-righteously.

"Stealing what?"

"Dirt."

Maddie stared at Liz for a moment, then broke into laughter. "You're kidding."

"I'm not." Liz lifted her chin.

"Okay. Why is that important to you?"

Liz slapped her forehead. "Now I get it. It was never about a vial of dirt. It was about the components and the structure of the soil. Gabe was already thinking of buying the Mattuchi farm. Once he got his hands on my soil samples, he knew he could possibly have a gold mine over there."

"Oh boy." Maddie's eyes narrowed. "If he planted grape vines in similar soil—"

"And with the Barzonni millions to back him up, he could put me out of business."

"Dirty rotten scum."

"The rottenest," Liz agreed.

CHAPTER SIX

POURING A FLIGHT of the vineyard's best aged cabernet sauvignons for a Chicago-based investment banker, Sam Crenshaw watched his granddaughter out of the corner of his eye as she spoke to Maddie. Sam had learned since the day Liz's father, Matthew, was born that a proper parent or grandparent needed to use high-level espionage tactics and have a boatload of intuition. Sam knew his granddaughter's body language better than anyone, including Liz herself, he'd bet. From her consternation, the way she ground her jaw and the way her eyes had turned from sky blue to stormy indigo, he knew something was very wrong.

That girl looks ready to kill.

Sam smiled at his customer, who peered down his nose over his designer eyeglasses at the paper Sam had slipped toward him. "Here's the list of your selections for this flight and a description of each wine," Sam informed him.

"Just let me know if you want to make a purchase," he said. He did not take his eyes off Liz, who had just walked Maddie to the door.

The man carefully rolled the second selection, an oak barrel–aged cabernet, in its glass and held it up to the light. He tasted the wine and smiled. "This one has a smooth finish. Nearly like velvet. Remarkable."

Sam turned his attention back to the customer. "Remarkable how? That you found such excellence here and not from a French burgundy?"

The man grinned merrily. "You're very observant."

Sam winked at him. "It's my job."

"I'll take a case of this one," the man said, sliding his credit card to Sam.

"Excellent taste. This is the best wine we've ever made. It's my personal favorite."

Sam continued to smile as he took the card, though he grumbled under his breath. The expensive sale should have made him happy. But he was much more interested in his granddaughter and her escalating irritation.

After the man signed his voucher, Sam used a walkie-talkie to call Aurelio in the warehouse. He would crate up the cases of wine for the customer and meet them at the front door.

Sam stepped outside and stood next to Liz under the porch roof to the tasting room. The rain was easing up. The storm clouds had nearly passed over them, and blue afternoon skies were beginning to poke through the cover.

Aurelio arrived with the cases just as Sam's customer walked out the door. The man popped the trunk on an arctic-blue BMW sedan.

Sam stood with his granddaughter and watched the man drive away.

"Did you just sell him a full case of your prized cabernet?" Liz inquired with a tone befitting a prosecuting attorney.

"I did."

"I thought you wanted to save it."

"No, I said I would only sell it to an aficionado."

She peered down the drive. "Really."

"I believe," Sam said proudly, "I have made a new friend. He'll be back. And often. If he has friends and they like our wines as much as he does, you and Louisa better get busy producing some prizewinners," he joked.

Liz scowled and the storm came back to her eyes.

"What is it?"

"Grandpa, we need to talk," she replied glumly.

"But later. All our customers will want to check out now that the rain is ending, so let's help Louisa first."

"I hate it when you say that. Is it me?"

"Not really. It's just that there's been a development." She patted his forearm, opened the door and went inside.

"Development? That's worse than 'we need to talk.'"

THE SUNSET BLISTERED the horizon while Liz and Sam sat in their white wicker rocking chairs on the front porch of the big farmhouse. Maria was in the kitchen blending garden basil, oregano, chives and garlic into an Italian tomato sauce for their dinner. The smell wafted through the house and onto the porch.

Sam held out a glass of cabernet to Liz. "Here. With a sunset this intoxicating, the wine will only pale."

"Stop being a poet," she replied, but she took the glass. She sipped the wine and exhaled in appreciation. "You shouldn't have."

"I can't let all the good stuff go to the semi-educated public."

"Maybe we should." Liz stared down into the wine.

"It's an indulgence. Now tell me whatever it is you have to tell me," Sam said.

Liz looked from the setting ball of fire in the west to her grandfather's kindly face. He had the same eyes as she. Crystal blue, like the melting snow waters running down a rock spring. He was still a strikingly handsome man and she could see why her grandmother, Aileen, had fallen for him when they'd first met. He was kind, thoughtful and levelheaded. Liz was counting on that level head of his to help them now.

"Grandpa, today I got the property tax bill."

"Ah," he said. "It's about that time again."

"Something happened last year and the treasurer's office never got our payment. We're in arrears over twenty thousand dollars."

"What?" Sam's eyes grew wide. "Impossible! I paid it with our cashier's check like you asked me to."

She shook her head. "Apparently not. I called and talked to Jane Burley. She said there was no mistake. I've been all over the office, in the truck, even in your desk."

Sam rubbed his face and sucked in a deep breath. "I know I paid it."

"Let's retrace your steps. First of all, I gave you the check the day before I left for France."

He snapped his fingers and his face brightened. "That's right! You were in France. I took you to the bus station the next morning."

"And then you were going into town to run errands—and pay the taxes. You had the check with you in the truck."

He looked at her quizzically with that cloud in his eyes she'd noticed lately. She had come to hate that look, and now she feared it.

"The truck. But I kept the check in my billfold."

"Of course you would! I hadn't thought of that. Maybe it's stuck behind that secret flap you use sometimes?" Liz felt hope rising inside her like a warm spring breeze.

"Right!" Sam put down his glass of wine and reached in his jeans pocket for his wallet. He riffled through the wad of bills and peeled up the old leather flap beside the cash.

Liz felt her breath catch in her lungs. She leaned over the arm of her chair and peered more closely at the wallet.

"Nothing," Sam announced.

Liz fell back in her chair and stared up at the porch roof. "It was my last hope."

"I can't believe I didn't pay it," he said guiltily.

Over the past year, Sam had been forgetting

things a little more than usual. He needed afternoon naps nearly every day. He told her he was slowing down, and she had assumed that was all it was. He was fully engaged in his life and in their business, so she hadn't considered there might be anything seriously wrong. Still...

"What did you do that day that would have caused you to forget?"

Sam was quiet for a long moment. "I was at the grocery store when Maria called me. She said the power had been cut—workers on the highway or some such. Our generator wasn't functioning, either, which seemed impossible. I drove straight home and met Aurelio. We called Burt Thompson, who came out and showed us the breaker had gone bad. Then that horrible storm came in. Nearly a tornado. We spent the rest of the week cleaning up downed trees and inspecting the vines. It was a week I'll never forget. Everything went wrong."

"I remember you telling me about it," she said. No wonder he'd forgotten to pay the taxes. He was trying to save the vineyard. And yet...a year later, they were facing a worse storm than a tornado.

"I'm sorry, Lizzie. Did you look in the safe?"

"Yes," she replied glumly. "I even went through the hanging files in the desk drawers.

The problem is that there's no way to know if someone else cashed it."

"I'm so sorry. This is all my fault," Sam apologized. "I have to believe we'll find the check."

"I hope we do!" Liz replied. "In the meantime, I have to call the treasurer's office and see what I can work out. The problem is the taxes for this year are due at the same time. We don't have that kind of money in our savings."

Sam looked down at his prized wine. "I'm glad I sold that case of my cabernet today."

"That will help," Liz said, patting his arm affectionately. "There's something else I need to talk to you about."

His left eyebrow ratcheted up. "Losing twenty grand isn't enough?"

Liz felt her heart flip. She hated seeing even the first smidge of consternation in his eyes. This man had meant the world to her almost her whole life. All she wanted was for him to be happy, and in the span of one conversation, she had hit him with two pieces of devastating news.

She knew Sam didn't have the enthusiasm or the energy for the kind of expansion Liz envisioned for the vineyard. Sam had worked hard on the land all his life, but her gambles on Louisa, the chardonnay grapes, the riddling and fermenting rooms—even the tasting room and the plan to make champagne—were all a crapshoot. A big roll of the dice. Sam had gone along with her not because he thought it was good business, but because he loved her.

Liz had to wonder what kind of twisted and sick blunder of fate would allow these catastrophes to befall them. Sam had walked the conservative route his entire life. He'd maintained the vineyard and ridden the roller coaster of drought and flood, and he hadn't lost the land. He didn't believe in banks, borrowing money or building for the future. He believed in holding on, but that was all.

Sam had often told her she would inherit everything when he died. His greatest fear had always been leaving her with a great pile of debt. But with Gabe Barzonni in the equation now, all bets were off. Liz's decisions alone could bring down Crenshaw Vineyards. With Gabe Barzonni as competition, they were about to enter the fight of their lives.

Liz crossed her arms over her chest as if she were afraid she'd be shot through the heart. Losing her vineyard, even a portion of it, would break her heart. She exhaled.

"Tell me what else is going on," Sam urged

her. "Because it sounds to me like this one is worse than losing the tax money."

"I'm afraid it is. Or could be. I just learned from Maddie that the Mattuchis sold their vineyard to Gabe Barzonni."

"Barzonni?" Sam repeated in disbelief. "What would Angelo Barzonni want with that cruddy little chunk of land half a universe away from his tomato farm south of town?"

Liz shook her head. "Not Angelo, Grandpa. Gabriel, his eldest son, bought it."

"Same darned thing. Trust me, the old man put him up to it!" Sam slammed his balled fist on the arm of his chair.

"That makes no sense. Besides, it was Gabe who was out here trying to take our soil. Now I know why he was here."

"Why?"

"It's so obvious. Our land has the same soil as Mario Mattuchi's. He grows Nebbiolo grapes, which are fine in Italy, but the climate here is all wrong for them. They have to ripen so late, even after our cabernet sauvignons have ripened. But he would never give them up."

"Mario is from the old country. He likes what he likes. Some years he did okay. But he never really sold his wine, anyway. I just don't understand why he would sell out to Angelo. Mario always told me he didn't like Angelo."

"He told you that?" Liz asked.

"He did. Many times, back when Matthew was alive and he and your mom…" Sam trailed off, clearly noticing Liz's pained expression. "Sorry. I didn't mean to bring all that up."

"It's okay, Grandpa. If we can't talk about Mom and Dad, who can? Especially now, when we're facing all this."

"Facing? What are we facing?"

"Gabe!" Liz answered much too quickly and with far too much emotion. Her voice rang with anger, fear and…excitement? Was that it? Liz hardly knew what was going on inside of her. How could she decipher the unfamiliar pangs and yearnings when she didn't even know Gabe's motivations for buying the Mattuchi land?

Sam's eyes narrowed. "Did you really have him in your gun's sight?"

"For a moment, before I recognized him."

"Well," Sam said thoughtfully. "Maybe he'll remember that and move cautiously around you in the future."

"Unfortunately, Grandpa, that future is this Saturday night."

"What's on Saturday?"

"Maddie and Nate's engagement party. It's going to be held at the Barzonni villa. Gina is putting on a big party for them."

Sam was silent for a long moment. "Gina, huh? At the villa?"

"Yes. I can't get out of it. I'm one of the bridesmaids."

Sam peered at her. "Who said anything about squirreling your way out of a command performance? Look, I have no idea what those Barzonnis are after, but this is the perfect opportunity for you to find out. I suggest you load both barrels and go in with guns blazing. No one's going to take us down without a fight."

"Sounds good to me, Grandpa. Just how do you suggest I do that?"

Sam picked up his glass, smirked and took a mouthful of the precious wine. "What you always used to do when presented with a dilemma. Go up to the catwalk."

Liz returned his smile, feeling the first inkling of peace descend upon her. "Of course. The catwalk."

CHAPTER SEVEN

THE "CATWALK" WAS the Crenshaws' name for the attic of the farmhouse. When Liz's parents, Matthew and Kim, had been alive, they had renovated the expansive area into a loft apartment with a walled-off bedroom complete with closets, built-in dressers and a master bath. A second bedroom across the landing at the top of the stairs had been Liz's room until her parents' deaths. After their accident, she'd moved into the guest room downstairs to be closer to her grandfather.

Along the entire north wall, Matt had installed three sets of eight-foot-high windows that, on a clear day, offered a view of Lake Michigan in the very far distance.

This was where her parents had made plans to expand her grandfather's vineyard. Through Matt's efforts, they had bought over a hundred acres of land to the north of the existing vineyard, which lay fallow to this day. It was Liz's most heartfelt dream to carry out her father's long-held goal and plant it all. Matt had wanted to prove that because of its geographic anomaly, his Midwest land was capable of producing wines as unique as anything California could offer.

Liz's passion to fulfill her father's dream had driven her for years. She'd been preparing the soil with her compost and had planted a parcel of peach trees to the northeast, which always turned a good crop. Liz believed that in the future, the fallow land would be perfect for their chardonnay grapes. Perhaps for some Limbergers, too. They were hardy and produced a high-quality wine.

All two hundred and fifty acres of her land, fully planted and abundant, was the only picture she would allow her imagination to paint. It was the same landscape her father had conjured in his mind over twenty years before. She would be the conduit from heaven to earth through which he'd make his mark on the world.

Liz could still remember standing at this window with him when she was only five years old, as he held her in his arms and pointed to the lake. "See that, Lizzie?" he'd said. "That gives life to our vines. That lake makes our land nearly like Sonoma, and the great vineyards on the west coast. There's nothing they do that we can't do. That lake isn't a lake, Lizzie. It's an inland sea. Let's call it the Michigan Sea."

"Yes, Daddy," she'd said, kissing his cheek, which had always been red from the sun. She'd ruffled his thick, honey-colored hair, the same hair she had. She remembered the smell of him, sun and wind and earth from working in the fields. And there was the smell of nature, she thought now, the scent of something ungraspable…like the memory she had of him. Real, still guiding her.

On either side of the windows were two huge desks, where her parents had worked. Her mother had handled the accounting and bill-paying, much as Liz did now, and she had also planned their trips to Chicago for lectures and visits to the food and wine conventions in New York and Aspen. Liz remembered her mother combing magazines for inspiration for the vineyard she and Matt dared to nurture in the middle of America rather than on the west coast, like all the other vintners in the nineties.

Liz watched the last of the setting sun.

Some people believed going to a cemetery would bring them closer to their loved ones, but not Liz. She knew the spirits of her parents were here in this room if they were in the house at all. Most of the time, she felt them when she walked among the vines and sang the same lullabies to the grapes her mother had sung to her.

Her parents had died in a car accident when she was only six. They had been in Sonoma, gathering vines, ideas and information to bring back to their piece of paradise. Despite the tragedy, Liz had never idealized them. They were her parents. Not saints. Not perfect. But they had taught her one thing.

To believe in her dreams.

That's what they had done.

Even though those dreams had killed them.

Tears nearly blinded Liz as she dropped her head and sat down in her father's desk chair. She and her grandfather hadn't touched the room since her parents died. Liz had come up to the catwalk all through her life to think, pray and dream. It was here she'd contemplated her trip to France and her decision to build the tasting room.

Liz had spent her early life in this loft. She'd learned to read while sitting on these rag rugs with her mother and she'd put puzzles together with her father. It had always been her haven.

How disappointed they would both have been if they knew what was happening to her

now. Losing the tax money. Giving in to her
fear of competition that hadn't even materi-
alized yet. Scrubbing her tears away, she remembered her grandfather's words earlier that
evening.

What was she doing? Giving up? "I can't
give up, can I, Daddy?" she asked the silver-
framed photograph of her father on his desk.
He was standing by a vine, holding a cluster of
prized pinot noir grapes, the first to be planted
on their land. Matt's intention had been to plant
the entire northwest slope of the property with
these grapes. It had taken twenty years, but Liz
had carried out his wish. She'd done it. She'd
fulfilled his dream.

And now this…this varmint…

Just thinking about Gabe riled her up. She
shot to her feet and slammed her fist on the
desk. "I won't give up, Dad. Mom. I promise."

Liz started to walk away from the desk, but
as she did her bare thigh caught on a protrud-
ing drawer. She sat back down and inspected
her leg—a piece of metal had cut the skin. She
was bleeding. *What in the world?*

She grabbed the drawer and yanked it. She
was certain she'd gone through the papers in it
at some point, but this time, she noticed a metal
separator had popped out, most likely when

she'd pounded the desk with her fist. Behind the separator were several journals.

With trembling, uncertain fingers, Liz opened the cover of the first notebook. "For Elizabeth— my Lizzie—from her parents on her first birthday."

Despite the tears welling up in her eyes, she turned the first page.

"You are the bubbles in our champagne, darling. We could not love you more."

The entries went on to describe her first words and steps, what foods she ate and at what ages. Liz assumed most young mothers wrote about these milestones in baby books. What was different was her mother had jotted down every single dish on the menu for each holiday dinner, and her father had chosen the white, red and dessert wines, along with the sherries and cognacs.

There were photographs of her grandfather holding her next to an enormous Christmas tree, and even a shopping mall photo of her with the Easter Bunny.

There were six journals in all, one for each year of Liz's life until their deaths. The journals were filled with photographs, tickets to vintage seminars and food fairs, plane tickets to Sonoma and more menus and wine lists.

But in the later journals, her father had begun what appeared to be stream-of-consciousness entries about his dreams and plans. He used the journals to put down thoughts he must have intended for her to see one day.

In the fourth notebook, her father went into great detail describing how he'd met Kim at a party at UC Davis. Kim had been a California surfer girl, blonde and tan and in love with beaches. Her wealthy parents had wanted her to become a lawyer. Kim wanted to live in France and be a vintner. She broke from her parents and worked her way through college, where she met Matt and fell in love. From that first party, they were inseparable. Her father had been blind to any other woman on campus.

Liz couldn't remember hearing her father expound upon his love for her mother, though he was always openly affectionate, and reading these tender and private words filled her with a longing to talk to him again. He was more than effusive with his praise for Kim and her accomplishments.

Most of all, Liz's mother had filled Matt's heart and soul with life.

Kim is like the air to me. I never knew I could be so happy just watching another person smile. Her laughter is loud and instanta-

neous, and though some people would be put off by it, it lights the day for me. She's the one person I know who has learned to live in the present. She lives for the moment. She never wonders if she should hold me or kiss me— she just does it. She must tell me she loves me a dozen times a day. I've always lived for the future. I'm better about that now, but when I was younger, I was always thinking "...after I graduate high school." Or "after college, I'll expand the vineyard. I'll make my dad smile tomorrow." My dad lives in the past, when my mother was alive. Kim has been good for him, too.

Matt's writings about her mother opened a door buried deep inside Liz. For the first time, she realized her life was lacking. She'd never felt love or longing for anyone in a ro-mantic sense. She missed her parents and loved her grandfather very much. When her parents left on that last trip to Sonoma, her father had picked her up, looked into her eyes and said, "You take care of your grandfather, Lizzie. He's your responsibility while we're gone."

"I will, Daddy," she'd replied. "I promise."

Liz felt as if those words had been burned into her psyche for eternity. *Take care of your grandfather*. She'd been doing that for over twenty years. He was all she had.

She was all he had.

This whole time, Liz had accepted that her life was just as it should be.

But now, she felt an emptiness she hadn't known was there.

Was she missing something important? Lots of people were single. And didn't more than half of all marriages end in divorce? So what was the point?

Her parents had true love and purpose. Was that why the universe had taken them so young? Had they experienced it all, leaving no more lessons to learn?

Like a thunderbolt hitting her, Liz realized she was terrified that if she let love into her life, death would soon follow. If she opened her heart completely, she would be devastated. Just as she'd been devastated as a child. She'd lost her world back then. And no matter what consequences one faced in life, death was irreversible.

Liz felt a throbbing from her heart deep into her soul. For so long, she'd covered up that aching, yawning hole with the love she'd given her grandfather and the love she'd received from him.

But the rhythm her parents had shared, as if

they were two artists painting the same landscape, seemed impossible to Liz. If she hadn't read her father's words, she wouldn't have believed in that kind of love at all.

She wondered if Sam knew about these journals.

Just then, she heard the dinner bell Maria rang to call them all in from the barns and fields. Liz picked up the stack of notebooks so she could continue reading them later in her bedroom, and a single snapshot fell out.

It was a picture of her mother wearing a white sundress. With her long blond hair falling straight down her back, she looked more beautiful than Liz remembered. The shot had been taken at a party of some sort. There were tiki torches and huge bouquets in the background.

The dress was gorgeous, with a handkerchief hem and a glittering belt around the waist. Her mother looked ethereal.

I wonder...

Liz rushed to her mother's closet. They had never cleaned out any of Matt's or Kim's clothes. Everything remained just as it had been twenty years before.

Liz shoved the T-shirts and work jeans aside, going farther down the steel rod to the Sunday dresses, velvet pants and jeweled sweaters her mother once wore.

Finally she saw a clear plastic garment bag that held the pretty summer dress from the photograph. Even in the dim closet light, the rhinestones around the square neckline, up the thin spaghetti straps and along the fanciful hem danced and sparkled. Slowly, Liz pulled the dress out of the closet. Her breath caught between her ribs. Chills ran from the roots of her hair onto her shoulder blades. "It's really here."

She whisked the dress off the hanger and held it up to her body. She and her mother were the same height. Same size. It was almost as if she could touch her. "Mom, thank you," Liz cried.

Liz believed her parents were guiding her by helping her find this lovely dress. She could be charming if she wanted. She'd learned that much about herself in France. Once she freed her mind from business and worries about her vines, she relaxed. And when Liz relaxed, she smiled more. She paid more attention to other people.

At that moment, she realized there was a significant difference between her and Gabe. When she was charming, it was because she was naturally curious about others. She empathized with them, making an effort to feel their joy and their pain.

Gabe's charm was fueled by aggression. He wanted something.

Liz needed a plan of action to deal with the Barzonni family. Not just Gabe, though he seemed like the place to start. He was a thief and a charmer. That much she knew. She would uncover his motivations soon enough. Liz walked over to a full-length mirror on the bathroom door. Holding the dress up and fanning out the skirt, she gazed at her reflection. Maddie's engagement party was not just any event. It would be an espionage mission. She needed to pull out every weapon in her arsenal to protect her family's land and her livelihood.

The Crenshaw baton had been passed to her. Her grandfather and their employees were counting on her. Finding this dress had been her confirmation she would triumph.

When Liz was a little girl, her mother had always told her she had a special guardian angel looking out for her. As Liz held the dress in her hands, she realized that angel was her mother.

Stinging with the pain of loss, Liz buried her face in the dress and let her tears flow.

CHAPTER EIGHT

THE BARZONNI VILLA sprawled across a low-lying hill south of Indian Lake. It was surrounded by over a thousand acres of farmland that produced exemplary tomatoes, corn, green beans, soybeans and a laundry list of other vegetables.

A brick drive, supposedly hand-laid by Angelo himself before the villa was even built, meandered up to the three-story Italian stucco house. Liz had heard it was an exact replica of a Sicilian manor Angelo had admired back in Italy. Though the sun had not yet set, the interior of the house was ablaze with lights. A stream of cars crept up the drive. Liz recognized several teenagers from Indian Lake who'd been hired for the evening as valets.

The front gardens were filled with an ocean of colorful impatiens, geraniums, black-eyed Susans and daylilies. Thousands of white crystal lights were strung through the limbs of the river birch and maple trees.

Liz was in awe. If this was a summer party, what did they do for Christmas?

She pulled her truck up to the front of the house and a dark-haired young man jogged up to her and opened the door. "Welcome to Villa Barzonni," he said.

"Thanks," she replied and slid out of the truck. She grabbed her pink sequin-and-satin clutch and smiled. "It sticks a bit moving into first gear. Just give it more clutch."

"Clutch?" He looked at her, terrified.

"Do you want me to park it?" she asked quietly so that no one else would hear.

"No." He swallowed hard. "It's been a while."

"Don't worry. You can't strip her. She's had rougher drivers than you."

"Okay," he said and hopped in.

Liz shook her head, chuckled to herself and gazed up at the house. It was imposing, and she felt intimidated. Lifting her chin and straightening her shoulders, she walked toward the front door.

"Liz? Is that you?" she heard behind her.

Liz exhaled and spun around. "Sarah! And Luke! How great to see you."

Luke leaned over and kissed Liz on the cheek. "Wow, Liz. You look spectacular. I

mean, I thought you were lovely as a bridesmaid, but this…"

Liz blushed six shades of crimson. Luke had
seen her dozens of times during all of his and
Sarah's wedding parties and dinners, so if she
could knock his socks off, Gabe was going to
be toast.

"Luke's right. You're absolutely stunning,"
Sarah chimed in.

"This dress was my mother's. I just found it."

Sarah nodded appreciatively. "Listen, girl.
Don't lose that dress again. In fact, I'd have
four more made in different colors. Can you
wear that in the tasting room?"

"Yeah, I bet you'd increase sales a thousand-
fold," Luke agreed.

"I'll take that under advisement."

Luke offered his left arm to Liz and his right
arm to Sarah. "Ladies, shall we?"

Liz grinned happily and slipped her arm into
Luke's. "Let's do it."

They stepped inside and followed a Persian
rug—covered hallway that led straight through
the house to a set of French doors, which
opened onto the back veranda.

Liz dropped her jaw. "Oh my…"

"You said it," Sarah gushed.

The Tom and Jason Big Band, dressed in

tuxedos, accompanied Dorothy Miles as she crooned the lyrics to a love song from the sixties.

A blue light illuminated the pool. A yellow-and-white-striped tent that matched the fabric on the wide lounge chairs had been erected at the south end of the terrace. Its interior was strung with another thousand Italian crystal lights in a mock ceiling drape that looked like a galaxy of stars. At the center of each large round table was a vase filled with pink and yellow roses, white orchids and trailing ivy.

Servers carried trays with glasses of wine and champagne among the throng of guests.

"Who are all these people?" Liz asked. There had to be at least two hundred in the crowd.

"I barely know any of them, except Nate and your girlfriends," Luke said, glancing around.

Liz lifted her arm and waved. "Oh, I see Mrs. Beabots with Maddie."

As they started to head toward their friends, Liz heard her name.

"Liz?" Gabe's voice rolled down her back like soft velvet. It was soothing, and that made it most unnerving.

Gathering wits at a time like this took staggering effort, Liz realized, as she tried to turn to face him. For some reason, her white linen espadrilles were caught between two veranda bricks. She wondered if Angelo had hand-laid them as well, so as to trip up his enemies when he needed them on their knees.

Gabe approached her.

His blue eyes were filled with appreciation as he looked at her, and the sides of his mouth crooked up into a pleased smile. He remained silent for a long moment, then blinked slowly as if trying to get his bearings. He swallowed hard. "You…you're…"

Mission accomplished, Liz thought. *Take that, Gabriel Barzonni.*

"You're dazzling," he finally said.

He was dressed in black tuxedo pants and a white linen dinner jacket, his tuxedo shirt open at the throat. His black hair glistened in the pink-and-lavender sunset, and she noticed his deep tan. His blue eyes bored into her with a killer gaze that turned her bones to gelatin.

Who's toast now?

Liz's quick mind filled with smart quips that would definitely have put her enemy in his place, but she chose the high road and decided to stick to her plan.

"So are you," she volleyed back.

This time his smile almost seemed genuine.

This wasn't fair. She'd just arrived and already she was having difficulty keeping her focus.

"Everyone is talking about the wine," he said, holding up a glass of red. "Maddie did a great job in choosing them. I bet you helped."

"I did."

He lowered his head and moved closer in order to whisper. "I never thought she'd pull it off. Mom had staunchly insisted on her favorite Italian wines—and some of my favorites, too, I might add. She and I think along the same lines on a lot of things. I just didn't believe Maddie would get her way with Mom so soon."

"Really?" Liz asked. "Maddie told me they haven't disagreed on a thing so far."

Surprise filled Gabe's face. "No kidding? Maybe Maddie has the magic touch. Good for her."

A waiter came by with grilled shrimp on top of tiny squares of puff pastry. Gabe reached over and took one of the hors d'oeuvres. "You have to try this," he said, holding it out to her. "They're my favorite."

Liz didn't move. He thrust it toward her, his arm outstretched.

If this was a test of wills, he was not about to back down. Liz knew it would be easier to give in to the small gestures he apparently demanded. She'd lie in wait for later.

When she finally took the proffered shrimp, his fingers grazed hers and sent a zing through her entire body. Liz didn't know why she was reacting to him so strongly. It made no sense. She was here to take him down.

She chewed the shrimp, and then tried her very own chardonnay, which was chilled to perfection. "It's good," she said. "Very good."

"My mom makes the best food." He grinned and took another sip of wine, never pulling his eyes off her.

"Your mother made these?"

"She made all the hors d'oeuvres."

"For all these people?" Liz asked incredulously.

"Yes. Oh, she's got a couple young girls she's teaching to be sous chefs, but pretty much, Gina did it all. She made all the food for the dinner, as well. All Nate's favorites, by the way. She hired a company to put up the lights in the trees, but she planted the gardens and urns. She arranged all the flowers for the tables, too."

"She did not."

He nodded. "I know. Intimidating, isn't it? She does just about everything. It's the Italian way, she says."

Liz was taken aback. She would have guessed Gina lived like a queen, doling out projects and commands. Gabe was telling her that Gina worked just as hard as everyone else on their farm. Or harder. Clearly, she had a talent for event planning. No wonder she and Maddie had bonded so quickly.

Liz's picture of the Barzonni family had begun to morph.

A brunette woman in a plunging, shockingly pink dress and excruciatingly high-heeled shoes brushed by them. She slowed long enough to trail her fingertips across Gabe's wide shoulders. "Hi, Gabe," she purred. "Nice party."

"Syd. Great to see you," he said, before turning back to Liz.

Syd appeared put off by Gabe's lack of attention. "Thanks for inviting me," she said and teetered away.

Gabe inclined his head in Syd's direction. "She's one of the managers at the canning company my dad contracts."

"I wasn't aware Maddie knew those people."

"She doesn't." Gabe chuckled. "I doubt Nate does, either. My father believes the first wedding in the family is a PR event for his business, not a celebration of love. So to avoid having all these people at the wedding, my mother suggested they invite them to the engagement party instead."

"Ah, that's where all these people came from," Liz said.

"Yeah. Appeasement."

"I'm liking your mother more all the time."

Gabe sipped his wine and peered at Liz over the rim. His eyes didn't waver.

"What?" she asked, feeling self-conscious.

"I have to admit I didn't think anything could be more arresting than you in those cut-offs holding a gun to my face, but this..." He waved his hand to indicate her dress.

"It was my mother's," Liz blurted, wondering why she'd revealed something so intimate.

"You look sad. Do you miss her?"

"You know about my mother?" Liz's eyebrow crooked in surprise.

"Yes. And your father. Mom told us about it when they died. Car crash, wasn't it?"

"Yes," she breathed, surprised that Gina would tell her sons such a sorrowful story. None of the Barzonni brothers would have been that much older than she was at the time, and to a kid, her tragedy would have been frightening. Perhaps the boys had heard about it on the news or read it in the newspaper first.

Liz herself had heard the radio reports as she and her grandfather had driven home from the funeral. Maybe the boys learned about it at school and asked their mom for more details. Few children lost both parents at once. Whatever had happened, apparently her story had impacted Gabe.

"We knew you were raised by your grandfather," he continued. "How old were you?"

"Six. Nearly seven." She looked down at her glass. "Sometimes it seems like it happened just a few weeks ago. Other times, I can hardly remember their faces."

"Was your mother as beautiful as you are?" he asked in that same velvet tone.

"More. She was more beautiful."

"I find that very hard to believe," he said. Liz didn't meet his eyes. He took the glass from her hand and placed it next to a nearby Roman urn. "I've made you sad, and this is supposed to be fun. Come on," he said, taking her hand and pulling her along.

"Where are we going?"

"To dance. Unless you'd rather go down to the stable and look at the horses."

Liz nodded. "That's right. I've heard stories about your father's Thoroughbreds. He still races them, right?"

"Actually, Rafe races them all now. My dad is slowing down. Usually when we have a party like this, the guests wind up with my dad down at the stable. He and Rafe love to show off their new prizewinners."

"Boy, Louisa would love that."

"Who is Louisa?"

"My *chef de cave*. She wants a horse so I'll quit riding my ATV between the vines. She says it disturbs them. At least that's what I think she says. Most of what she says is in French."

"You have a *chef de cave*?"

"I do. She was in the tasting room the day you came to the vineyard…"

When you stole from me, she wanted to say, but she didn't. This was a night for discretion and fact-gathering. Not for finger-pointing, which would only put her opponent on the defensive.

Gabe smiled his most charming smile, the one Liz already knew not to trust. She felt a warning bristle creep up her back.

"Liz, you are a woman of a hundred surprises."

"Okay, so here's another surprise for you, Gabe," she said. "I don't dance very well."

"Ah, nothing to it. Just hold on to me. I'll be your guide. I learned from the best."

"Who would that be?"

"My mother. She taught all of us boys to dance."

"You're right. She does do everything."

Gabe pulled Liz close enough that she could feel his heartbeat beneath his jacket and smell the fresh scent of lime and fabric softener. But there was something else, something spicy and masculine she couldn't put her finger on. All she knew was that no man had ever made her feel giddy and light-headed simply by being close to her. Liz had put her life into the vineyard and taking care of her grandfather. She'd certainly never danced with a handsome man, under the stars, to a live orchestra.

Gabe's arms were strong as he moved to the rhythm of the Italian love song. He talked about his mother, but Liz didn't quite catch every word he said. She knew she should pay closer attention, that whatever he told her might serve a purpose in her future dealings with him. The problem was she felt oddly safe in his arms, as if he were the kind of man a woman could surrender all her troubles to. Liz had never bargained for her emotions to turn against her.

Then the thought struck her. Gabe must be romancing her deliberately.

Why?

The music ended, but Gabe didn't release her. "You weren't so bad." He chuckled. "In fact, I could dance all night with you."

"Why?" Liz uttered her favorite word without thinking.

Peering at her with narrowed eyes, he dropped his hands to his sides. "Because I like dancing with the prettiest girl at the party."

She matched his piercing gaze. "I'm curious, Gabe. Why are you flattering me so much?"

"I didn't know I was. Trust me. It's not flattery."

Liz *didn't* trust him. He answered one compliment with another. There was only one way to ferret out the truth from a scoundrel, and that was a surprise attack.

"Gabe, did you just buy the Mattuchi farm?"

"I…"

Maddie and Nate came rushing up to Liz and Gabe. "There you are, Liz! Sarah told me you were here, but I hadn't seen you." Maddie hugged Liz, then stepped back to take in her outfit. "Luke was right. You look gorgeous!"

Liz shook her head. "Maddie, you've seen me nearly every day this week. Surely…"

Gabe interrupted. "I've been trying to tell her that all night. Nate, help me out here. Doesn't Liz look amazing?"

Nate hadn't taken his eyes off Maddie in her teal chiffon cocktail dress. "Next to my fiancée, truly amazing."

Maddie grinned. "Oh, Nate. How diplomatic. I love you." She kissed him soundly.

Just then, Gina stood near the orchestra and announced that dinner was about to be served. She asked all the guests to move to the dining tent.

"That's our cue," Maddie said. "You guys sit with us at the head table. Gabe, you're next to Nate, and Liz is next to you."

"Wonderful," Gabe said, holding his arm out to Liz. "Shall we?"

Nate extended his arm to Maddie, who pulled him close as they walked. When they'd been in high school, people in town had commented on how Nate and Maddie could walk down the street arm in arm and appear to be one person, they were so close. So in sync.

Liz had never understood that closeness. She wondered what it would be like to get a thrill just from being next to someone.

On their way to the tent, Liz stopped to give Mrs. Beabots a hug.

"You look like a princess," Mrs. Beabots told her, glancing at Gabe. "He's a charming prince, that one," Mrs. Beabots whispered in Liz's ear. Then she leaned toward Gabe. "Come give me a hug, Gabriel Barzonni, and don't pretend I haven't known you since the day you were born."

"How are you, Mrs. B?" Gabe hugged her and kissed her cheek.

"Sharp as a brand-new tack, and don't forget it. Now," she said, shaking her finger, "I see how you look at my little Liz. Just remember how protective I am of all my girls. She's precious cargo."

"I wasn't doing a thing," he said defensively.

"Is that what you call it?" Mrs. Beabots teased. Then she smiled. "Have a good time, my dear. And, Liz, tell your grandfather to give me a call."

"I will," Liz assured her with a little wave.

Gabe held out the chair for Liz. The members of the wedding party sat in chairs draped with garlands of ivy, yellow roses and white satin ribbons.

A waiter came and placed poached salmon with hot dill and hazelnut sauce in front of each of them. Liz looked at Gabe. "Gina made this, too?"

"The whole family loves her salmon," Gabe said.

A tapping of silver against crystal ended the many conversations as Angelo stood and raised his glass. "A toast to my son Nathaniel and to his lovely bride, Maddie. May your lives be blessed with abundance. *Bon appetit.*"

"To Nate and Maddie," the crowd shouted in unison.

Gabe did not toast. His face had gone dark, and he remained silent.

Though Liz knew she shouldn't reveal any of her growing empathy toward him, since he had avoided the one question she'd come here to pose to him—she told herself it was just curiosity that spurred her to ask, "Something wrong?"

His eyes blazed a bitter, angry blue, and she was certain they could cut through ice. "Not much of a toast, was it?" he grumbled. "Yes, Liz. I bought the Mattuchi vineyard. I didn't buy their entire farm."

"But why?"

He lowered his voice and took on a purposeful tone. "Why do you think? I intend to go into the wine business."

"And you just happen to want to do that next to my vineyard," she retorted.

"Exactly," he said harshly, his eyes darting to his father. He picked at his salmon.

"So when I found you on my land, you really did want to steal my dirt. Did you already know you were going to buy from them?"

"Yep."

"And what? You just needed validation?"

"Yep." He pushed his chair back slightly so he could look at her face fully. "That's really good wine you make, Liz. A few more years, and it'll start being written up in the wine magazines. Maybe win some prizes."

"I should hope so," she replied. "That's the goal, anyway."

"Yeah," he said, his eyes sliding back toward his father. "That's the goal."

Liz sensed an undercurrent of suspicion and even jealousy in Gabe, but then, she had to admit she was the one who had come to this party with ulterior motives. Perhaps she was filtering everything through her earlier mindset. She had wanted to delve deeper into his reasons for buying the Mattuchi land, but maybe it was just as he'd said. He wanted to grow some grapes. She knew the Barzonni land was ill-suited for a vineyard. It was a gold mine for its current crops, but that was all. For wine, the vines needed Lake Michigan. Just as her father had told her.

"Are you okay?" Liz asked.

"Sure," he said, patting her arm. "Do you like the salmon?"

"I do. But you didn't like the toast."

"You'd think he would mention the word *love*, wouldn't you? It is an engagement party after all."

"Maybe he was nervous or not used to giving speeches," she offered.

"I don't make excuses for him. You don't have to, either," Gabe grunted. Then just as suddenly as the dark mood had descended, Gabe's eyes brightened and he smiled his Mr. Charming smile at her. "Promise me one more dance before you go tonight?"

"Okay."

Gabe appeared to relax once he had her answer.

Liz couldn't help but wonder exactly how practiced Gabe's smile was. What was he hiding? And why was his tone so often underscored by bitterness and anger?

Glancing around at the incredible beauty Gina had created for this party, Liz felt as if she were living in a fairy tale. But she wondered if, like in some fairy tales, there was something wicked hiding behind a magic curtain.

CHAPTER NINE

IT WAS AFTER midnight when Liz drove up to her farmhouse and found all the lights still on. It had been a long time since Liz had been out late enough that her grandfather would have felt the need to wait up for her.

"Grandpa?" she called as she set her evening bag and truck keys on a dark walnut table in the foyer.

"In the living room," he called.

She could hear the rustle of newspapers as she entered the room. He always complained he never had time to read the daily news. Judging by the stack of papers at his feet, he'd been reading all night. "You didn't have to wait up," she said, bending down to kiss his cheek and pat his shoulder.

"Sure I did," he replied. "I want to know what happened. And you know I'm not talking about the food they served." He shot her a purposeful look.

"You want to know about Gabe."

"Yes. And what he's up to."

She untied her espadrilles and took them off. Then she tucked her feet under her skirt as she sat down on a sofa across from him. "He bought the Mattuchi vineyard, just as we'd heard. He told me he plans to go into the wine business."

Sam tilted his head back and closed his eyes. "We're doomed."

Liz pursed her lips into the pout she'd practiced since she was a child, meant to display her disdain. "We are not. He's a novice. He doesn't know a thing about wine. I think he's playing."

"Playing?"

"Sure. Just like his brother Rafe, who plays with racehorses. This is Gabe's...folly, I'm going to call it. I, for one, intend to beat him at his own game."

Sam shook his head. "You don't understand. No matter what the game, they can play for higher stakes than we can. They can stay at the table all night long. They have so much money, Liz, that I..."

She clamped her hand over his forearm to arrest his protests. "I'm betting he doesn't get off the ground. Oh, let him buy some equipment and pretend he's in the wine business. This life takes all your heart and soul—"

"And then some."

"It certainly does, Grandpa. We know that. Dad knew that. And that's how we'll outlast him. He can spend some money, and when his new toy loses its shine, he'll toss it aside and go on to something else."

"How can you be so sure?"

"I watched him at the party." She shrugged. "He impresses me as the noncommittal type."

"How's that?"

"Call it female intuition. There were a lot of women there who stole his eye too many times. Maddie and Sarah told me he's never had a serious girlfriend in his life. If he's that way with relationships, he'll be that way with this business."

Sam rubbed his chin, but he remained silent.

"What are you thinking, Grandpa?"

Sam took a deep breath. "Not sure. I don't know anything about him except that he's Angelo's son. And that bit of knowledge bothers me. Angelo has never made a move that wasn't successful. He's wily, smart and focused, and he never misses a trick. I've heard other farmers say Angelo cheated them out of their farms in the old days when he was buying up land.

That's how he came to own so many acres south of town. He bought out his neighbors."

"How could he cheat them?"

"Technically, he couldn't. They lost their land because Angelo won all the canning contracts. Their crops weren't as good as his, so they weren't able to sell their crops, and they went bankrupt. Once they were on their knees, Angelo moved in for the kill."

Liz's eyes grew round. "Do you think that's what's happening to Mr. Mattuchi?"

"I don't know. I haven't gotten wind of it. If so, he's being very quiet about it. But it makes sense to me that Gabriel learned his father's tricks. Once Gabe gets a foothold in the wine market over there and takes a few of our vendors from us, we start to lose customers. Then when we're desperate, he tries to buy our vineyard from us."

Liz bolted to her feet. "Well, we're never selling. Ever! This has been Crenshaw land since you were a young man. Despite this situation with the taxes, we'll figure it out. We'll make more wine. But we will never leave this land, no matter who tries to take it from us!" She pounded her fist into her palm.

"God love you, Lizzie." Sam rose from his recliner and put his arms around her. "I agree wholeheartedly. I wish your daddy could see you now. Matthew would be so proud of you."

She smiled at him. "Thanks for that, Grandpa. I wish he were here to give me advice."

"I know exactly what he'd say," Sam replied.

"What's that?"

"Take no prisoners." Sam leaned over and kissed Liz's cheek before climbing the stairs. "Good night, sweetheart. Sleep well. We have a busy day tomorrow. Should be a lot of tourists."

"Good night, Grandpa."

Liz studied the rhinestones on the hem of her skirt as they gleamed in the lamplight. Was it only an hour ago she was dancing in Gabe's arms? She'd felt so comfortable, she could have danced with him all night and then some. The hours after supper had passed with lightning speed. She hadn't wanted the party to end.

She had sensed his power and confidence, yet she'd gotten a dozen conflicting impressions, as well. There was no question he loved and respected his mother, but when the conversation had turned to his father, he had immediately grown tense. Or worse, clammed up and remained silent. Was he angry with Angelo? Why?

What if the stories her grandfather had told her about Angelo were true? Allegedly he had taken advantage of his neighbors back in the sixties when he'd first come to Indian Lake. Was he ruthless? And had he taught Gabe to be just like him?

Liz rubbed her forehead, hoping to swipe away the questions that continued to flog her when it came to Gabe. It would be easier to define him if she weren't attracted to him. It took a lot of courage to admit to this very serious flaw in her equations.

She was attracted to Gabe.

But now that she was aware there was a problem, she could fight it.

How easily she'd seen him as the enemy before the party. She'd been prepared to charm him. She was supposed to wrangle information out of him. Luckily, she'd managed to find out that he did intend to go into the wine business. He was going to be her competition.

That alone should have made her despise him on the spot.

But it didn't.

She'd been intrigued, if anything. It would take several years for him to get his vines up and growing, to let the wine ferment, to age the bottles and finally to get the wine to market. And that was just the beginning. Success in the business was so complex, so dependent on a thousand nuances of weather, skill and knowledge, and on educated associates like enologists and agronomists, that Liz believed Gabe would be disheartened within the first year.

Tenacity. Passion. That's what a vintner had to have.

Liz's passion was practically inbred. But what of Gabe's?

Was he becoming a vintner on a whim? Did he have any idea what such a life would be like? Was this his bid to build something of his own, or was he simply bored with tomatoes?

Liz thought of even more questions she should have asked Gabe but had not. At the time, she'd been too mesmerized by him to think.

Some spy she'd turned out to be. It was a good thing she'd never applied for a government job. She wouldn't have lasted fifteen seconds. But then, she'd never reacted to a man the way she had to Gabe. It wasn't his tuxedo or the music or the moonlight, either. She'd felt the same magnetism when she'd aimed her gun at him.

Reason told her it was just chemistry, like the fermentation that took place in her tanks and the aging that occurred in her oak barrels. Chemistry was not the same as trust or respect.

Gabe had done nothing to win either from her. In fact, his actions had indicated the opposite. The problem, Liz finally realized, was not with Gabe at all. The problem was with her.

She had to put these feelings into perspective, she thought as she rose and picked up her shoes. They served no purpose. They wouldn't help preserve her vineyard. The party had been a one-off. After all, how many out-of-this-world parties like that was she going to attend in her life?

Liz grabbed her evening bag and crossed to the staircase. She placed her hand on the newel and looked up to the stained glass window at the top of the stairs. It showed a vineyard with the sun shining down on the grapes. Sam had told her that the history of winemaking was as old as man. That was probably true. Sumerians, Assyrians and Babylonians had made wine eight thousand years ago. Wine was part of the civilized world. Liz liked that she was carrying on an ancient art. She took a great deal of pride in that. Just like this old house and the land they owned. There was history here. Family. A sense of tradition. She liked all that, as well.

On her way to her room, she passed her

grandfather's closed door. She could hear him snoring quietly.

She continued down the hall and opened her door, picking up the damp towel she'd used to dry her hair and tossing it in her white wicker hamper.

She pulled her phone out of her purse and saw there was a text from a number she didn't recognize.

Gorgeous. I had a wonderful time tonight. Let me know that you got home all right. GB.

What?

Why would Gabe care about her safety? He barely knew her. She'd never had a man ask about her trip home before. Because Liz was a private person, her first reaction was suspicion. But oddly, she didn't feel as if her privacy had been invaded. She didn't feel violated. In fact, she felt a strange sense of calm and reassurance. There wasn't the first trace of alarm. Instead, she liked it.

She felt protected, as she had when she used to tuck her hand into her father's and he would gently squeeze it to let her know he was there. Caring. Shielding her from harm. She'd always felt safe when he was around. And tonight, she'd felt safe in Gabe's arms. She hadn't expected that.

He had been a surprise to her. And a conundrum.

A man like Gabe had reasons for his actions. She didn't believe for a minute any of his words were uncalculated.

She stared at the screen and her back stiffened defensively. The animosity and suspicion she'd tamped down minutes before rose again. She tapped out a message.

How did you get my number?

His reply was nearly instantaneous.

I confess. I told Maddie I needed your number so I could ask you about those fantastic wines you selected.

"Sneaky!" she grumbled aloud. Then she wrote another message.

You could have just asked me.

She stared at the phone. The reply, this time, was not immediate. Good. Maybe he'd think twice about who he was dealing—

Can you blame me for feeling a bit intimidated? You're the most beautiful woman I've ever seen, Liz. I just thought the night ended too soon. I could have gone for one more dance.

Liz chewed her bottom lip, wondering if answering him was a wise move. She chose to be logical.

The orchestra left. Remember?

Who needs music?

He was doing it again. Sucking her in. She could so easily allow herself to fall into his romantic trap. Liz had managed all these years on her own without the snarls and heartbreak of romance. She intended to maintain the status quo. She had to stop Gabe. Now.

Good night, Gabe.

Good night, Liz.

Liz exhaled and collapsed onto her bed. She wondered if she would get any sleep at all. She had too many visions of Gabe in her mind.

CHAPTER TEN

GABE SLID HIS FINGER across the screen of his smartphone and felt a smile warm his face. The cleanup crew was folding the rented chairs and the orchestra breakdown team had just carted away the last of the sound equipment. He leaned his head back and looked up at the glittering sea of stars overhead. "Stellar night," he mused and crossed his hands behind his head.

Gabe was baffled at how quickly and how often thoughts of Liz invaded his head. Before the party, he'd been curious about her, especially because he was interested in her land. He'd had several opportunities tonight to ask her bluntly if she would consider selling. But he hadn't.

He'd held back.

After dancing with her and confessing the truth about the Mattuchi deal, which he hadn't even shared with his parents—a first for him, since he always blurted his secrets to his mother—Gabe had to admit he was enchanted with Liz.

Definitely enchanted. At the very least.

He'd noticed Liz's spine stiffen when he declared his plans to build a proper vineyard on the property. She obviously regarded him as competition, and he knew he could be slitting his own throat by revealing why he'd wanted to test her soil. She was smart. He hadn't fooled her for a minute. Still, he was helping the Mattuchis. No one else in Indian Lake would have agreed to such a preposterous real estate deal. Anyone with any business acumen would have forced Mario to sell the entire farm, not just a piece of it, and then booted the family off the land.

Gabe wasn't sure how effective he'd been in turning Liz's opinion of him around, but he'd made a dent in her very apparent armor. He supposed that telling her he was going into the wine business might have reinforced her negative opinion of him, but it was his bet that Liz was the kind of person who cut her teeth on challenges. He liked that about her.

"She's fearless."

"What was that?" Angelo said as he sat down in a chair next to his eldest son. "Who is fearless?"

Gabe's eyes narrowed. "I thought you'd gone to bed."

"No. Your mother is asleep." Angelo watched the workers tie up trash bags. "This is my favorite part of a party. When it's over."

"I thought you liked Mother's parties."

"I indulge her," Angelo replied in the patronizing tone Gabe had grown to despise.

"She worked very hard. I think everyone, especially Nate and Maddie, appreciated it."

Angelo shrugged and undid his bow tie. "You didn't answer my question."

Gabe paused, mulling over the wisdom of telling his father about his personal life. For years, Gabe had struggled to keep his friends, decisions and goals to himself. His father's controlling nature had been intimidating when he was younger, but these days Gabe simply believed that what he did in his own life was none of his father's concern. Still, since Liz was one of the bridesmaids in Nate's wedding, his father would find out about her sooner or later.

"Her name is Liz."

"Is she from around here?"

"Yes. She and her grandfather own the vineyard north of town."

"Crenshaw?"

Gabe swore his father's intake of breath was so sharp it could have cut crystal. "Yeah. Sam Crenshaw. You know him?"

"I do," Angelo replied, a steel edge to his voice.

Gabe sat up straight. "How do you know him?"

"I just do. And you are not to have anything to do with his granddaughter. Do you understand me?"

"Are you giving me an order?" Gabe asked disbelievingly.

"Precisely," Angelo said firmly. "I'm the head of this household, and I forbid you to see her."

Gabe shook his head. "Who I see is my personal business. There's no good reason—"

"I have lots of reasons." Angelo was nearly fuming. "I've known Sam Crenshaw since I moved here. He is vermin, I tell you! When I was first establishing this farm he tried to malign me."

"Sam? I find that hard to believe," Gabe said.

"He told lies about me all over town. He said I was cheating the farmers and stealing their land. Lies!" Angelo spat. "I forbade your mother to have anything to do with him or his family."

"Mother?"

Angelo cut the air with his palm. "He was very angry after his wife died. Some people said he was insane. He was a recluse, they said. In the beginning, I didn't care because I was too busy building my own empire. Sam lost several crops. Money got tight. Then I heard the rumors about me. I knew he had started them."

"But why? It makes no sense. Did you do anything to him?"

"It was jealousy. I was becoming rich. He was poor. The bank turned him down for a loan. Harold Kramer told me that himself at the Feed Store."

"Who's Harold Kramer?"

"He was the bank president. He also told me Sam had asked him if he'd heard the stories about me cheating my neighbors."

Gabe looked at his father. "But Harold didn't say Sam had started the gossip."

Angelo rammed his fist on the chair arm. "Nitpicker! It was Sam, I tell you. Back then, I drove out to Sam's vineyard and had it out with him. I warned him I would destroy him if he ever spoke to Gina or you boys ever. A person that evil could contaminate a young mind permanently. I had to protect my family."

"You had a showdown with Sam Crenshaw?"

"Yes." Angelo exhaled forcefully.

"And you never resolved it?"

"There is no resolution when you're dealing with the devil." Angelo shot to his feet and pointed his finger at Gabe. "And his granddaughter is never to set foot on my land again. Do you understand?"

If Angelo's story had been about another family, Gabe would have thought it bizarre, but considering how tyrannical his father was, he believed it. Or at least portions of it. Intuition told him something was missing in his father's version. The truth lay beneath layers of anger and a near-pathological need for control. Angelo was judgmental, and he held grudges for decades. "Like I said, she's a bridesmaid and I'm a groomsman for Nate's wedding."

"Make sure that's all it is."

Gabe pressed further. "What are you talking about?"

"I watched you dancing with her. I saw the way she looked at you and you looked at her." He tapped his temple. "I know the look. It was the look of love."

"Love?" Gabe chortled. He admired Liz, respected her expertise, but he wasn't in love with anyone. The suggestion was ridiculous.

"Not her, Gabriel. Any woman but her."

Angelo tromped away, making certain he had the last word. As he always did.

CHAPTER ELEVEN

LIZ TOOK THE early-morning South Shore to Chicago and got off near Randolph Street station. Though it was a distance, Liz preferred to walk to the Merchandise Mart. It was a rare treat for her to leave Indian Lake and get to the city. Her life was not easy—her vines and vintages were demanding. They left no time for frivolity or vacations. This day in the city was something she'd had planned for months, ever since she'd heard about the symposium of international wine editors and tasters. Liz walked up Michigan Avenue to Wacker Drive and then headed west. It was a perfect summer Saturday morning in the city as she crossed the Chicago River on the Wells Street Bridge and looked down at the tourist boats as they chugged through the water. The city seemed to glisten in the sun, refracting light from polished steel and newly washed skyscraper windows. A day like this, with profusions of summer flowers billowing from streetside urns, planters and window boxes, was enough to make anyone believe they had entered dreamland.

Liz pulled the ticket and brochure out of her slouchy leather purse and checked the address of the meeting room.

The ticket had been expensive, and though Liz had attended only one of these lectures in the past, her recollection was that the audience had been mostly composed of winemakers. This lecture was particularly interesting to Liz because in the past year, small harvests in western Europe, Australia and South America had caused the price of wines to rise substantially. There was no question in Liz's mind that across the globe, vintners were improving the quality of their products. Sheer volume was no longer the objective. It was excellence. And that was precisely what Liz aspired to. She didn't care if her vineyard ever logged more than fifteen thousand cases in a given year, which would be a real stretch for them, even now. She cared that someday, her pinot noirs, chardonnays and eventually champagnes—and possibly some merlots—would rate ninety points from the experts. A rating of ninety points or more brought in close to a hundred dollars a bottle for wine in France. In California, the price was closer to eighty-five. Illinois was still down at the bottom with states like Washington and Oregon, where vintners could only hope for forty-five to fifty dollars for their finest bottles. But Liz knew better times were ahead of her.

She and her grandfather had not yet released his prize cabernet sauvignons. Sam had sold some to a few wine buffs whom he trusted, but mostly, Sam kept his bottles under lock and key. This season they would sell pinot noirs. This year they'd hold back their chardonnays.

But it was on the fallow land that Liz's greatest dream lived. She intended to create a product as renowned as the incredible Pétrus wines of Bordeaux. If they could create history with their merlot and cabernet grapes on only twenty-eight acres of land, so could she and Sam.

Walking this close to the Chicago River, Liz could feel the summer air turn cool. She noticed ominous storm clouds to the west, barreling toward the city with a vengeance. Liz realized she hadn't checked her weather app in the past several hours, as she normally would have, since she wanted to take as much of a break from the vineyard as possible.

She was only a block away from the Merchandise Mart, with its imposing Art Deco design. The wind swept down the river, rustled leaves and then swooped around the corners and up the sidewalks. If she was lucky, she'd make it to the glorious bronze-and-buff lobby before she got drenched.

Just as she stepped inside, the skies opened up. Shoppers and tourists raced past her into the safety of the lobby.

Liz had to laugh to herself. In her giant French satchel, she had a small folding umbrella. She was prepared.

Liz went to the security guard near the bank of elevators.

"I'm going to the eighteenth floor," she told the dark-haired man, who wore a sour, bored expression. She couldn't help but wonder if he had been hired for his very apparent indifference.

"Last car. Let me see your ticket. That's an exclusive meeting," he said, surveying her summer dress and lime-green linen jacket.

She handed over her ticket and kept smiling at him, hoping to melt his judgmental exterior, but apparently the man had never been the beneficiary of a smile in his life. He continued to frown at her.

She walked away and pressed the elevator button, then rode to the top of the building.

The meeting room was small, with four

dozen chairs set in neat rows. Along the walls were long tables covered in white cotton cloths and sparkling clean red-and-white wineglasses. She saw clusters of corkscrews, aerators and stacks of paper cocktail napkins. There were cases of wine stacked on the floor, and next to them were portable "wine cellars" filled with white wines. *Chilled to a very proper forty-five to fifty-five degrees, no doubt,* Liz thought.

There were a couple dozen men in the room already, most of them wearing business suits or expensive summer golf shirts with expertly cut slacks and Italian shoes. They watched her as she entered. She was the only woman at the symposium so far. Liz put her purse on an aisle chair and stayed standing for a moment, hoping to make eye contact with anyone who looked like a vintner. Finally, giving up, she sat down.

Within a few minutes, two elderly gentlemen and an attractive woman in her early forties walked up to the front of the room with arms full of brochures, papers and a laptop. As if someone had hit a gong, all the men scrambled for a chair. Several more people arrived, and among them were three more women. Liz was relieved that she wasn't the only woman here, though she wasn't sure why that would have bothered her. All these people were potential buyers and customers. For that, she realized, she was very happy.

The lights in the room dimmed slightly. By now, all the chairs were full except for the one directly across the aisle from Liz.

Just as the lead speaker turned on his microphone, the door opened and one more man, drenched to the skin, rushed in. His loafers squished when he walked, as if he'd jumped through mud puddles on his way here. His white linen jacket, sky-blue shirt and twill pants were plastered to his skin.

He swiped his hand through his wet hair and took the last seat. Across from Liz.

He smiled at her.

"Gabe?"

Jabbing his thumb toward the door, he said, "It's pouring out there." He chuckled.

"I can see that," she whispered as the first speaker, a wine expert from New York, began his welcome speech. Of all the people in the world she could meet at this exclusive and not-all-that-well-advertised symposium, here was Gabriel Barzonni. She blinked. He wasn't supposed to be in Chicago while she was here on her mini break.

She'd been fortunate that he hadn't texted or called in the week since she'd dismissed him after the party. She'd told herself she was rid of him, that he'd understood she didn't want anything to do with him. She'd convinced herself Gabe was simply being polite when he'd inquired about her safe arrival home. There was nothing romantic going on between them.

Gabe had been courteous toward her, dancing with her as one of Maddie's bridesmaids. Many groomsmen felt such things were their duty, and she knew better than to read anything more into it than that.

Yet here he was, soaking wet, having braved the summer storm to attend the same lecture as her. Distrust buzzed through her entire body. "What are you doing here?"

He leaned across the aisle and grinned charmingly. "Learning something, I hope," he whispered back. Then he winked at her.

Liz sat up straighter. Now she knew he was up to something. He was being too cute. Why did he do that? Didn't he know she would *never* fall for his magnetism?

And that was another thing. What was wrong with her that she felt so drawn to him? Even now, she couldn't help but try to catch a glimpse of him. He was smiling as the speaker began, completely absorbed.

Perhaps Gabe's interest in winemaking was

as deep-rooted as hers. If so, she was wrong to judge him so harshly. She shouldn't think the worst of him and his motives.

Liz focused on the lecturer. He was saying that all twenty thousand of their tastings that year had been held under blind and controlled conditions.

"How can they do that?" Gabe asked Liz, leaning into the aisle again.

The man sitting in front of her turned around and gave her the most withering look she'd ever seen. She wanted to stick her tongue out at him—no, that was childish. It would have felt good, but she didn't give in to the impulse. Instead, she twirled her finger. "Turn around and pay attention. You'll miss something."

"Not with you talking all the time," the man growled.

Liz lifted her chin haughtily and stared past him at the speaker.

Just then, Gabe rose and stood over her. He tapped the arm of the man beside Liz.

"Pardon me. Do you mind switching seats with me? I had a meeting and couldn't get a cab."

The man stared blankly at Gabe.

Gabe didn't miss a beat. "It's my girlfriend's birthday," he said, putting his hand on Liz's shoulder. "I promised her I'd meet her here. Do you mind?" Then for emphasis, Gabe flashed the man a wide, disarming smile.

"Sorry," the man whispered, gathering his briefcase. "Be happy to."

Gabe stood back and let the man pass, then he quickly sat down, took Liz's hand and kissed it.

As the man sat in Gabe's chair, his face screwed up into a grimace. He lifted his thigh, touched the back of his pants and realized the chair was wet. He shot Gabe a nasty glance.

Gabe lowered his eyes and kissed Liz's cheek as if he hadn't seen the man's predicament.

Liz turned on Gabe and shook her finger at him. "Don't you be nice to me," she whispered. "Anyway, that was a horrible thing to do. That poor man."

"I'll buy him some new slacks."

"That's what you do? Use money to get you out of scrapes?"

"This wasn't a scrape."

"It was certainly a lie."

"A white one. Besides," Gabe whispered, "I couldn't spend the entire lecture having that guy be mad at you because of me." Gabe wrinkled his nose as he glanced at the man in front of Liz. "Sourpuss."

Liz had to smile. Then she bit her lip. "Well, he's right. You are disturbing the lecture. I paid a lot of money to hear this."

"So stop talking to me and listen. That's what we're here for," Gabe retorted. He crossed his ankle over his knee and leaned back, his eyes on the podium.

The expert from Burgundy was a boring speaker, but his information was fascinating. Liz found herself in a nearly rhapsodic state as he discussed the 2010 wines from his home region, the most elegant in twenty years.

Ninety minutes into the lecture, the speakers announced a ten-minute break. Half the audience bolted for the restrooms.

Liz turned to Gabe. "Isn't it wonderful?"

"It is," he said, taking a mini recorder out of his jacket pocket. "Luckily, I'll never lose a single word."

Liz admired the recorder. "I wish I'd thought of that," she said. "I could have played it back for Grandpa. It's all as good as I hoped it would be. I can't wait till the grafting expert talks."

"I'm here for the tasting," Gabe said. "I have so much more to learn, and some of these new blends coming out of South America fascinate me. The Malbecs are really catching on."

"Is that what you're going to grow on the Mattuchi land?"

"I am," he said.

She pointed to a thin man with even thinner hair who was fiddling with a stack of notes near the front of the room. "Professor Argus is going to address Malbecs."

"He's another reason I'm here," Gabe said flatly. "I called him when he was in Buenos Aires two years ago. We talked for quite some time."

Liz's eyes widened. "I'm…impressed."

A cynical smile lifted a corner of Gabe's mouth. "No, you're not. You don't believe me. You're surprised, if anything. You think, like everyone else, that my little vineyard is a joke."

"I never said that."

"You didn't, but others have. In Indian Lake, they talk about what I'm doing like I had a lobotomy. It's a natural progression, if you ask me. I'm already a farmer. I'm just changing crops is all."

"*All?* There's a lot more to it than that, Gabe."

"I'm aware, Liz. You know a lot more than I do. You were born on the vineyard, weren't you?"

"Yes, as a matter of fact."

"So you think it's your birthright. It's part of your genetic makeup."

"My grandfather and my father, even my mother, were all vintners."

"That's great," he breathed, with a respect she could nearly take and carry home in her pocket. "But what I'm trying to say is that there are those of us, not born among the vines, who have come to it like it's our destiny, like we were given this special talent or purpose. It's hard to explain."

"It's a passion," she said quietly.

His blue eyes, the color of the Mediterranean Sea, pierced hers. "That's exactly right, Liz. Passion. It's a yearning so deep and so profound I can't ignore it anymore. No matter how idiotic everyone else thinks I am, it's important to me that you understand that about me."

"But why?" she asked, shaking her head and wishing she hadn't asked the question. It seemed impossible to her that this person she'd only recently come to know—first by nearly shooting him and then by dancing with him all night—should give a whit about her opinion.

"Because, Liz… Because you—"

A bell rang and everyone rushed back to their seats.

The speakers went to the tasting tables and started uncorking bottles.

"Ladies and gentlemen, we will begin the event that has compelled most of you to attend this conference. The blind tasting. First, our own editors will demonstrate their expertise, and then we'll open the tasting to anyone who wants to test their skills. We will have everything from a Chambertin burgundy to an Oregon chardonnay."

Gabe stood up and held his hand out to Liz. "Shall we?"

She took his hand. When she stood they were nearly nose to nose, so close she could feel his breath on her lips. It was all she could do not to impulsively kiss him. Instead, she said, "You didn't answer my question."

His expression was serious. "Because you're a great deal like me. And frankly, I find that intriguing."

CHAPTER TWELVE

THE MALBEC LECTURE ended and was followed by two hours of wine tastings. Each of the editors demonstrated their unique ability to discern currant from blackberry flavor, mushroom from lavender, cassis and rosemary undertones, and to compare the subtleties in a French burgundy from 2010 to one from 2013. When the editors asked for a volunteer from the group, only Gabe came forward. No one else wanted to look foolish, but Gabe was a good sport about it all. And he amazed the audience—Liz included—by correctly identifying an Italian Soave, an Argentinian Malbec and a South African shiraz.

When the symposium was over, Liz gathered her purse and headed for the back doors. Gabe was preoccupied by his conversation with one of the editors.

Liz rode down to the lobby and saw it was still pouring rain outside. She took her umbrella out of her satchel.

"Can I give you a ride home?" Gabe asked, jogging up to her from the elevator bank. He was shoving his arms into his jacket sleeves and hoisting it onto his broad shoulders. He fixed the collar.

"I…er…I'm not going home right now," she said, glancing around nervously.

Gabe smiled broadly. "Gonna play hooky?"

"Well, I…"

"Look," he said, pointing to the rain outside. "You don't have to make excuses. There's no work back at the farm on a day like this. Let's steal the rest of the afternoon together. What did you have in mind?"

"Steal?"

He shrugged his shoulders. "It's an old saying we had in the family. We'd steal time to do something fun. My mother would bring us here to Chicago to shop or go to the museums."

"Shopping?" The corner of her mouth curled up. "I guess that habit started early."

"What? Dressing well is important. And I loved shopping with my mom. She was always fun. Mostly we went to the toy departments while she looked for our school clothes. She'd take us out for Chicago-style pizza or really sloppy burgers. She made sure we saw all the new exhibits at the museums. She said it was educational. I remember her fighting with the teachers when she wanted to take us out of school for one of our 'expeditions.' Sometimes we'd see a play. She loves musicals."

Liz was touched that Gabe appeared to have a very strong relationship with his mother. She hadn't expected him to be so verbal about it. Clearly, he was a man who didn't shy away from revealing his feelings.

"Your mother sounds like a wonderful person," Liz said, allowing the fleeting memory of her own mother to come to rest in her mind for a cherished moment.

"She is. I hope you get to know her better. I think you two could be friends."

"Friends," Liz repeated. Friends with Gabe. Friends with Gina. It was an idea she hadn't really pondered until this moment. She'd been too busy being suspicious and wary. Judgmental. She'd allowed herself to fall into her bad habit of categorizing people without really knowing them.

Still, her grandfather was concerned that Gabe was positioning himself to try to buy their vineyard. Or "steal" it after nearly driving them out of business.

But was that possible? The Crenshaw Vineyard was established, though she hadn't forgotten about the lost cashier's check. She wanted to believe she would find it and that the money hadn't been stolen. She worried about their unpaid taxes, and they were still in debt from building the tasting room. Gabe didn't know that, though. Not yet.

"So, where are you off to?" Gabe asked.

"Well, I'm not going shopping." Liz gave him a tight smile.

Gabe tilted his chin. "I get it. Must be top secret. Well," he said, leaning over and whispering in her ear, "no matter what it is, I won't tell a soul. Discretion is my middle name."

"I doubt that." She chuckled and hoisted her purse strap onto her shoulder.

His jaw fell open. "I'm wounded. Truly."

"You are not." She punched him lightly on the arm. "All you're trying to do is wrestle an invitation from me. Why, Gabe?"

"I thought that was obvious," he said earnestly. "I want to spend time with you."

"Why?" she nearly whined, but she managed to keep her frustration in check.

"I like you, Liz. There, I've played my hand. So can we be friends and get on with getting to know each other?"

Liz opened her mouth and he held up a finger.

"Don't even think about asking me why

again. Now, come on. Share your umbrella with me and tell me where we're going."

She glared at him. "You're not going away, are you?"

"Nope." His handsome face beamed at her.

Liz exhaled. "Fine. I promised Maddie I'd visit her new café that just opened last week. I couldn't make the grand opening, so I thought this would be a good chance to check it out. She said she'd be there every Saturday for the first few weeks to make sure it's all going well and the staff is properly trained. I thought that was wise."

"I agree. Now," he said, taking her umbrella and opening it as he pushed through the door, "let's begin our time heist."

THE CUPCAKE AND CAPPUCCINO CAFÉ was located just up Wells Street from the Merchandise Mart. It was the first of Maddie's franchises to be built and opened. Liz and Gabe huddled under the umbrella as they made their way to the café. They'd gone about half a block when Liz realized how easily they'd fallen into step with one another. It reminded her of dancing with him—everything flowed naturally. She should have been suspicious of a man getting this close, almost hip to hip. Especially Gabe.

She couldn't understand the delight she felt when she was with him.

Was she really smiling this much? Was that laughter bursting forth when he made his jokes? Suddenly, she was very glad he'd insisted on spending more time with her this afternoon.

"Here we are," Gabe said as they came to a halt.

They stood in front of a luxe storefront with high glass windows surrounded by black and brown granite pillars. Across the top of the front door, in brass with backlights, was the name Cupcake and Cappuccino Café.

Liz was in awe. "Maddie has talked about her café so much, but to be here and see this... wow!"

"Wait till you see the inside," Gabe said, closing the umbrella. He placed his hand on the small of Liz's back and held the door for her. "You're going to love this."

"When did you see it?"

"I came up a couple times this summer when I could get away. After Nate and Maddie got engaged, I kind of hung out with them on a few of their trips to Chicago."

"Really?"

He nodded. "After seven days a week on the farm, month after month, I try to take a few hours' break when I can. Plus, there are some great wine bars nearby. Nate and I would go there to talk sometimes, and I was able to do a lot of research."

Once inside, Liz was speechless.

"You don't like it?"

"It's just that it's…so different from her café in Indian Lake."

"Yeah." Gabe motioned to the elegant Italian lighting, faux painted walls and marble floors. "This is the city version of 'down home.'"

The sitting area was filled with square tables and Italian-style chairs. Under the huge window were three love seats upholstered in yellow-and-white-striped fabric, and a modern glass-top coffee table in the center of the setting held a squatty vase of yellow roses.

The focus of the café was the enormous vintage copper-and-brass cappuccino machine in the center of a dark walnut coffee bar, where baristas were making lattes. Behind them, three young women in yellow-and-white-striped aprons piped different flavored icings onto cupcake bases.

"It's wonderful," Liz gushed as he led her over to a love seat.

"What would you like?"

"I can get my own," she said. She started to rise, but he put his hand on her shoulder.

"Are you implying that I can't afford it, or that you don't want me to know your secret cravings?"

She stared at him.

"That's it. You're really a closet cupcake addict and you don't want anyone to know." He laughed heartily and flopped down next to her. "You are so much fun to tease."

"Oh, stop," she said and pushed his arm playfully.

What was she doing? Was she flirting with him? And why did that not bother her at all?

Just then Maddie came out of the back storage room with Nate, who was carrying a stack of paper cups. They both stopped dead in their tracks.

"Hi, Liz," Maddie said with a warning wave.

Liz stood immediately and wiped the swoony expression off her face. "Maddie!" she exclaimed, feeling like a kid who'd just been caught red-handed.

"How was the lecture?"

"Great!" Gabe said, jumping up off the sofa to give Maddie a hug and slap his brother on the back. "It was one of the best I've ever been to. Plus, they had a tasting event at the end."

Gabe kept up a lively chatter about the wines he'd tasted that afternoon and how lucky he'd been to identify each vintage correctly. "I tell you, I surprised even myself."

"I'm glad," Nate replied. "Maddie, why don't you show Liz around? She hasn't seen the place. I'll hang with Gabe for a minute."

"I'd love to see it all," Liz said, her eyes still sparkling with admiration.

Maddie grabbed Liz's arm and smiled. "I'm so glad you came. I love showing the place off."

As the two women walked away, Gabe realized he was *still* smiling and *still* had his eyes glued on Liz. He was surprised at the warmth he felt.

"Hey, what's with you, man?"

"Huh? What?" Gabe got to his feet. "Wait. I want one of those German chocolate cupcakes you brought home last weekend."

Nate pressed his brother back into the sofa. "Not till you tell me what's going on."

"Going on?"

"You know what I mean. Between you and Liz. When I walked out of the storage room you both looked like starry-eyed teenagers."

"We did?" Gabe glanced over at Liz. She and Maddie were carrying on an animated conversation punctuated with giggles and hugs.

"So how long has this been happening?" Nate asked. "I thought you two just met at my engagement party."

"That was the first time we danced. Not the first time we met."

"So when did you meet?"

"When Liz tried to kill me."

"Stop horsing around," Nate groaned. "It was a simple question."

"Okay, so I was being dramatic. But she did have a shotgun. She carries one around on her ATV. You can ask her."

"I think I will. Maybe I can get a straight answer out of her. You always do this, Gabe."

"What?"

"Evade. You always answer questions with more questions, or you change the subject entirely."

"That's not true. I never evade the subject with Mom."

"You do with Dad," Nate grumbled.

"That's different," Gabe said harshly. "It's how I…cope."

Nate's eyes scanned his brother's face. He put a hand on Gabe's shoulder. "I wish you didn't have to do that anymore, Gabe. You've been running Dad's business since the day you left Davis. He issues orders to you every morning and you do it all and then some. I may have been gone for ten years, but I saw what was happening and I see even more of it now. How much longer can you keep this up? Being his lackey and barely getting an ounce of appreciation from him?"

Gabe stared at his hands, oxygen burning holes in his lungs as if the years of resentment and anger had turned his breath toxic. "I wish I didn't have to do it anymore, either, Nate."

Nate exhaled. "You have no idea how good it is to hear that. You need to leave him, Gabe. He's a thankless boss and an even worse father."

"I know. I should."

"But you haven't."

Gabe felt his insides clutch. He'd never confided in Nate, or any of his brothers, for that matter. Gabe had shouldered a lot of responsibility because he was the oldest. He felt a familiar wave of protection toward his mother.

"I'm all Mom's got, really. I don't think any of you have seen her cry when she thinks we aren't looking. Maybe because I'm the oldest, she's always confided in me."

"You've always been loyal to Dad, too," Nate countered. "To the farm. To his business. I know you love Mom, but there's going to come a day when all this will overwhelm you, Gabe. I know it."

"Is that your medical opinion?"

"You think I'm kidding? I'm a cardiologist. If you don't use your heart correctly, it will turn on you."

Gabe chuckled. "That's funny."

Nate shook his head. "These days, the medical community considers it a fact."

Peering at his brother seriously, Gabe dropped his banter. "I think I'm learning that." His eyes slid toward Liz. "I'm not involved with Liz at all, Nate. You know how much I've always wanted to be a vintner. Maybe there's a chance Liz would consider selling a parcel of land to me. I'm not sure. But the truth is we're friends."

Just then, Liz looked away from Maddie and straight at Gabe. Her smile lit the room more brightly than the expensive Italian chandeliers.

Nate's eyes ping-ponged from Gabe to Liz and back. "That's not the smile of a *friend*."

"Sure it is, Nate. But frankly, I wouldn't know. I don't have all that many friends."

"I know the feeling. None of us has ever had the time," Nate mused. "Career commitments. And, for you, exhausting hours on the farm."

Gabe was pensive. "Do you think lack of time is why Dad's always been so uncaring?

Or is there something missing in his character that he doesn't give a rip about any of us? Dad was never very sociable, when you think about it. He's always stayed on the farm, hardly going beyond our property lines except to go to church."

"I never thought about it, but you're right," Nate agreed. "Mom's the social one. Service League plays, her church sorority. Remember when she was our Cub Scout den mother? And she always went to town for exercise classes. Now it's Zumba."

"Dad's never really liked people," Gabe said. Then something popped into his mind. "Hey, have you ever heard Dad say anything about Sam Crenshaw?"

Nate shook his head. "Should I have?"

"Not really..." Gabe's eyes darted to Liz again.

"You're talking about Liz's grandfather, right?"

"Yeah. It's just that he said something strange the night of the party. But thinking back, it was just too out of the blue to be taken seriously."

"After our engagement party? I wouldn't take anything he said that night seriously."

"Actually, you're right. Dad's not happy if

he's not barking orders, and when he doesn't have workers to boss around, he's gotta find someone else to shout at. Mom tuned him out long ago."

Gabe stood up and pasted a bright smile on his face. "Let's join the women," he said and walked over to Liz and Maddie.

"I'll buy anything you want, friend," he told Liz. "The sky's the limit."

CHAPTER THIRTEEN

AFTER SPENDING AN HOUR with Maddie and Nate at the café, Liz felt she couldn't decline Gabe's offer to drive her home. Insisting on taking the train back to Indian Lake sounded absurd even to her ears, so she gave in. He'd parked his Porsche in a garage halfway between the café and the Merchandise Mart, and Gabe had set out to trudge through the rain with Liz's umbrella while she stayed dry at the café with Maddie.

Liz listened to Maddie complain about the new stainless steel shelving that hadn't arrived and the fact that she was still training the new manager. Nate spent a good amount of time on his cell phone returning phone calls to patients. She was impressed with the deep concern in his voice as he calmly answered each question, adding a bit of humor to ease their fears and concerns.

Liz saw Gabe drive up and waved through the large window. She turned to Maddie and hugged her.

"Don't forget that you, Sarah and I are going to look for bridesmaids' dresses on Wednesday," Maddie said. "Audra at the Bride's Corner called and said the winter collection has just arrived."

"Winter." Liz glanced outside at the summer rain that was just beginning to dissipate. "Seems forever away. Thank goodness. I hate the cold and the long, silent months at the vineyard." She took in Maddie's glum expression. "Sorry. I bet you can't wait for your wedding to get here."

"No kidding. But the house has a long way to go, and I'd like to have a place to actually live together once we're married." Maddie frowned. "I think building our supposedly uncomplicated lake cottage is more work than running my café."

Liz, Nate and Maddie said their goodbyes and Liz headed out the door.

Inside Gabe's Porsche, Liz took a moment to appreciate the luxurious interior. Her 1978 Ford pickup with a clutch and four-on-the-floor transmission, an AM radio and hand-crank windows was about as utilitarian as it could get. Although Gabe's car was over a decade old, he kept it in pristine condition. She wondered if he waxed and polished it himself. She glanced over at his large biceps, which strained against his linen jacket. Yep. No question he did the work himself. His car was important to him, and he obviously took a personal interest in his belongings. She liked that. A lot.

Gabe synced his phone to the car to return three calls, all of which were business-related. Apparently, they were also urgent. Gabe apologized for the calls, but Liz noticed he apologized even more to his family for taking the afternoon off.

They were going through the tollbooth on the Skyway when he finally turned his phone off. "I bet it's like that for you, as well. Always being in demand. They probably can't live without you and your guidance at the vineyard."

"You're right. But today was special and they all knew it. So I turned my cell phone off."

"That's brave," he said.

She closed her eyes and inhaled deeply as she sank back in the luxurious seat. "I wanted to make sure I absorbed every scrap of knowledge I could. I've looked forward to this symposium for months."

"I know exactly what you mean. Stealing time to do the things we want to do is getting harder by the day."

Liz watched the trees stream by as they exited the busy interstate for the much calmer traffic on Indiana Toll Road.

"I'm curious, Gabe," she said. "You're clearly swamped with all the work you do for the farm. How are you going to manage the time to build a proper vineyard on the Mattuchi land?"

He cocked the right side of his mouth into a lopsided grin. "Caffeine."

"I'm being serious," she said.

"I've found ways to carve out time. Plus, I've hired an excellent manager for the vineyard who will live in a used trailer I've bought for the first year."

"Do I know him?" she probed.

"Probably not," Gabe answered but didn't offer any more information. Then he glanced at her. "I'm not going into this thing on a whim, Liz. I'm committed to building one of the best little vineyards in the country. This has been my dream forever, and I'm going for it. Nate taught me that."

"Nate? I don't understand."

"He was only nineteen when he took off and joined the navy. He wanted to be a doctor rather than the farmer my father expected all of us boys to become. As far as Dad was concerned, there were no options for our futures.

In order for Nate to take charge of his own destiny, he had to lie to us, break Mother's heart and let the entire city of Indian Lake believe he was a monster for leaving Maddie the way he did. I actually wanted to deck him for all those reasons and more. But he did it. He got his degree and went to med school and became a doctor. Now look at him. He's got the world by the tail."

"And you don't?"

He stared straight ahead and ground his jaw. "I will," he said with tangible determination.

Liz understood his tenacity. To be a vintner took more than sweat and toil. It took superhuman grit and resolute faith—you had to believe the vines would give back, eventually, no matter how long the wait.

"Have you always felt like that, Gabe? About the vines and the wine, I mean?"

"Ever since I went to Davis. I had applied for a scholarship without my parents' knowledge. I don't know why I chose Davis, except that it was as far away from Indiana as I could get. My grades put me on the dean's list in high school. I must have written one heck of an essay for that application, because I got pretty decent funding. How could my parents *not* let me go?

"Anyway, about a month after I'd started my boring freshman courses, I went on a long weekend holiday to Sonoma. I can't tell you the feeling I had. It was like dying and then being reborn. I have never felt as at home as I did touring the vines. I couldn't stand it. I wanted to lie down and sleep among them. I don't know what exactly happened to me, but my explanation since then has been that I found my destiny. I went back to school and signed up for an elective in viticulture. I was hooked. Then, after my junior year, Nate took off. My dad went ballistic, essentially. He demanded I finish my degree at Purdue so I could help at the farm."

"And you've been working for your father ever since?"

Gabe nodded with a look so solemn and steely she thought it would cut the windshield. *"Au revoir, le vin."*

"And you figured that buying the Mattuchi land would be your breakout, like Nate's running away?"

His eyes slid from the highway in front of them to Liz's face as a perceptive smile creased his lips. "That's part of it. I had promised Mario not to say anything to anyone, but the truth will be all over town soon."

"The truth?" She shook her head. "I don't understand."

He patted her knee. It wasn't a patronizing gesture, but a reassuring and understanding one. She liked the feel of his hand against her knee. "You of all people deserve the real story, Liz. Nearly six months ago, Nate told Sophie Mattuchi, during one of their surgeries together, that my dream was to be a vintner. Sophie had just learned her father had cancer. The Mattuchi family had okay, but not great, insurance, and his treatments were going to wipe out their savings and then some. To me, Sophie proposed I buy some of their land to help them out financially. You can guess how excited I was. But I had no idea how good or bad the soil actually was."

"So that's when you started spying on me?" Liz turned in her seat to look at him squarely.

He exhaled his exasperation. "Why are you so suspicious, Liz? Do you do this to everyone or just to me?"

"What?" she asked innocently.

"You think I'm out to hurt you for some reason. I'm not. When you found me that day, I had been over at the Mattuchis. I had my test tubes in my trunk because I'd tested their soil. I was committed to buying the land to help

Mario, and because common sense told me that since their land butted up to yours, there had to be some good qualities and nutrients I could bank on. I was curious about your soil, I admit that. It was the first time I went to your place. I didn't even know you had more land. Liz, honestly, I'm sorry about not asking you if I could test your soil. It was very wrong of me."

The sincerity in his voice touched her. She chose to believe him. "Accepted and forgiven. Would you agree with me that we need to put that behind us?'

"I agree. By the way, how much unplanted land *do* you have?"

"A hundred acres."

He whistled. "I had no idea it was that much. Then that means the largest part of your vineyard hasn't been tapped yet."

Liz gazed out the windshield but all she saw was her father's face, beaming at her. "That's right. Only about fifty acres is planted now. My fallow land is my inheritance. My grandfather owns the rest of the vineyard, but the fallow land was deeded to me. It's my father's dream. He told me exactly how to plant it. Nowhere in the Midwest, not even in Michigan, is there a stretch of land like that one, and it's right in our own backyard. The air currents, the wind off the lake bringing the humidity, the rich soil… it's perfect for chardonnays and champagnes. That land is the reason I went to France. I'm going to turn it into something incredible and I won't stop until I do."

Gabe reached for her hand, but before he touched her, he retracted it. Liz saw his hand slide back onto the steering wheel. "Sorry. I get carried away sometimes."

"I know just how you feel. We share a love of the land. The only thing we do not share is the heritage."

"My father's dream is the most important thing in my life," Liz admitted.

Gabe pursed his lips. "I wish I could have known him," he said sincerely.

"I wish I could have known him longer. I like to think we would have had fun working the vineyard together."

Gabe smiled. "Well, I think it's pretty cool that you and I will be working nearly the same land together, trying to make some really great wines. So, since we'll be work neighbors, do you think you could possibly dial down your distrust of me?"

Liz tore her eyes from him and looked at the highway. "I do have a suspicious nature, don't I?"

"Yes. You do. Why is that?"

"I've always been that way. My grandfather says my first word was *why*, and I guess I haven't changed since then."

Gabe rubbed the back of his neck and shot her a thoughtful look. "That's just natural curiosity. But when it comes to me, you jump to the worst conclusions."

Liz didn't like how discerning Gabe was. How was it possible he'd come to know her better than she knew him in such a short period of time? Didn't it take hours and hours of conversation and working on problems and projects together to really get to know a person? She had known her grandfather all her life and she was still learning new things about him all the time.

Gabe was dead-on this time. She hadn't trusted him in the least. She questioned everything about him, from his motives to his charming smile. She was convinced he wanted something from her. Now that he'd explained how his purchase of the Mattuchi land had come about, she truly believed he hadn't had any ulterior motives when she'd caught him on her land. He'd just wanted to find out what kind of soil he'd be working with.

That, however, didn't account for why he appeared to be manipulating events and circumstances so they could be together more often. It had been Gabe's idea for the two of them to be paired up for Maddie and Nate's wedding. That was circumspect, wasn't it?

Liz folded her arms across her chest. "Maybe that's because you do things that aren't always so straightforward."

"Oh, yeah?" He guffawed. "Name one."

"Fine," she countered. "You manipulated your brother into appointing yourself as my groomsman for his wedding."

"I merely suggested it." He smiled to himself and glanced at her. "Aw, c'mon, Liz. It was a great idea. How else was I going to get you to dance with me in the moonlight?"

"That's why you did it?" she demanded. "You wanted to dance with me?"

"I sure did." He chuckled. "And it worked."

Part of her was flattered that Gabe had gone to all that trouble just to dance with her. But she wondered why he felt he had to work so hard to get what he wanted, when all he had to do was ask. He could have asked to test her soil. He could have asked her for a dance. Now that he'd told her so much about his relationship with his father, she guessed that Gabe had learned the hard way that asking permission only opened him up to rejection and dismissal.

Liz peered out the windshield and noticed the light was fading. "We should be back in Indian Lake soon."

"Uh-huh."

They were silent for a long moment. "Gabe, how long have you been looking forward to today's lecture?"

Gabe gripped the steering wheel. Liz had a feeling she wasn't going to like his answer. "About a week," he confessed.

"And I've had my ticket for months," she said quietly. "How did you find out about the lecture? Don't tell me. From Maddie?"

He nodded. "Yep. And she mentioned you were going to visit her afterward. I knew Nate was going to be in Chicago, too. I just thought—"

"What?" she interrupted. "What did you think, Gabe?"

The exit for Indian Lake loomed ahead. Gabe signaled and left the toll road. "I thought it would be a great way to see you again, and if I got lucky, maybe you would talk to me and spend some time with me."

"Is that so?"

"Oh, yes, Liz."

Liz's mind was reeling. On the surface, Gabe's actions seemed controlling. Yet at the same time, her heart told her that wasn't the truth. She'd felt his passion for winemaking as if his words came from her own soul. He'd told her a great deal about his relationships with both his parents, good and bad...certainly more than she'd revealed about herself. She actually found herself empathizing with him for never having experienced the kind of love she'd had with her father. One moment, she felt compelled to reach out to him with comfort. The next, she wanted to withdraw. Why was he so insecure when it came to her? Was she that off-putting? The only thing she knew for certain was that these tangled vines of uneasiness and caring had planted themselves deep within her.

She'd never felt these feelings before Gabe. Ever. And she wasn't sure what they meant.

By THE TIME they arrived in Indian Lake the rain had stopped and the clouds had cleared enough to create a striking sunset.

"I have an idea," Gabe said, turning onto the gravel drive to Cove Beach. "Let's steal just another minute to watch the sun go down."

Liz checked her watch. She was stunned to

see it was nearly nine o'clock. "I really should get home."

She realized she couldn't wait to get away from him. If she stayed with him any longer, she might like him more. And then what? Throwing aside the fact that he intended to become her competition, there was something else that threatened her. Something that could change her forever, if she let it.

"Five minutes. What difference can five minutes make now?" he said, parking the car and turning off the engine. He opened his door. "Come on. Sunsets are always gorgeous reflected in the lake. I never get to see them like this. I'm always at the farm."

"Okay," she relented, opening her door.

Gabe jogged around the front of the car and took her hand.

"Let's go over there," he said, pointing to the picnic table closest to the water's edge. There was a thicket of cattails to the right, and swirls of lake weeds wove around the stalks, glittering in the pink light.

They sat on top of the table rather than on the bench. Gabe let go of Liz's hand and she was surprised by her disappointment. Why should she feel snubbed? They'd just spent the entire day together. They'd exchanged some private information about themselves and shared their intimate histories. Had she thought they'd become closer? Was she getting more emotionally involved with Gabe? Was she actually growing to like him?

Maybe he believed they were just two people who'd gone to a lecture together and met friends for coffee. Or perhaps she had wounded him by being distrustful. Maybe he was feeling guilty for going to the lecture and crashing her café date with Maddie.

Liz had told herself for weeks she didn't want a romance with Gabe. Or with anyone, for that matter. Love was dangerous territory for her, and the risks to her heart weren't worth the benefits, as far as she could see.

It was one thing to be a bridesmaid to his groomsman, and to be working neighbors. But that was all. It was really best that nothing romantic happen between them.

Gabe appeared to be totally absorbed by the lavender, pink and orange striations ribboning the horizon. As the sun sank, the clouds above them morphed into pink puffs against an ever-darkening sky. It was nature's light show. Until the day she died, Liz would never tire of watching sunsets.

"Beautiful, isn't it?" she said softly, hoping not to disturb his thoughts too much.

"Amazing. And there are never two alike. I must have a thousand photographs of sunsets on my computer. I use different ones for screen savers." He chuckled and turned to face her. "There's nothing more…beautiful…"

Without warning, Gabe kissed Liz. It was a quick kiss, and as he abruptly pulled away, Liz heard him breathe in sharply, as if something had shocked him. Then he kissed her again. He cradled her face in his strong hands and held her close.

Liz placed her hands over his. Though his lips were soft and full against hers, she felt the same power and purpose she'd seen in his eyes when he'd talked about his vineyard. With her eyes closed, she felt as if she were floating into space. Liz felt emotions she had long ago forgotten—longing, comfort and building excitement, as if she were sailing out of a stormy sea into a safe harbor. But just as quickly as she had found pleasure, she was filled with a biting terror that made her pull away from him.

She would have been lying if she said she didn't like his kiss, but she would also have been lying if she allowed him to take another.

"I'm sorry," he said. "I shouldn't have done that. It was just the sunset…and you're so beautiful…" He looked into her eyes.

Liz knew instinctively that he was asking for another kiss. "Apology accepted," she said tersely, straightening her back. "I need to get home. I left my truck at the train station. Can you drop me off there, please?"

"Don't be mad." He hopped off the table and held out his hand.

Liz didn't take it. "I'm not mad at you," she said. "It's just that this isn't a road I want to go down with you."

He put his outstretched hand in his pocket. "You really are mad."

She started walking toward the car. "Gabe, I'm not like the other girls you take out. I'm not going to fall into your arms. I'm not going to become some clinging vine until you decide to uproot me. So it would be best if you save the charm for someone else."

He rushed up to her and grabbed her arm. "You've got me all wrong."

She cocked an eyebrow. "Really?"

"I shouldn't have done that. And you're right. You aren't just any woman to me. I was hoping we could become friends. I really like you, Liz. I was hoping you would like me, too."

She exhaled, dropping her shoulders. "I do."

"Truthfully?" He brightened, but only a bit. "That's good news."

"But even as I stand here, Gabe, I still get the feeling you're after something. You want something from me. If it's not a kiss, then what is it?"

Gabe swallowed hard. It was now or never. "Liz, would there be any circumstances under which you would consider…er…selling your fallow land?"

Liz dropped her jaw and gaped at him. "You're serious?"

"I could be."

"The land I just told you that my father, whom I loved more than life itself, put all his heart and soul into…you want me to sell it to you? A novice vintner?"

"Liz, I'm very good at what I do. You saw that at the blind tasting. I know wines better than anyone. Maybe even better than you."

"Thanks a lot," she fumed.

Anger was the last reaction he'd wanted from Liz. Her passion for making wine was a carbon copy of his, and it just seemed natural that joining forces would benefit them both. Obviously, she didn't feel that way. She was possessive and controlling, and she thought he was an intruder. Again. If he didn't make himself clear to her, he was going to lose her friendship and trust completely.

"I didn't mean it that way. I was trying to say your land would be in capable hands. I would do it justice, and I have the money set aside to build it into what I can only guess your father envisioned for it. I've worked hard all my life. I don't bet on my brother's horses or blow my money on stupid stuff. I've invested wisely and it has paid off. I've always known what I wanted. I'm ready to make my move, Liz. You could help me."

"Help you? I hardly know you. This is too much, Gabe!" She strode away from him.

Gabe raced after her. "Liz, please. Listen to me. This could be good for both of us."

She whirled around, her eyes blazing at him with an anger he'd only seen when facing himself in a mirror after a fight with his father. "Get this straight, Gabriel Barzonni. I'm not selling my land to you or anyone else. I don't need you. I don't need your money! Grandpa and I have been just fine all this time without any help from anyone. You got that?"

"Why would I think I was helping you? I was talking about a straight-up business deal," Gabe said. "What's going on here, Liz?"

She clamped her lips shut and glared at him. "I just want to go home." She marched over to his car and tried to open the door, but it was locked.

"Talk to me," he demanded.

"No."

"Fine. Don't. If I can't get around that wall you've built, then there's no use."

He hit the remote to unlock the car. Liz got in and slammed the door.

Gabe started the car and spun gravel beneath his tires as they left the cove behind.

LIZ HAD NEVER ridden silently in a vehicle with another person before, and she didn't like it. Gabe was stoic and she knew there was nothing she could say.

If this were a "straight-up business deal," then why were they both so emotional about it? She slipped her eyes toward him and saw the hurt look on his face. For the life of her, she couldn't understand why she would be so concerned with his emotions when she hadn't deciphered her own yet.

Gabe was right.

She *had* kept a barricade around her heart. For years. But this…feeling she had when she was with Gabe was growing in strength, and it frightened her. Her first impulse was to eliminate the cause of the fear. If she didn't see Gabe again, if she didn't kiss him again, she wouldn't be so afraid.

They pulled up to the train station and Gabe parked his car next to Liz's old pickup. He kept the engine running.

"Thanks for the ride," Liz said, feeling oddly guilty.

"I really meant it when I said I was sorry, Liz. I shouldn't have kissed you, but I'm not going to say I'm sorry for liking it so much." His tone was sincere. "But I didn't mean to upset you so much."

"Okay," she said and got out of the car.

She walked around to her truck and drove away while Gabe remained behind.

Liz glanced at him in her rearview mirror. He sat still, watching her. Waiting patiently.

Today he'd huddled with her under the umbrella, brought his car around to Maddie's café so she wouldn't have to walk in the rain and given her a ride home. Now he was waiting to make sure she was safe.

It was her guess that by the time she got home, she'd have a text from him to make sure she made it without incident.

As she drove out of the train station, she shook her head.

Gabe's offer had stirred her ever-present fears. She still had not found the cashier's check, even after going through all her purses and Sam's desk drawers for a third time. The weight of the pending tax bill was forcing her to think out of her comfort zone. More than anything, Liz had wanted to fulfill her father's dream of planting the fallow land. But that dream was quickly fading.

If she sold the land, the profit would dig them out of debt and give them a small reserve to make it through the winter.

Selling the land would solve their financial problems, but the idea made Liz uneasy, even incensed. If she were honest with herself, though, the real cause of her growing anger was that it had been Gabe who'd brought up the idea. They'd had a lovely afternoon together, but was his romancing just a ploy to get her to sell to him?

She felt her insides twist, and an acrid taste filled her mouth. Betrayal always tasted rancid, Sam had once told her.

Had Gabe been after her land this whole time? When he'd said he liked her and wanted to get to know her, she'd believed him. He'd seemed absolutely sincere, sharing intimacies about himself and his parents, and she'd actually bet her own emotions on it. But this put a new slant on every word he'd said to her. She felt as if she was looking at Gabe through a cloud of dark smoke.

Right now, Liz felt plain stupid. She should have seen through him, figured out his game plan before he'd let it play out. He'd used her, and though she knew he needed her to attain his goals, she felt diminished nonetheless.

None of her real friends had ever made her feel this bad about herself.

Clearly, Gabe was not her friend.

CHAPTER FOURTEEN

LIZ ARRIVED AT HOME and saw all the house lights burning as she parked the truck, reminding her of her late-night return from Maddie and Nate's engagement party. The tasting room had been battened down, but Louisa's lamp in her attached apartment was still on. Though it was not even ten o'clock, she'd expected her grandfather to be asleep as he usually was by this time.

As she walked in the front door, she was careful that her heels did not hit the old oak floor and make noise. She needn't have bothered.

"It's about time you came home," Sam grumbled from the living room, where he was sitting in his recliner.

His hands were on the arms of the chair as if he were ready to spring forward at any moment. "You don't need to get up, Grandpa," she said.

"Where were you?" he asked angrily. "I've

been worried sick all day and when you didn't answer your cell phone…"

"My phone?" Liz slapped her palm against her forehead. "I completely forgot! I turned it off when the lecture started and never turned it back on." She dug in her purse and pulled it out. The screen was black. She looked back to her grandfather. "I'm sorry—" she began, and then stopped abruptly. "You knew I was in Chicago."

"I knew nothing of the sort. Why would I? You didn't leave a note or anything." He was frowning, but as he cocked his head to the side, Liz detected a flicker of guilt in his expression. He remained silent and blinked slowly and deliberately, as he often did lately. Liz didn't know exactly when this habit had started, but she had realized it was indicative of his need to concentrate. Liz didn't know if he was purposefully trying to keep her attention focused on him, or if he had truly lost his train of thought. She wasn't sure which was worse.

"You knew where I was," she retorted with a raised voice.

"I most certainly did not," he countered, scrunching his eyebrows together.

She put her hand on her hip and cocked her head. "You have known about the lecture for months. This morning I gave you a hug before I left. You told me to take good notes and tell you everything I learned at the lecture. You even said that next year you want to buy a ticket for yourself."

"What lecture?" Sam asked sheepishly. He visibly dialed down his anger.

It was happening again. "You forgot."

"I did?"

"Uh-huh. I bought a ticket to this symposium and wine tasting months ago." She turned her cell phone on and glanced at it. There were eight missed calls from her grandfather. If she hadn't been with Gabe all afternoon and evening, she would have thought to check her messages. But she'd been caught up in her emotions and, honestly, in trying to forget the vineyard for a day. Her neglect had caused her grandfather great distress. "I'm really sorry, Grandpa. I should have thought to call to check on you."

"I don't need to be checked on," he said defensively.

"I didn't mean it the way it sounded." In the past, when she'd caught him in one of his senior's moments, she'd tried to pretend it was funny, as he did, and laugh it off. But this was much more serious. He'd spent the day worrying about her unnecessarily. That kind of concern wasn't good for him, and she didn't deserve this cloak of guilt that descended on her every time he forgot her whereabouts or misread her actions.

What frightened Liz most was the possibility they were headed down a dead-end road if her grandfather was developing Alzheimer's or something similar. She loved him with all her heart, but already she could tell she was ill-equipped to deal with a disease as debilitating as dementia.

Liz would need guidance and counseling in order to cope with the challenges, heartbreaks and day-to-day expectations of being Sam's caregiver.

Immediately, she thought of Nate and his connections at the hospital. Surely he would know where she should turn. She made a mental note to call his office on Monday morning.

For the moment, just being patient, caring and practical seemed the best course of action.

"I never meant to worry you, Grandpa. Did you ask Louisa or Maria about me? They knew where I was."

"I did not," he said emphatically and with an air of self-possession. "Louisa went to town to shop and Maria spent the day in the vines with Aurelio."

"So you didn't even try to find them?"

"No," he replied with chagrin. "I thought you would call me."

"Here's what I think, Grandpa. From now on, we should have some new rules. When you can't find me or I don't answer my cell, which could be for a lot of different reasons, you promise to talk to Louisa, Maria or Aurelio. I never leave the vineyard without making certain every single person knows where I am."

Sam stared at his own phone. "Okay."

Liz exhaled. "Then tomorrow morning, I'll tell them the new rule. How's that?"

"Fine."

"Grandpa," she said, kneeling on the floor next to his chair, "I don't want you to ever worry like this again. It's not fair, and it's unnecessary. I was fine all day. I was in the city, and after the lecture, I went to Maddie's new café."

"Maddie?" He raised his head and looked at her blankly.

Liz felt her blood turn to ice. This couldn't really be happening to them. Sam wasn't that old, and he was the picture of excellent health.

"Maddie Strong. Her new franchise café is in Chicago. You remember?"

He smiled and tossed his head back. "Of course. Her new place in Chicago. I couldn't figure out what you were talking about. How you could be at Maddie's café in town and the lecture in Chicago at the same time."

Relief flooded Liz like a summer rain after a killing drought. Sam was fine. They'd just had a misunderstanding. Her nerves were on edge, no doubt due to Gabe having kissed her and then having offered to buy her father's land. She was reading too much into the situation with her grandfather. He'd been alone in the farmhouse all day—he just hadn't thought to call anyone else. That's all it was. Wasn't it?

Liz squeezed his hand.

He grinned broadly at her. "So, how was it? If I do recall correctly, there was going to be a tasting. How did you do?" he asked as if he hadn't missed a beat.

"Okay, I guess. But it was Gabe who bested even the editors." Liz stopped herself immediately. She'd said Gabe's name without even thinking. It had just come out.

"Barzonni was there?"

"Yes." She got up and sat on the faded gold brocade sofa across from him.

Sam leveled a pointed gaze on his granddaughter and folded his arms across his chest. "I find that very interesting. I've never heard of him showing up at one of those lectures in all the years you've been attending them."

"Grandpa, I only go to one a year. They're so expensive. Besides, Gabe is a vintner now, and he's planning to make a fine wine in the years to come."

Sam harrumphed. "That'll be the day. Mario Mattuchi never grew diddly on that land of his."

"He never really tried, according to Sophie. His land is like our fallow land. It's just waiting to be nurtured." She watched her grandfather's eyes focus on the front window, tracking from the dark yard to the tasting room apartment, where Louisa's single lamp was still lit. Liz couldn't tell if his mind was wandering or if he was in deep thought, but she waited for him to continue.

"Yours is one of the best palates in the Midwest," he finally said. "Probably even better than your father's was, and that's saying something. I would have liked to have seen you take all those experts on." He smiled to himself. "That would have been something. But you didn't try?"

She shook her head. "There wasn't time."

"Barzonni stole the show."

"I suppose."

"Actually, that was very smart of you."

"It was?" she asked.

"From this day forward, we have to be aware that Barzonni is our competition. Maybe not this year or next, but in the future. He's new to the game and needs someone—you, for instance— to guide him." Sam nodded as if confirming his own suspicions. "I think you were wise to play your cards close to your vest. Tell him nothing. Though even the tourists learn a great deal on their visits." He tapped his temple. "The rest is up here. Past experience. You remember that."

Liz lifted her chin in assent. "Right, Grandpa."

She was thoughtful for a long moment. One half of her was swimming in a warm blue sea of unfamiliar romantic dreams, and the other part of her was siding with her grandfather.

Something had to be wrong to make her feel this conflicted. Her grandfather was right. Gabe was competition. It was in the best interest of her vineyard for her to wheedle as much information as possible about his exact intentions for his vineyard. Two could play at his game. If he planned to plant only Malbecs, as he'd told her, then there was no need for real concern. Liz and Sam had never planted Malbecs, so they wouldn't be direct competitors.

In the future, Liz had to be more cautious than she'd been today. Now that she knew Gabe wanted to buy her land, she understood how serious he was about winemaking. She couldn't reveal any more about her processes, marketing or future plans. She carefully scrutinized the conversations they'd had earlier and was relieved she hadn't given away anything vital.

She'd failed miserably by enjoying their kiss. She had no idea if he'd enjoyed kissing *her*, since he'd apologized, but there had been an odd, stunned light in his eyes that made her wonder.

"I don't know what to make of him, Grandpa," Liz finally said. "When we drove back to town, he talked an awful lot about his childhood and his family."

Sam held up his hand. "Whoa. Back up. Did you say you drove back home with him?"

She bit her lower lip as she had when she'd been caught mischief-making as a little girl. "I did. It was pouring rain, and the train station was a long way away. I didn't see any harm in it."

Sam leaned forward and clasped his hands in his lap. He stabbed her with a very seri-

ous look. "Actually, that was smart. The best
way to infiltrate the enemy is to go undercover.
Good job. Did you learn anything significant?"

Liz considered the wisdom of talking to Sam
about Gabe's offer but decided against it. Right
now, Sam was feeling guilty and contrite about
the loss of the cashier's check. Maria had told
Liz he'd gone through all his dresser drawers and emptied them completely. He'd even
cleaned out his closets, which Maria had never
known him to have done.

If Sam found out Gabe was interested in
buying their land, he might urge her to consider the sale because of the lost check. Liz
knew that Sam was content with the vineyard
just the way it was and he didn't feel it was necessary to expand the fields to include Matt's
land—her land. The fallow land was a young
person's dream. So it made sense that the acreage would appeal to someone like Gabe. Gabe
had the kind of energy and vision she guessed
her father had had all those years ago.

"Liz?" Sam pressed her. "What else did you
learn from our enemy?"

Enemy? It sounded vile when Sam said it,
but was that the truth? Right now, Liz believed
Gabe had wooed her with moonlit dances and
an unforgettable kiss in order to convince her

to sell her land to him. "Like I said, he talked a lot about his family. For instance, he's very close with his mother."

Sam sat back and rubbed his chin. "Since he's practically running their farm, I would have assumed he and his father were one and the same."

"Apparently not." She looked out the window thoughtfully. "I may be stepping out by saying this, but I get the impression Gabe has real issues with his father. He seems to be on edge when his father is around, or even when he comes up in conversation."

"Hmm. Close with his mother, huh?" Sam's voice dropped nearly to a whisper. "She doted on him."

Her grandfather's eyes had a faraway look as he spoke. How did Sam know Gina doted on Gabe? Liz had barely told him anything about Gabe. For a long moment, Sam appeared to be in another world. Then, quite suddenly, he jerked his gaze back to her.

"What else did he say?"

"That's what he said," Liz interjected, not paying attention to the faraway look in Sam's eyes. "She used to take him and his brothers to Chicago to see the theater and art galleries. The museums. He loved it."

"So did you, when I took you. Do you remember the aquarium and the planetarium?"

"I do, Grandpa." She smiled, feeling the last vestiges of her former fears about his memory and mind vanishing. "Those were wonderful times."

"Yes," Sam replied. "Wonderful. After Matthew and Kim died, I tried to make life as normal for you as I could." Sadness marked his tone. His voice caught on the final word.

"Oh, Grandpa!" Liz jumped up from the sofa and hugged him. "You did just that. I was so lucky to have you. I still am. Don't ever think otherwise. I had all the love and affection any child could ever want from a parent. And you were both mother and father to me. It must have been so hard on you."

He touched her long hair and smoothed it. "It's been my pleasure, Elizabeth. Every minute of it."

Liz looked up into her grandfather's loving blue eyes and winced at the thought that one day he would be gone. His loving presence would never be replaced by that of another person on earth.

CHAPTER FIFTEEN

GABE SAT AT the computer in the large walnut-paneled study that led to the back veranda. He was going over a new canning contract. They were about to have a bumper crop of Italian green beans they'd never grown before—what Gabe had thought would be an experimental year was turning out to be a productive one. The weather had been on their side, and because they'd received the right amount of rain on the exact days they'd needed it, his little crop was going to make them an extra ten thousand dollars. It wasn't much for a farm that pulled in hundreds of thousands of dollars a season, but Gabe believed that each time he could profit from a fallow piece of land, he was ahead of the game.

He pushed back in his chair and gazed out at the pool area, where his mother was spreading a colorful linen cloth on a table. She'd just come back from the hairdresser, who had trimmed her hair neatly to shoulder length and restored her dark brown color. There were times when Gabe looked at his mother and marveled at how little she had aged since he was a child. She had worked just as hard as Gabe's father all her life, yet she looked twenty years younger than she was. Gabe attributed this to her outlook on life: she believed that no matter what, every moment of every day was precious. She lived in the moment and never took anything or anyone for granted.

For the first time in his life, Gabe felt he'd found that same attitude in another person.

Liz.

Gabe stood, shoved his hands in his pockets and walked away from the window. Then he walked back. He sat down again, his mind filled with visions of Liz. The feel of her lips against his. The icy chill she'd given him when she'd turned down his offer.

He'd made some miscalculations in his life, but that kiss had to go down in his personal history as the worst.

And if that weren't bad enough, he'd blurted out that he would like to buy her land. He hadn't known the Crenshaws owned anything more than the fifty or so acres they had planted and worked. Once he'd realized that Liz and he were practically writing the same wine journal, he jumped at the idea of aligning forces.

It seemed natural to him.

But Liz had swung the opposite way and looked at him as if he were a terrorist, not a potential business partner.

He swiped his face with his hand then rubbed the back of his neck. "Well, you've gone and done it this time," he chided himself. "What were you thinking?"

Liz the woman and Liz the business partner were going to be not only frustrating to deal with but impossible to predict. At this point, he wasn't sure if she'd ever talk to him again, after the glare she'd thrown him when she'd driven away last night.

And despite all his strategizing about how to convince Liz that working together would benefit them both, his thoughts kept going right back to kissing her.

He turned off his computer. Just as well. He couldn't remember a word of the contract.

He picked up his cell phone, thinking he'd send her a text. *And say what?* He'd missed his chance to call or check in on her last night. He knew she'd liked it when he'd texted to make sure she'd gotten home safely after the engagement party. He'd had an opportunity to do that again yesterday, and he hadn't taken it. Not that he expected her to talk to him after what he'd said and done at the cove.

Gabe watched his mother carry a tray of food out to the table she was setting. She tossed a green salad inside a large wooden bowl, and then she began slicing a large loaf of Italian bread. He couldn't tell from this distance if it was her garlic bread, smothered in butter, minced sautéed garlic, parsley and basil, but he hoped so.

The bright summer sun glinted off the pool, and the sunbeams hit Gabe's eyes. Again, he immediately thought of sitting on the picnic table at sunset and kissing Liz. How was it possible that a simple kiss had affected him so deeply?

He'd met Liz when he was ten, but he knew from their talks about their pasts and the death of her parents that Liz didn't remember him from those days.

But he'd never forgotten her.

Gabe had struggled to tell Liz that his mother had taken him and his brothers to her parents' funeral, but each time he'd thought to broach the subject, he was afraid she would question his motives. Most of the time, Liz seemed to think he was some kind of carrier monkey.

And yet, at other times, he would swear that no woman had ever treated him with more genuine concern than Liz did. She was the first person he'd ever met who was truly interested in his dreams of winemaking. Perhaps it was because Liz was the first female vintner he'd known.

Gabe rubbed his chin. Now that he thought about it, that wasn't entirely true, either. He had met female winemakers and sommeliers in the past. It was Liz's attentiveness that was different. When she listened to him, she gave him all her concentration. She didn't blow him off or belittle his ideas.

In many ways she was so much like him.

The biggest difference between them was the fact that she'd grown up under the weight of grief and loss. Gabe couldn't begin to imagine how difficult that must have been for a little girl.

Gabe distinctly remembered his mother arguing with his father about taking the boys out of school for the funeral. None of his brothers understood why it was so important for them to attend, but they were all so happy to play hooky that they'd gladly gone. That funeral was the first memorial service Gabe had ever been to. Being the eldest, he'd been expected to make Rafe, Mica and Nate behave. But all of the boys had easily fallen into line when they'd sensed how solemn the day was.

What had impressed Gabe the most was his mother's stoic silence nearly all morning. She'd seemed to be in another world as she'd driven them back to school from the graveyard.

He remembered Gina talking to them about the sorrow of death and the misfortune of little Liz.

All these years, Gabe had kept a picture of Liz in his head, a gangly six-year-old with a river of honey-colored hair flowing past her waist, fanning across her back like illuminated angel's wings.

She'd held her grandfather's hand all day, and though the old man had cried openly, Liz had never broken down. Gabe had wondered if she'd been in shock, or if she had been trying to stay strong for her grandfather. Gabe knew that if his mother died, he would never be able to stop his tears.

Being emotional was probably a flaw of Gabe's, but his mother had told him once that he laughed joyfully, shouted his anger and cried out his sorrow because he cared about life so much.

Over the past seven or eight years, Gabe feared he didn't care about anything enough.

He'd started to feel dead inside. Working on the farm—the business contracts, the ledgers, the marketing plans—just wasn't exciting or fulfilling. He was following in his father's well-worn footsteps and the ruts were so deep they were nearly impossible to step above.

Gabe was at a crossroads, and this past year, he'd decided he had to do something about it or he'd wither from the inside out and blow away.

Being the eldest Barzonni, Gabe had precise responsibilities. It was his duty to oversee all that Angelo had built. To carry on the family name and business and to provide for the next generation.

Angelo had roamed the streets of Naples as an orphan, stealing, begging and scraping for every morsel of food, so Gabe supposed becoming a landowner in America, where no one knew him, was his father's brass ring. Life circumstances had molded Angelo into a survivor—no matter the cost to his family life. Gabe was well aware of the stories about how Angelo had come to own all the farms around his villa. When he was just a boy, Gabe had dismissed them as gossip or sour grapes. Now that he was older, he wasn't so sure.

Angelo had been blessed by being in the right place at the right time. He'd come to Indi-

ana right when a terrible drought had put most
farmers out of business. He'd had money saved
from years of working seven days a week at
every job he could find.

Once in Indiana, Angelo had bought several
farms for back taxes due, which many people
saw as stealing the land from his neighbors.
Other parcels and farms he negotiated squarely
with the owners or their estates and heirs as
time passed.

There was not a harder-working man on
earth than Angelo Barzonni, and he had
taught all of his sons diligence and persever-
ance. What he didn't ever acknowledge were
the dreams his sons fostered for themselves.

Angelo cared about sustaining his own
dream. Oh, he connected with Rafe because
of their racing horses, and he and Mica bonded
over Mica's inventive ideas to make the farm
run more efficiently. But his father's inability
to nurture his sons' needs and goals had cut
him off from them. Now there was nothing
left of their relationships but cordialities—the
respect an employee would give an employer.

Gabe had lost sight of his own dreams until
he'd had the chance to buy the Mattuchi vineyard. For the past six months as he'd worked
with the attorneys and Mario to finalize the

deal, his ambitions had come back to him one by one.

In the process of harvesting his passion, Gabe had realized that one day he would be forced to break his father's heart. He wasn't sure how many years he could run the farm and see to his vineyard at the same time. He told himself he was young and energetic and could do anything. If his father could build up his land and business to the degree he had, surely Gabe could work two jobs. At this phase, his little vineyard felt like moonlighting anyway.

But later…

Once the wines had been aged, once the vines had doubled and then tripled, he would have to tell his father he was moving on. He would have to quit the farm.

What kind of firestorm would erupt on that day? Would Angelo disown him? And would his mother side with him against his father or would she take Angelo's side? Would Gabe lose his whole family because he wanted— no, needed—to make a name for himself on his own terms?

Gabe needed to become his own person. When he made decisions, they needed to be his own. They would affect *his* business and not his father's farm.

He raked his fingers through his hair and stood stock-still as he thought of his little vineyard next to the Crenshaws'.

Mixed up in the turmoil about his future was Liz. Her image floated across his mind at least a dozen times a day. Okay, three dozen. Gabe didn't understand. He'd met stunning women before. But he'd only met one Liz Crenshaw.

He should have known better than to have kissed her. What had he been thinking? That he could grab some of that radiance for himself? Some of her courage?

Getting to know and understand Liz had fueled his new desire to be with her. His feelings for her were making him act totally out of character. He was usually secretive, but he'd told her about his childhood and his issues with his father. Gabe had bumbled and stumbled his way into her life, hoping simply to get to know her, and then crazy as it was, he'd continued to stumble right into a romantic trap.

He actually did care whether she got home safely. He did care what opinion she had of him. He wanted her to like him. He wanted her...

Gabe felt as if he'd been stabbed with a pitchfork. Could he be falling in love with Liz?

If he was, that would mean he should not

and could not pursue a land deal with her. But now that he'd calculated those precious acres into his own ambitions, letting the idea go was painful.

If he wanted Liz, really wanted her, he would have to give up his dreams—maybe for good.

Sure, he could make some wine on the Mattuchi land, but he'd always known it was just a start.

He could still buy grapes from foreign countries and blend and ferment to varying degrees. His wine would be good. But superlative? Probably not. And that was his goal.

He tried to conjure up the long-held vision of himself holding a bottle of award-winning, in-a-class-by-itself wine, but the image was slowly erased by the compassion for him in Liz's eyes.

For years, he'd vowed to himself that once he'd ventured onto his own path, nothing was going to stop him. Now he wasn't so sure.

Suddenly, he had two dreams he knew he couldn't live without. And the one with Liz in it was gaining ground, fast.

Gabe knew he'd blown it with her. Though he'd apologized to her for the kiss, she'd pushed him away as if he'd been carrying a deadly virus. Then he'd made matters worse by asking her about the land sale.

That was a hot button if ever he'd seen one. But why?

The answer was there somewhere in their conversations. He went over every word they'd said to each other. He could only surmise that her need to fulfill her father's dream was just as vital as his need to pursue a dream different from his own father's—to pursue a career as a vintner. If her drive was anywhere near as strong as his, he realized suddenly, Liz could easily be obsessed. And obsession was something Gabe understood in spades.

Gabe had ached to have a life of his own, and yet, he'd always felt he lived on the tenterhooks of his duty to his family and the sense of responsibility he felt toward his mother. He'd obsessed over how he would move out on his own and not break his mother's heart.

It was ironic, the way fate maneuvered two people together and then pulled them apart by using their own ambitions against them.

He didn't know if she'd ever want to see him again, but he hoped to heaven she did. If he was going to salvage their friendship, much less move to the next phase of their relationship, he'd better come up with something more than flowers with which to apologize.

He would also have to figure out a way to bring his father around to the idea of him spending time with Liz. And that was bizarre, as well. Both the things Gabe wanted most, Liz and his life as a winemaker, would create another rift in his already shaky relationship with his father. Ever since the night of Nate's engagement party, Gabe had been careful not to mention Liz or her grandfather around either of his parents, even though his father's prejudices made no sense to him.

It had been a long time since he'd pushed his opinions on any of the boys. Angelo had simply reverted to old behaviors that night.

But what has he got against Sam Crenshaw?

At that thought, a vision of young Liz at her parents' gravesite flashed across his brain.

He drummed his fingers thoughtfully on the doorjamb as he stared blankly out the window. He saw nothing but visions from the past. *Why would Mother take us to that funeral? Did she know Liz's parents all that well? Why was it so important we all be there? Why wouldn't she just go by herself?*

The more Gabe pondered the past and its connection to the present, the more questions he had about it. Something must have happened back then to cause his father to lash out against Liz now. As far as Gabe was concerned, it didn't matter. His father could rail all he wanted, but Gabe intended to see Liz whenever she would allow it.

Sadly, Gabe didn't need Angelo in order to botch his chances with Liz. Gabe already had his hands full convincing her he wasn't the bad guy.

Gabe looked out the French doors again and saw his parents as they shared their lunch. Suddenly, his mother rose frantically as if to move toward the house. Angelo shot out his hand and clasped her wrist to pull her back. He shook his head as he said something to her.

Gina opened up a cloth napkin and poured a glass of ice water into it, then placed it on Angelo's forehead. She gently pressed his head downward until it was between his knees.

Gabe opened the door and darted onto the terrace. "What is it?" he yelled.

Angelo waved his arm at Gabe. "I'm overheated is all. It's nothing. I'll be fine."

"He said he was dizzy," Gina replied. "Gabriel, open the umbrella so it gets the sun off your father's face."

Gabe cranked the umbrella until it cast its full shade over the table. "How's that, Dad?"

"Fine," Angelo replied. "I'm better already. I'm going to get back to work."

"Nonsense. You are not going on that tractor again this afternoon. Gabe, you take over for him. I want him to go in the house and get some rest," Gina commanded.

"Okay, Mother." Gabe studied his father. "Should we call a doctor?"

"No doctor!" Angelo growled. "I'm just slowing down. Anyway, I have to help Rafe with the horses."

"All right," Gina relented. "But after a nap."

Gina put her arm around Angelo's waist and walked with him into the house. Gabe turned around and headed toward the tractor, which was parked beyond the horse barn.

He would have to think about his dreams for a future full of Liz and Malbecs some other day.

CHAPTER SIXTEEN

LIZ STARED DOWN at her cell phone that sat on the wooden counter in the utility shed.

Thinking of you. What are you doing?

Why are you thinking of me, Gabe?

Liz thought of a dozen questions she could ask him, but each one would have elicited more banter, which she didn't have the time or patience to pursue. As she started to reply, she was surprised to see her hand was shaking. What did *that* mean?

She'd be lying if she told herself she hadn't been thinking about him. The fact was she couldn't get him out of her mind.

Liz scrambled for answers to her questions about love and her life's direction.

Had her mother been alive, Liz would have gone to her immediately, but she didn't have that luxury. What she did have were her parents' journals and a small cache of her mother's letters to her father. Because she'd been a child when she'd read the letters the first time, they'd all seemed romantic and idyllic to her. Reading them now as an adult, her interpretations would be more insightful. And she still had so much to learn from the journals her parents had written.

Even back then, Matt had been concerned about Sam's moodiness and occasional lack of concentration. So the behavior Sam had displayed when she'd gone to the lecture in Chicago clearly wasn't new. Sam had often forgotten things when her parents were alive, and it had been up to Matt or Kim to right the wrongs, finish the projects Sam had started and make hard decisions without including the older man.

Liz found one particular journal quite inter-esting because it was filled with her father's re-flections about the history of the vineyard and contained many details about Matt's young life, his mother's death and Sam's grieving process.

Apparently, after Liz's grandmother died, Sam had floundered in a sea of grief. It took a great deal of work on Matt's part to bring Sam back to the present and keep him focused. Then, in the summer of 1979, it was as if Sam had rejoined the living. In the vineyard, he was unstoppable. Matt was sixteen and had already honed his passion for winemaking. By the next summer, Matt had been accepted into UC Davis, and though he attended high school classes and clubs, he spent all his free time tending the vines and maintaining the cellars alongside his father.

However, Liz also read that in the spring and summer of 1980, Sam drove into town three or four times a week. This was unusual behavior for the older man. Still, Sam seemed happier than he had since his wife died. He smiled more often, and on several occasions, Matt had caught him singing to the vines. But no matter how many times Matt tried to elicit an explanation for his father's newfound happiness, Sam clammed up about it.

"It doesn't concern you," was all Sam had said.

Matt also wrote that Sam had taken to sitting in the rocking chair on the front porch nearly every night during the sunset. He'd abandoned his nightly news programs and sitcoms in favor of nature.

Between his homework, chores and constant study of winemaking, Matt was always too busy to join his father. Still, the quiet ritual had impressed Matt.

Liz realized that since Gabe had stolen his

way into her life, she had stopped watching television completely. Her head was too full of thoughts about Gabe during her leisure time. Mercifully, she was able to accomplish all her tasks around the vineyard with the same precision she'd always had. But the moment her jobs were done, her mind wandered to one place and one place only. Gabe.

Sam had been despondent over her grandmother's death, but it was possible that after a long period of mourning, his mind had just snapped back to reality. Liz had grieved for her parents for a year, but after that she'd been so busy with school—learning new things and making new friends—that the void she'd felt after their sudden death had been filled by her grandfather's love and her new friendships.

Suddenly it hit her. Sam had grieved until a new person had filled the void left by her grandmother.

Matt had only been sixteen when his mother died, so Sam would have been in his late thirties. It wasn't all that difficult for Liz to imagine Sam as a younger man. He was still robust, and she guessed that back then, he would have been a great deal like Gabe. Ready to take on the world, do new things…and make new friends.

But who?

Liz's phone vibrated in her hand. It was another text from Gabe.

Where are you?

"Will you stop, please?" she grumbled to herself.

Working.

I know that. But where, exactly?

I was cleaning my gun in the utility shed.

It's not loaded, is it?

No. But it can be. Why?

She grinned widely at her own joke.

Because I'm coming in.

Liz lifted her head at the sound of the door opening. Gabe's tall, wide-shouldered frame was backlit by the midday sun. He was wearing an old pair of jeans, work boots and a navy T-shirt that left not a single muscle to the imagination.

"Hi," he said, holding up a brown paper bag. "I bear gifts."

Liz chuckled as he walked toward her. She was always struck by his handsome face, and when he smiled at her, she knew his magnetism could crack a Geiger counter. "What kind of gift?"

"The apology kind. I can't stand you being angry with me."

"Anger would imply—"

"That you have feelings for me like I have for you?"

"Maybe. Or you could just be a pest. Like a horsefly or a mosquito."

"Good one. But I'm not buying it." He moved closer.

Liz felt her heart thrum in her chest. Each time she was near him, something happened to her that made her lose all reason.

Inhaling deeply to reset her reality rudder, she asked, "So, what are you doing here on a workday?"

He plopped the bag on the workbench and put his hand on his hip. "Face it, friend. For us, every day is a workday. If we don't take time to smell the roses, our entire lives will be wasted."

She pursed her lips and glanced at the brown paper bag. "Is this another one of those 'stealing time' things of yours?"

"Yep." He grinned mischievously. "I thought we could go on a picnic."

She shook her head. "No can do. I really do have an awful lot of work—"

"Don't go there," he warned.

"But it's true. I can't."

"Yeah, you can."

"No, Gabe. Besides, you should have called first."

"No way. You'd just have turned me down."

"Oh? Like I'm doing now?" She flipped her braid over her shoulder for emphasis.

He moved closer. "Now, listen to me. I brought my mother's famous Italian chicken smothered in marsala wine. There's also some Italian bread with olive oil for dipping, and some fresh parmesan. If you're really good, we can share her extraspecial hazelnut, cream cheese and raspberry torte."

Liz's eyes widened. "Like the one we had at Maddie and Nate's engagement party?"

He nodded. "The same. I figured since I

brought all these bribes, you could contribute a bottle of wine."

"Oh, you did?" She tried to fight a smile of delight but failed. "So, you admit to wanting to bribe me. That must mean you want something I would otherwise be unwilling to give you."

Gabe sucked in a breath and peered into her eyes. "That goes without saying," he said quietly.

Liz stood still, wondering how long she could go without initiating a kiss. She could plant a surprise one on him, as he'd done to her. But if she were smart, which she had promised herself she would be around Gabe from now on, she would pull back and remain in the safety zone.

"Well," she said, swallowing hard, "I'll get a pinot gris to go with the chicken."

"Not a chardonnay?" he asked, sounding wounded.

"Sold out. The next round of fermentation won't be done for another year. But you know that already." She cocked her head and shot him a suspicious look. "Or did you want to taste it while it's young so your apparently perfect palate can register its aging process?"

He grinned. "I hadn't thought of that, but

that's an excellent idea. I'll go for the chardonnay."

"Forget it," Liz replied sharply. "You get the
gris."

"I don't care, Liz," he said. "I'll drink water
as long as you come away with me. Just for an
hour. That's not so bad."

Liz jammed her hand onto her right hip.
"Something tells me that if we don't have this
picnic today, you'll just be here tomorrow."

"Probably." He smiled and grabbed the bag.
"Shall we?"

"Where are we going? The beach?"

"I thought we'd stay here."

"Here? In the utility shed?"

He burst out laughing. "This is too scary for
me, what with all your weapons close at hand.
I meant out in the vineyard."

"I know just the place," she offered. "I'll get
the wine."

ACROSS THE BRILLIANT azure sky, fleets of enormous white clouds sailed at high speed, mo-
mentarily blocking out the sun.

From the top of the hill, Liz and Gabe
could see past the farmland valleys and catch
a glimpse of the sun's rays bouncing off Lake

Michigan. A summer breeze gently moved the warm air.

Gabe had not only brought the lunch, but also paper plates, cutlery, plastic wineglasses with little twist-in pedestals and a saddle blanket, which Liz assumed he'd swiped right off the back of one of Rafe's horses.

"Looks like you thought of everything," she said.

He peered into the brown bag. "Everything but a bottle opener."

"No worries," Liz replied, whipping a corkscrew out of the pocket of her jeans. "I'm always packing," she joked.

While Liz opened the wine and poured it, Gabe turned on his iPhone and played a French song.

Liz held out the wine and stopped. "I know this song. I heard it when I was in France."

Gabe took the wine. "I love this album. I listen to it when I'm in the fields."

"Like today?" She looked down at his dirty work boots.

"Precisely."

"What were you doing?" she asked, taking her first bite of chicken. She smiled appreciatively as the flavors of garlic and marsala wine burst in her mouth.

"We're starting the plans for vine placement." He held up his hand to stop her protests. "I know. It's too hot to do the actual planting. I've been growing rootstock and graftings in my small nursery on the farm. They'll be even stronger by next April, when we plant them."

He chortled. "Boy, you should have heard the blowup between me and my father over that one."

"Tell me."

"I've always tinkered in my little nursery, but Dad didn't know I'd filled the pots with grape vines until he went to the Grange meeting and heard about me buying Mario's land. Dad said he didn't believe it until he went into my nursery and saw what I was doing."

"Then what happened?"

"He called me a lot of names. Fool and idiot among them. Needless to say, he was very angry that I hadn't told him outright and that he had to find out from the gossips. My counter was that we'd never shared much with each other, so why should we start now. I think that's what I said." Gabe shoved a piece of chicken into his mouth and chewed thoughtfully before he went on. "In the end, he said he didn't much care what I did as long as it didn't interfere with my work for him."

"So you didn't tell him that by next spring, you'd be pretty occupied with the vineyard."

"Like I said, I'll have a manager who will do most of the day-to-day work. I'll have to ride the fence for a while to keep peace in the family."

"That's important to you," she offered.

"Yes." He carefully wiped his fingers on a napkin, studying it.

Gabe took another bite of bread and, gazing out over the acres of Crenshaw land, said, "So, how long have you—or rather, your father—owned all this?" he asked, sweeping his arm in the air.

"My father bought it the year before he died." Liz felt her eyes mist over.

"It's beautiful," Gabe said. "You still miss him, don't you?"

"Very much. You know, it's funny. Because of you, he's come back to me, in a way."

Gabe's blue eyes flew open. "I reincarnated the dead? How'd I do that?"

She laughed softly. "I was angry with you for stealing the soil that day, and I went up to my father's study. I found his old journals and started reading them." She pushed the chicken around on her plate but didn't take another bite. "He went to UC Davis, just like you did."

Gabe stopped chewing. "He didn't."

She nodded. "That's where he met my mother. They must have been quite the couple back then. She was tanned and blonde and a self-proclaimed surfer girl. She didn't have a serious thought in her head until she met my dad. Legend has it, she told him once he had enough passion for the two of them." Liz smiled and wiped a tear from the corner of her eye. Then she looked up at the sky. "He was like you in some ways. He wanted to make his mark in the world of winemaking. He wanted to be known for doing the impossible. He not only wanted to create a good vintage, but he wanted to do it here in the middle of the country. Most people thought he was a fool when he bought all this land."

Gabe stared at her. "They think that of me."

Her eyes locked on his. "I'm sure you're wrong, Gabe. You're just stretching your wings. That's a good thing."

"I think so," he replied, nearly in a whisper. "It's what I have to do if I want to keep my sanity."

"Most people never had any sanity to begin with, so how can they judge?" She laughed.

Gabe was silent for a moment. Then he looked up. "I saw you—that day at the graveyard. I saw how you stayed strong for your grandfather when he was falling apart. You'd just lost your mom and dad and you didn't flinch. All those people talking to Sam and to you, and you held his hand so tight..." Gabe's voice caught in his throat, but he kept going. "I don't think I've ever seen anyone behave as bravely as you did, and you were only six."

"You remember all that?"

"I'll never forget it. You impressed me." He paused again. "It's funny—now that I think about it, I'm not sure I actually knew your name. All Mother said was that the funeral was for a friend. I assumed our mothers knew each other. They'd have been about the same age, right?" He pressed on without waiting for her answer. "As the years passed, I asked my mother about the little girl who'd lost her parents, and she would just brush off my questions. After a few tries, I gave up asking. It wasn't until I saw your blue eyes peering at me over the end of a shotgun that I put two and two together."

His expression was serious as he continued. "I stopped asking about you, Liz, but I didn't forget you. On that day, I knew I wanted to be your friend."

"And now you're making up for lost time?" she asked.

"You might say that."

Liz guessed there were a thousand thoughts rumbling around in Gabe's head, and oddly, she wanted to know what they were. "Did you ever want to live in the city, like your brother did?"

His eyes sparked with ambition and impatience.

"Never," he answered. "I wouldn't know what to do with myself if I couldn't feel the dirt under my boots or breathe in the electrically charged air when a storm is coming."

"Me, too," she said honestly.

"I find that very refreshing." He stretched out on the blanket and propped himself up on his elbow. "I've never known a woman who understood a farmer's life. All the women I've known want to go to parties and get their nails done. When they realize what hard work it is to labor on a farm, they run the other way."

Liz threw her head back and laughed. "Oh, and that's why you're so womanless at the moment? I'd venture to say it wasn't that way a month ago."

"Well, Miss Smarty Pants, you'd be wrong. There's never really been anyone..." He lowered his tone. "Well, there hasn't been anyone in over a year."

"Is that so?" she teased, tossing a paper napkin in his face.

"I envy you," he said seriously. "Following in your grandfather's and father's footsteps is what you really want to do."

Her father's footsteps? She felt as if she'd truly lost step with her dad. She'd jeopardized their well-being by not finding the cashier's check. She wasn't so sure it was Sam's fault at all, but hers. She had to have put it someplace safe before going to France. In the frenzy of leaving, she'd simply forgotten to give it to him.

Now that she'd nearly resigned herself to the fact that the cashier's check was lost, she almost wished she'd never gone to France or brought Louisa back. She had probably risked their financial well-being by borrowing the money to construct the tasting barn. Suddenly, Liz felt unsure of just about every business move she'd made.

Perhaps it was synchronicity that had brought Gabe to her life right now. He was going through all kinds of changes and being forced to make hard choices with his family, and he had chosen her to be his confidant. He appeared to genuinely trust her. Why else would he tell her about his discordant relationship with his father?

The more Gabe drew her into his world, the more she found herself really listening to him—with her ears, and her heart.

"I feel like I've barely begun," she replied, gazing across the expanse of unplanted land. She exhaled deeply. "My father put his heart and soul into this acreage. I have drawings and blueprints of precisely how it should all be planted. For instance, down there where the hill drops to that little valley, the temperature plummets twenty degrees and the soil is perfect for blueberries. Those blueberries he and I planted are still there. I want to blend that flavor with a new merlot vine I've ordered from California. Every time I come up here, it's as if I can reach out and touch him. I can feel my dad leading me, talking to me, showing me the way. I know it sounds silly to a lot of people, but I believe that."

"He's alive to you up here," Gabe offered. He tapped her head gently.

"Yes. Very much." She smiled.

Gabe knew the smile was for her father. Not for him. She carried her heart in the corner of her eyes. He could see so much love in her gaze, it nearly hurt to witness it. He wanted to burn this image into his memory—her thinking of her father. Loving him. Gabe wondered what that would be like, to be loved by Liz unconditionally.

"He would be very proud of you, Liz."

"Do you think so?"

"Yeah. I know I would be. I am. You want so much and you have the talent to do it all. You're going to make this place legendary. I can feel it."

She blushed. "I don't know about that. I thought I would have been further along by now. Unfortunately, it's going to take a great deal of money, which we really don't have… especially now."

"Now?"

"It's a long story. I don't want to bore you." Liz longed to share her worries with him. He'd trusted her enough to bare his problems. Friendship was a two-way street. Friends helped each other, and right now, she needed comforting.

He reached out and touched her hand and then kissed her palm. "Believe me, you could never bore me."

"We had a mishap. I thought I could take care of it, but it's not turning out to be that easy. We got behind on our taxes, and when I

called the assessor's office, they told me that
I'd have to make double payments. Though it
helps not having to pay it all in one big chunk,
it's very difficult. That's why there's no chardonnay. We're selling everything we've got."

"I'm so sorry, Liz. How can I help?"

"It's not your responsibility."

"But I want to help you. I do."

"Why, Gabe?"

She was looking at him with eagerness and
yearning. She wanted the truth from him. It
seemed that she wanted to trust him.

Gabe realized he'd fallen in love with Liz.
He would do anything for her. He'd move
mountains for her. Taxes were a sticky problem. If she was in deep, the situation could turn
dire. Was she in over her head with her new
tasting room, as the Mattuchis had said? Was
she in danger of losing her land?

There was no way Gabe would allow that to
happen. Lord only knew who would come in
here, pay off the taxes and then kick her and
Sam off the property. That very thing could
easily have happened to the Mattuchis if Gabe
hadn't stepped in. Sophie had said he'd been
their savior.

But would Liz see an offer from him in the
same light?

Would she think he was a guardian angel, or a devil?

Gabe believed there was only one answer for Liz and that was for him to buy her land. Not an outsider.

No, for Liz's dream to become reality, the best option for them both was for him to buy and plant those acres. He would be helping the woman he loved and her family, even if she didn't know about his feelings. Maybe then she would come to trust him. Even love him.

As far as Gabe was concerned, his idea could right all the wrongs in her life—all the wrongs between them—and if the fates chose to shine on him, Liz might come to see how good they could be for each other.

"You'll find a way, Liz," Gabe finally said, dipping his toe into the precarious waters he intended to tread.

"Yes, Gabe. I will find a way," she said resolutely.

Gabe touched her cheek and moved a long strand of hair behind her ear. The urge to kiss her nearly wiped out his courage. "I could help you if you'd let me."

"Help me?" She bristled.

"I could buy this land from you. You could pay the taxes and whatever mortgages you

have. You'd be solvent, and then we could—"
He stopped abruptly. Her blue eyes had turned
to ice.

She slapped his hand away from her neck,
where he'd been caressing her. "So that's your
plan!" She jumped up and planted her feet sol-
idly to steady herself.

"Liz, don't look at me that way! It was just
a thought. An idea to help you."

"You have no intention of helping me or my
grandfather, Gabriel. You're just after what can
help *you*. You saw my fallow land when you
checked into the Mattuchi farm. Admit it."

"Well, yes," he said, rising to stand face-
to-face with her. Despite the fact that he was
half a foot taller than she was and outweighed
her by fifty pounds, he realized she wasn't intimidated in the least. He would bet she would
keep up with him in a tussle, armed only with
adrenaline. "But I had no idea how large it was
until you told me. And now showed me."

"And since then, you've been trying to figure out just how you could wangle your way
into my life and get on my good side, or out-
and-out romance me like you've been doing.
But don't worry! I blame myself, too. I should
never have told you about the back taxes. I'm
an idiot." Liz felt more than just stupid. She was

hurt and disappointed that Gabe still wanted her land more than he apparently wanted her. Tears threatened to spill over, but she beat them back and glared at him.

"No, you're not. It's like I told you. I've admired your courage since you were a kid. Since I was a kid."

"I'm not buying it, Gabe. You probably made that story up. It was a pretty good one—I'll give you that."

He took a deep breath. "Now you're twisting everything around. I just wanted to help you."

"Why?" Part of her felt gutted, raw and seeping. The other part was begging for the truth. Did he have any feelings for her at all? Was it possible she had been moved to her core by his kiss, and he hadn't? Did he sleep all night through without thinking of her? Was she the only one falling in love?

She kept asking "why" because she needed to hear his reasons for continuing to come around. Even now, heated by her anger and feelings of betrayal, she still wanted him. She was more in love with him than she'd thought possible and it terrified her.

"Honestly, Liz, I have never met anyone as pathologically paranoid as you are. Do you do this to everyone you meet, or just to me?"

"Do what?" she demanded in a voice one decibel below a shout.

"Distrust. It's written across your face. You don't believe a thing I tell you. Not even that, as a child, I thought you were courageous. Maybe you weren't courageous after all. Maybe you were just scared stiff like you are now. It's a lot easier to label everyone in the world as a liar or a thief than it is to actually trust a person. So that's what you do to stay safe. You lock the whole world out. Then you can't get hurt. You're untouchable. I may have been too busy or too picky to have ever had a relationship, but what's your excuse? You've never had one for the reason I just hit on."

"You haven't hit on anything," she said. "Your behavior is textbook projectionist. All narcissists do that. They shine the spotlight of blame onto someone else so it never shines on them. You're only angry because your ploy didn't work. I called you on it."

He shook his finger at her and then let his hand drop. "What's the use? I'm out of here."

He leaned down and gathered the food, cutlery and plates he had brought. He shoved it all into the paper bag.

Liz stood frozen to the spot as he gathered up the horse blanket.

Holding the rolled-up blanket under his arm, Gabe stopped long enough to stare her straight in the eye. "Goodbye, Liz."

Liz watched Gabe tromp down the hill and cross the flat land to the gravel parking area. Liz watched him toss his things in the trunk and then drive away.

"Good riddance, scumbag," she said, feeling her anger deflate until she was completely drained. The heat that had threatened to sear her insides was replaced with a hollow void. The saplings of hope she'd unearthed as she'd gotten to know Gabe were now withered and dead. She felt the same way she had when she'd first stared down at her parents' graves.

Today, she'd lost a new friend.

As she trudged down the hill from her father's favorite place, a new fear sprang to life.

Selling her land to Gabe would solve all their financial issues. She could pay the back taxes and current taxes and still have enough to finish buying the equipment she wanted. But selling to Gabe would mean she would have to face a deeper loss than ever before. She would have to lose her father all over again. His dream would be gone and with it, her own plans and goals. She'd buried both her mother and father once. Gabe had said she'd been brave and strong back then, but Liz knew she could never do it a second time.

That second death would be so painful and everlasting, she knew it would be her undoing.

CHAPTER SEVENTEEN

THE DUST FROM Gabe's tires had barely settled in the driveway by the time Liz reached the tasting room. There were three cars in the parking lot, all with out-of-state plates. Liz caught Louisa's eye as she grabbed her apron from her office.

She went to the counter, where Louisa had just poured a flight of reds for three men in shorts and expensive golf shirts. "What can I do to help?" Liz asked.

Louisa nodded toward the far corner of the room, where a woman was sitting near the windows. "That lady wants a cheese plate. I haven't been able to get it for her."

"I'll do it. What else?"

Louisa leaned her head close to Liz's ear. "I saw Gabe with you. You should be smiling but you look terrible. *N'est-ce pas?*"

Liz forced a grin as she turned around and went to the refrigerator to pull out a selection of cheeses. Taking a white pottery plate out of the cupboard, she placed cheese, crackers, pita chips and a fresh daisy on the plate.

"Can I get you anything else?" Liz asked as she set the plate in front of the auburn-haired woman.

The guest glanced up from her tablet and smiled. "I would love another glass of wine, but I have to drive back to Chicago. I'd like to buy a bottle of the cabernet I tried. It's wonderful," she said. "It's expensive, isn't it?"

"Very."

"I still want it. I'd also like a case of the pinot grigio and a half case of your ice wine."

Liz tilted her head and peered at the woman. She was immaculately dressed in an expensive navy suit with white piping. She wore high-heeled navy shoes and had a classic Chanel bag that shouted style. "You look familiar. Have you been here before?"

"Yes. Just a few weeks ago. Your tasting room is so cozy, and I adore Louisa. She's turned me onto some very good wines that my friends in Chicago just love. I had no idea all this was here." She waved her hand toward the window overlooking the vineyard. "Actually, I grew up in Indian Lake. I've passed through here several times lately. I'm looking for a new home base for our company."

"And you're considering Indian Lake?"

"Among others, yes." She stuck out her hand. "I'm Katia Stanislaus."

"Liz Crenshaw." Liz shook hands with Katia. "Did you go to Indian Lake High School?"

"I did. But I'm sure you were in grade school back then." Katia paused. "When I drove up I could have sworn I saw Gabriel Barzonni driving away."

"Yes, you did. Were you a classmate of his?"

"No. I was a senior when he was a sophomore. But I remember watching him play football. We all thought he would go pro. He was that good. What's he doing now?"

"He works for his father on the farm."

Katia nodded with understanding in her eyes. "Yeah. His future was pretty well carved out for him, wasn't it?"

Liz chewed her bottom lip thoughtfully. "You must have known them all pretty well."

"We all knew Angelo," Katia said. "I always felt sorry for those boys."

Liz had to concentrate in order to keep from dropping her jaw. Pity for a Barzonni? What didn't she know? Gabe had been pouring his heart out to her for weeks and she was realizing through this one conversation with Katia that she hadn't been paying close enough attention. Liz had been so focused on her own problems and anxieties that perhaps she hadn't been fair to Gabe. Gabe was right. He'd been doing the majority of the friendship-building. He'd made a generous offer and she'd crucified him for it. She really was paranoid—in addition to a long list of other faults.

She realized it was her turn to apologize. Clearly, there were depths to Gabe she had yet to explore—beyond his desire to buy her land.

"I suppose having an inherited career can be a good thing." Katia smiled widely, her eyes glittering.

Liz couldn't help but wonder what it was like to be so beautiful.

Katia continued. "It was very lucky for you, wasn't it? I mean, your vineyard was here when I was a little girl. My mother and I used to come and pick our own apples and pears. I have some very happy memories of this farm. I guess it's a vineyard now. But can people still pick their own fruit?"

"No, we pick them ourselves and use some for ciders. It's so nice to hear we were a part of your life."

Katia sighed wistfully. "Your place is like home to me. You have no idea. It's lovely."

Louisa walked up to Liz and whispered, "I need two cases for those guys over there." Louisa indicated to the men at the counter for whom she'd been pouring flights. "I hate to take you away, but Aurelio isn't answering his phone."

"No problem." Liz turned to Katia. "Excuse me, Katia. It was a pleasure to meet you."

"Same." Katia smiled back.

Liz pulled her cell phone out of her pocket. There were no calls and no texts.

No Gabe.

Liz felt her stomach turn. The sour taste of guilt rose in her throat.

She hid her face as she flew out the door toward the fermenting barn and aging cellars, hoping Louisa would not see her tears.

Angrily, she crossed the parking lot, wishing she could stop Gabe's words from echoing in her head.

Untouchable.

Paranoid.

She opened the barn door and flipped on the fluorescent lights. She walked past the steel tanks, not seeing anything but the look on Gabe's face when he'd assaulted her with his opinions.

He'd appeared to be more stunned than

angry. And had that been genuine concern she'd read in his eyes?

To keep herself from falling under his spell completely, she had to protect herself. Gabe said he wanted to be her friend, but at the same time, it seemed as if he wanted more. Why else would his eyes continually fall to her lips? Why did he move so close to her to ask even the simplest questions?

Gabe was invading her space. Making her feel uncomfortable. And he was doing it on purpose.

His goal was to try to buy their vineyard. Or at least a large chunk of it. And she had given him the ammunition with which to pursue his goal, guilt-free.

She felt off balance and weak in the knees. How could she have fallen in love with such a con artist? How desperate she must look to him now!

She had to pull herself together. She had an entire summer's and autumn's worth of wedding-related events to endure with him. He'd humiliated her already. She couldn't let her girlfriends know how much he'd duped her. Used her.

Soon, Gabe would be out at the Mattuchi vineyard nearly every day.

A few short weeks ago, she'd been in power, controlling her own business, vineyard and life.

Along with the shock of the lost cashier's check, Gabe had appeared, and everything had been inverted. She didn't know up from down anymore. The worst part of it was that she'd fallen in love with him, and as a consequence of that she had to keep him at arm's length, to push him out of her life. She wanted her world to go back to the way it had been before he'd stumbled into it.

But it wasn't working out that way.

He'd accused her of being paranoid.

Gabe standing next to her—so close she could feel his breath on her cheek—pointing out her flaws, should have crushed her on the spot. But somehow, she'd stood up to him. She hadn't blinked or cried. She'd withstood his flogging and watched as he'd walked away.

She'd found the courage to pretend he had not hurt her. To act as if his words would have no lasting impact. But it wasn't true.

Here, deep in the earth, where no one could see or hear her, she could shout, scream, yell and curse him.

But she didn't.

Because he was right.

I am paranoid. I am afraid.

Until an hour ago, Liz had allowed herself to believe that Gabe saw past her fears and accepted her the way she was.

She had been wrong. He'd wanted her land. Not her.

And what if he had actually wanted Liz? The land came with her. What would he do if she didn't have it? Would he want her then?

The ache in Liz's heart was agonizing. But her anger was stronger—it grew and burned away the pain of her heartbreak.

Tears had been streaming down Liz's cheeks, though she had remained unaware of them. She'd been used. She'd told Gabe private things about her parents and her love for her grandfather. Had told him her goals for the vineyard. She'd shared her dreams with him. And worse, she'd told him her fears.

You must have lost your mind! she chided herself. *Well, it's the last time. This can't happen again. Ever.*

Everyone on the vineyard depended on Liz. Her strength, energy and passion kept the vines alive and the company's hopes thriving.

It was up to her to erase Gabe Barzonni from her life. She would find a way to pay the taxes and she would find a way to fulfill her father's dream.

She would do it.

And she would do it on her own.

CHAPTER EIGHTEEN

LIZ SAT IN the kitchen staring at the vineyard ledger on her laptop and feeling gloom seep into her veins. She'd paid yet another large check on the back taxes, finished the payroll for the skeleton crew of day workers they absolutely had to hire for the harvest and covered the month's utility bills. There was less than five hundred dollars left in the account. Liz had drained the savings two weeks before to pay six thousand on the current property taxes and mortgage. Though their summer sales had been strong, the tourist trade was going to drop off in the fall. Two days ago, she'd landed a small grocery chain account down county, and that would help them through to the winter holidays.

They'd always managed to make it through from one year to the next. She reminded herself that both Sam and Aurelio had predicted a bumper crop this harvest, which would yield a third more bottles of wine than last year. If that came to fruition, they could make it, but barely.

Still, only having five hundred dollars for groceries, gasoline and essentials for the rest of the month made Liz uneasy.

She turned off the computer and looked over at the pretty present she'd wrapped for Maddie and Nate's couple's shower at Mrs. Beabots's. Even her precarious financial situation didn't fill her with as much trepidation as the thought of tonight's party.

It was mid-September—nearly a month since she'd last heard from Gabe. She knew in her heart her initial assessment of him as a thief had been correct. He had never wanted her. He'd only used her to try to buy her fallow land.

She'd revealed her innermost aspirations to him—making Crenshaw Vineyards as productive as any California vineyard. Gabe knew of Liz's devotion to Sam and her concern for his well-being. These were the priorities in her life. Had he not heard her? Did he honestly believe she would consider selling to him?

For all his protestations that he just wanted to be her friend, what he really wanted was to plunder her. Perhaps Gabe was following in his father's footsteps in more ways than one. Angelo had coerced many farmers into selling to him when times had been tough. Maybe Gabe had thought he would give his father's tactics a try.

Liz had avoided Gabe completely since that day on the hill. She had successfully kept to the vineyard, occupied as she had been with end-of-summer duties, including bringing in the harvest.

Tonight, her asylum ended. Not only was Liz expected to be present at the shower, but Sam had talked about nothing else for two weeks. He'd bought a new white shirt and sport coat for the occasion. Liz had considered making a last-minute excuse so she didn't have to go. She could always give Maddie her gift later, or send it with Sam. But Maddie would have been very disappointed if any of her friends wasn't with her. Maddie's only family member was her reclusive mother, and Babs Strong had not been invited to the wedding. Liz wanted to be a loyal friend, even if seeing Gabe tonight would be like facing the devil. Liz steeled herself for the showdown.

"Grandpa!" Liz shouted. "Are you ready?"

"What?" Sam answered from the living room.

"Are you ready to go?" she asked, picking up her gift and carrying it down the hall. Sam was sitting in his recliner, watching the weather channel with the sound muted. "Why are you still wearing your work clothes?"

He looked up at Liz, who was dressed in a midnight-blue cocktail dress with a sequined and beaded cardigan to match. On her feet she wore gold, low-heeled sandals. "Where are you going?"

"*We* are going to Mrs. Beabots's shower for Maddie and Nate."

"That's tomorrow."

"This *is* tomorrow."

Sam's eyes flew open and he nearly hopped out of his chair with more energy than she'd seen in him in years. "Give me twenty minutes."

"Don't forget to shave!" she said as he whisked past her and slammed the bathroom door.

Mrs. Beabots's grand Victorian home was ablaze with lights. Enormous Boston ferns hung from the porch ceiling. Soon, Mrs. Beabots would take them indoors and nurture the plants until the January furnace heat destroyed them. Liz wondered offhandedly if Gabe's nursery, where he fostered his grape vines and grafted rootstocks, would offer the right climate in which to prolong the life of Mrs. Beabots's ferns.

Liz parked half a block from Mrs. Beabots's. Sam got out of the truck and nearly bolted down the sidewalk, stopping halfway to the house. "C'mon, Lizzie. Take the lead out of those shoes."

"My goodness. If I didn't know better, I'd say you had a hot date waiting for you."

"Don't be silly. But Emma is the best cook in town."

Liz walked up to him and put her arm through his. "Emma, eh? I don't think I've ever heard anyone call her by her first name."

Sam grinned. "She was a real beauty in her day."

"She still is. And she's sharper than you are."

"Honey, everyone on the planet is sharper than I am," Sam joked.

As they climbed the steps of the front porch, Liz glanced up the boulevard and noticed both sides were filled with cars she recognized. Including a newly polished black Porsche.

She swallowed hard and touched her earrings. It wasn't like her to feel self-conscious, but she did now. She couldn't understand why she would be feeling this way. Wasn't she trying to thwart Gabe's romantic moves? Wasn't she trying to signal that she was off-limits? Wasn't she still livid with him? She was the one who had been wronged. She would have to hold her ground and not buckle.

He only wants what you represent, Liz. He doesn't want you. Never did.

As Sam rang the bell, they could hear music playing and laughter inside. Lots of laughter.

And then the door flew open.

"Emma!"

Mrs. Beabots was dressed in a vintage black knit Chanel suit with gold buttons and gold braid trim, just as the designer herself would have worn in 1945. Her hair was meticulously coiffed in a sleek, chin-length cut that, though gray, looked very much like Coco's. However, Liz seriously doubted the famous Parisian designer had possessed as much sparkle and energy at eighty-one as Mrs. Beabots did.

"Liz, don't you look scrumptious." She held out her arms for a hug.

"Thank you for hosting this party, Mrs. Beabots. I know Maddie is so happy and thankful." Liz felt tears in her eyes. "You are her real family."

"I know, pumpkin. I know. But you're her sister, as well. And don't forget it. That's what we all are here in Indian Lake—family for each other."

Then Mrs. Beabots turned to Sam, who was patiently waiting for recognition. "Sam," she said in a gentle whisper. "I'm so very glad to see you."

Sam leaned down, hugged Mrs. Beabots and lifted her up off the floor.

"Oh, you crazy boy. Put me down." Mrs. Beabots giggled.

Sam set her back down on the floor.

"Now come in and join the others."

"Is there anything I can help you with?" Liz asked as she and Sam followed the older woman inside.

"I always have jobs for my girls. Would you supervise the gifts? Lands above, but yours is the prettiest one here, Liz. I put them all in the front parlor since the buffet is in the dining room and the guests are all gathered in the living room. The front parlor was always Maddie's favorite, Sam. It seemed appropriate to me that Maddie and Nate open their gifts in there. It's small, but we'll all peek around the corners. What do you think, Liz?" Mrs. Beabots rambled.

"We'll make it work. We could even film

them and conference call everyone on their smartphones."

"Are you speaking in Martian, dear?" Mrs. Beabots asked, leading them to the dining room.

The long table was covered with platters of appetizers, from crab rangoon to sugared bacon bites to tiny red potatoes filled with feta cheese and chives. Liz knew Mrs. Beabots had made all the appetizers herself, and each bite would be cooked to perfection. Her grandfather was right. Mrs. Beabots was Indian Lake's best cook. She wasn't about to let her reputation dim.

At the far end of the room a large round table held five antique epergnes filled with Maddie's signature cupcakes, iced in a rainbow of colors. Illuminated icicles, silver snowflakes and crystal stars were suspended above the cupcakes, and Liz guessed this was going to be the aesthetic of Maddie's winter wedding reception.

Sam proudly poured himself a glass of Crenshaw merlot, while Liz helped herself to some champagne.

Taking in all of Mrs. Beabots's careful preparations for the party, Liz felt a lump of emotion deep in her throat. When Mrs. Beabots said that Sarah, Maddie, Liz, Isabelle and Olivia were like daughters to her, she was more than serious. They were her family. They were all orphans of one kind or another. Emotionally, they had all needed a mother, and Mrs. Beabots had been that to each of them. She had been their lifeline when they had needed one. Even in her vintage Chanel suit, she was full of homespun wisdom. She was worldly and small town at the same time. She was more than just a friend—she had been a mentor, guide and supporter for all the young women in Liz's group.

"Liz?"

Liz's mind slammed into the wall of reality.

"Gabriel."

He was shockingly handsome in an indigo suit that must have been custom-made—no store-bought garment could have skimmed a man's body that expertly. But it wasn't the suit or the white shirt or the silk tie that made her weak. It was the look in his eyes as he gazed at her. She saw pain, contrition and regret in those blue depths, and for an instant, she felt guilty for putting those feelings there.

Then she felt adrenaline shoot down her spine and turn it to titanium. She lifted her glass of champagne. "Here's to the happy couple."

"Barzonni," Sam grumbled, sticking out his hand. "I assume your family is here?"

"Yes, sir. My brothers are in the living room with my father. My mother is in the kitchen helping with something or other."

"Gina would do just that," Sam said, immediately putting his glass down on a table and walking toward the kitchen.

Liz peered at her grandfather curiously. "How does he know…" She never finished her question, as Gabe moved in beside her and she lost her train of thought.

"How are you, Liz?" he asked. The nonchalance in his tone sounded forced, and his face was filled with unease.

She folded her arms across her chest. "Fine, thanks," she said cordially, as if they were distant acquaintances. As if they had never kissed.

"Still hating me, I see."

Liz peered at him. He was standing unnervingly close to her. She wondered if he knew the dramatic effect his movements had on her. And if he did, was he using that to manipulate her?

She had to brace herself to keep from getting caught in his game, because right now all she could think about was his scent and warmth. She ached to put her hand in his.

Liz lifted her chin haughtily. "And do you blame me?"

"Liz." He breathed her name in a way that made her breath catch.

"No, Gabe," she said, her better sense prevailing. "I don't hate you. I haven't given you a second thought."

"Oh. That bad, huh?" He looked away and then leaned in so that his eyes bored into hers. She had no choice but to gaze into their depths. "Liz, you have me all wrong. You misunderstood everything I was trying to say."

"Oh, and you're so innocent," she shot back sarcastically. "I suppose that's why you sent me all those emails and texts." She regretted the words as soon as they came out of her mouth. She'd tipped her hand, revealing that she had expected, even wanted, to hear from him. She hadn't played this very cool at all. In fact, she needed to just stop talking altogether in order to prove to him he didn't matter to her in the least.

Gabe rolled his eyes. "You're honestly telling me you would have read anything I might have sent?"

"No. I'd delete them."

"I figured."

She pulled back from him like a turtle going into its shell. "I'll tell you what, Gabe. You go your way, I go mine. It's for the best. I'll see you at…at however many of these things we have to attend for Maddie and Luke's sake."

"Liz," Gabe said in a low, serious tone. "I wanted to help you, not hurt you. I still do, but you're jumping back from me faster than a jackrabbit from a predator. And I have to constantly ask myself why that is."

"I don't know what you're talking about."

"Sure you do," he said, placing his hand around her wrist. "Right now your pulse is beating like a war drum. You act like an animal that's caught in a trap. I'm not the enemy here, Liz."

"You're not my friend, either."

"I'm trying to be, Liz. Maybe you've never had a real friend before…"

Angrily, she snatched her hand from his grasp. "I have lots of friends," she replied tersely.

"Sure, girlfriends. Who all have their own lives and loves. But what about you? Don't you ever ask yourself if you'd like the same thing?"

"Look who's talking," she said, jamming her forefinger into his chest. "You're the original love-'em-and-leave-'em lothario."

"Wrong. Sadly, I didn't love them in the first place. I didn't take the time. This is different."

Liz sucked in her breath. "Different? What are you saying?"

"What I've known for some time now is that you mean a lot to me." He mussed his hair with his fingers. "Frankly, you make me nuts. I can't get through a single hour without thinking about you."

He smiled slowly, with warmth and sincerity, and for an instant, Liz almost fell into his trap. She had to get away from Gabe and her love for him. No good could come of it. Just the idea of giving in to her feelings for him shot terror through her veins. If she fell for him, it would end eventually, just as all real love stories did. Liz didn't believe in taking chances. She believed in keeping everything precise, orderly and manageable, just like her rows of grape vines.

Giving Gabe access to her heart would be a disastrous move. It could only end in heartbreak. Even if things worked out between them, they'd eventually have to face the greatest loss of all: death. Just as she had had to do at a very young age.

Liz could feel the panic building. "This… scenario you're trying to manufacture…"

"Manufacture?" He shook his head. "Liz, you don't take me for that much of a fool, do you? There's already something going on. You wouldn't have kissed me the way you did if you didn't feel *something* for me."

"That was before I discovered your true motivation. You just want my land."

He pulled back. "Get off that, will you? It's true that your land would be a dream come true for me. But wanting that doesn't negate my feelings for you or what I think is happening between us. Besides, I already have a vineyard."

"A playground. A patch. That's all that little space is." She waved her hand in the air. "That's not enough for you and we both know it."

"True. I'll find more land. Maybe I'll go up into Michigan. Yours isn't the only vineyard around the lake," he replied harshly. Then he ground his jaw. "Fine, you just go on pretending I'm the bad guy. That'll keep you all safe and secure. If that's the way you want it, you got it." He put his champagne glass down. "I'll see you around, Liz."

"Thanks," she said and watched him walk away from her for the second time.

Liz didn't know how it was possible, but this second departure was more annihilating than his first one had been. They were in a house.

He had only gone into the next room, and yet he could have been on Mars. It suddenly felt as if they were light-years apart. She'd finally gotten through to him. She knew this time he wouldn't bother her again. She should have been washed in relief, but what she really felt was inexplicable sadness, as if she'd just lost something very valuable.

CHAPTER NINETEEN

BEYOND MRS. BEABOTS'S two-story carriage house, which had been recently refurbished, was a well-maintained walking garden. It had been Mrs. Beabots's pride and joy ever since she came to live in this grand dame of a house on her wedding night.

In the center of the garden was a row of flowering fruit trees, which were now heavy with pears and apples. A faint gilding had brushed the edges of the leaves to signal the end of the growing season. Along the south-facing side of the garden were several trellises with lush climbing roses, passion flowers, mandevillas and night jasmine. Beneath the trellises were hundred-year-old marble and stone benches. Most modern homeowners would have installed path or solar lights, and maybe even "moon" lighting up in the trees, but Mrs. Beabots was old-fashioned. She insisted on carrying a kerosene lantern or flashlight with her whenever she ventured out into the dark.

Liz followed the red brick pathway to the gazebo at the back of the garden, where she could see a lantern glowing. Two figures sat inside—a man and woman.

As she drew closer, she could hear them laughing, and from their soft, hushed tones, she sensed camaraderie.

Sam and Gina?

Suddenly, Liz felt as if she was intruding on a private moment. Questions came at her like bullets, each one opening a new wound. Their whispers and soft laughter suggested a deep, emotional connection that went far beyond friendship. Had they been in love once? Were they in love now? When had it all started? And why were they seeing each other now?

Sam had his arms around Gina, and she'd laid her head on his shoulder. They seemed comfortable and familiar in each other's arms.

Liz couldn't stand any more second-guessing. "Grandpa? Is that you?" she said as she marched forward.

"I'm here," Sam replied. Gina slipped out of his embrace and stood a foot away from him. "What's up, *ma petite*?"

"Dinner is being served." Liz paused at the bottom step to the gazebo. She looked directly at Gina. "How are you tonight, Mrs. Barzonni?"

Gina smiled softly. "I'm good. Very good now, actually." She reached out her hand to Sam. "Thank you, my friend. I will never forget this night."

"The pleasure was all mine," he said, taking her hand and kissing it.

Gina shot Liz a meaningful glance. "I'll see you both inside."

She walked away, the full skirt of her white chiffon dress swishing. As she passed through the dappled moonlight beneath the autumn trees, the sequins and seed pearls on her sweater sparkled like dewdrops, making her appear ethereal.

"Gina is so beautiful," Liz said.

"She sure is," Sam replied admiringly. "That's exactly what I thought the first day I met her."

Liz spun around. Was she actually going to get the truth? If Sam had caught her redhanded, she wasn't so sure she'd have told him the truth about Gabe. In fact, she hadn't told any of her friends about what had been going on between the two of them. Not that he'd kissed her, nor that he'd told her he wanted to be more than friends. She certainly hadn't told anyone she'd been fool enough to think he'd been telling the truth. She'd kept his invasion of her life a secret. Was it because she was ashamed of him? Ashamed of herself? Did she think herself weak for having fallen for him? Or had she kept her mouth shut because she wanted to get rid of him before he had a chance to cause any real damage?

"And when was that, Grandpa?"

"About two years after your grandmother died. It was the summer of 1979."

"But she was married!"

"No, she wasn't married, but she was engaged. Angelo had been in Indian Lake for about eight years by then. He lived in a trailer on his farm. He'd already started buying up the surrounding land. Times were tough for all of us back then. Interest rates were sky-high. Winters were brutal. Summers were worse—drought, diseases. The government had banned all the good pesticides and hadn't come up with anything to replace them with. Most farmers thought it was the end of the world. I was buried in grief and depressed. I'd taken to coming into town on Saturday afternoons to see the science-fiction double features at the Roxy Theater. Your dad was about sixteen then, and on every other Saturday, he took off to the beach and I went to town. I saw Gina coming out of the ladies' shop next door one Saturday. She was the most beautiful woman I'd ever seen. She was much too young for me. She was only twenty-seven and I was forty-three. But she was just learning English. She was renting a room at Hazel Martin's house."

"Hazel still rents rooms. Maddie has lived there for years."

"No kidding? I thought Maddie lived above her café."

"She rented it to Lester MacDougall. Ann Marie Jensen wanted Lester to have a good experience here in town so he wouldn't run away again."

"Ann Marie was always wise," Sam said, sitting back down on the stone bench. "Anyway, I drove Gina around Indian Lake—showed her some places to shop, the Civic, the beaches, the ballet and symphony. I told her where to send her children to school when the time came."

"Shouldn't Angelo have been doing all that for her?" Liz asked.

"You would think so," Sam said. "But Barzonni was too busy building his empire. He didn't have time."

"Wow, it's a miracle they met in the first

place." Liz glanced back toward the house. "Do you know how they did meet?"

"She said it was almost like an arranged marriage, but without the family doing the arranging. Angelo was an orphan. Somehow he'd amassed a fair amount of money in Sicily before he came to the States. Anyway, Gina was one of six girls, and she met Barzonni just before he came to Indiana, at some friend's birthday party. She was only fourteen or fifteen at the time. I guess Angelo kept bragging that he was going to America and that someday he would be very wealthy, own a big house and throw great parties of his own. Gina told me she was young, naive and hooked. She fell in love not with Angelo, per se, but with his dream of the future. He left Italy but they always stayed in touch. Gina didn't want to become another Italian housewife. She wanted to live an adventurous new life in another country. She loved growing things. She knew she would make him proud with the lovely garden she would keep, and the dinner parties she would throw using her own fresh ingredients as the bases for her meals.

"So, when she was twenty-six, he sent for her. She made him promise they would not get married until after she'd spent at least six months in the US so that she would know if she liked it."

Liz tried to imagine what her grandfather had looked like back then, when he was in his early forties. He would have been fit from working the vineyards every day, yet vulnerable because his wife had recently died. Liz guessed that back then, Sam could easily have put sparkles in Gina's eyes. "And she fell in love with you?"

"No. I don't think so."

"What? How could she not fall in love with you? You are the best ever. Was it the age difference?"

He smiled at her then took her hand and patted it. "Sometimes, life is so complicated. Even if something seems right or natural, it doesn't always happen the way it should."

"But you fell in love with her?" Liz ventured.

"I did. I always told myself it was just a crush. But tonight, seeing her, smiling at me with so much life in her eyes, I swear, I think I lost my heart all over again."

"But, Grandpa, this time she really is married."

"Don't I know it," Sam groaned.

Liz rubbed her temples. "How is it possible

that everything has gotten so thorny all of a sudden?"

"Really? I thought things just got straightened out," he said.

"How's that?"

"I had a chance to really talk with Gina. Over the years, we've seen each other around town or at the symphony or on the Christmas candlelight tour, but I've never really been able to tell her how I felt. I mean, she had the boys to raise…"

Liz put her hand on his arm. "What do you mean, tell her how you felt?"

"I wanted her to know that I'm her friend and she can always count on me if she needs me. With or without Barzonni, I'm there for her."

"You said that?"

"Yes. I did."

"That's really…courageous, Grandpa."

"Because I'm so old?"

"Well, yes," Liz replied. She didn't want to hurt her grandfather's feelings. He was still the most precious person in the world to her and she would never want him to think he wasn't first on her list of priorities.

"Liz, it's precisely because I am this old that I decided to speak up. I can't tell you how many times I've stayed awake all night and wondered 'what if…'"

"What if what?"

"What if I'd told Gina I was in love with her before she married Barzonni. What if she'd fallen in love with me, too? My life might have been very different. It might have been fuller. Richer. The land and the vines might have meant even more to me than they do now." He paused and peered deeply into her eyes, his own filled with sincerity and regret. "You see, we have these dreams of making the best darned cabernet in the United States, but it just won't be enough if you don't have someone to love and someone for you to love back. It's love that makes the vines sing and the grapes want to create for us. It's love that brings out the magic in the wine. We weren't put on earth to sleep and eat and talk on our cell phones. We were put here to be with the people we care about."

"I believe that, Grandpa. I have you," Liz said, with tears in her eyes. She threw her arms around his neck. "I love you so much."

"I love you, *ma petite*. I always will." He smoothed her long hair with his palm. "None of us knows what tomorrow will bring. I don't know if I'll be gone tomorrow or if I'll live to be a hundred. But I do know I had to take this chance to tell Gina I care for her. And if I see her next week by some coincidence, I'll tell her that again. It saddens me that an amazing woman like Gina may have gone all her life without having been truly loved."

"Oh, Grandpa…"

"I don't want that to happen to you, either, Liz. You keep your eyes and heart open. Don't close them off, like I see you doing."

"I'm not doing that."

"Sure you are. You've always done it. You're afraid that if you fall in love, madly in love— like your dad did with your mom—that something terrible will happen. That you'll lose your lover like you lost your parents."

Liz started to protest, but Sam quieted her quickly. "Don't deny it. I've known that about you for a long time. You have to ditch the fears, Liz. Just think about what I've said."

"I will," she told him.

"Promise me."

"I promise." She smiled.

Sam stood up. "Let's go in for that scrumptious dinner that only Emma can make."

"Just one more question, Grandpa. Do you hate Angelo because you never told Gina that you love her?"

"It's not him I'm mad at. I'm mad at myself for not stepping up when I had the chance."

"So you think he's an okay guy, then?"

"I didn't say that. I still don't trust him. Those Barzonnis have always got a secret agenda."

Liz chewed her bottom lip thoughtfully as she took her grandfather's arm and began to walk toward the house. One thing was for certain: Gabe had an agenda when it came to her.

Her grandfather had loved Gina Barzonni nearly half his life. Liz wondered if she would be able to forget Gabe and live hers without him in it. Or would she be like Sam and only gain the courage to be honest with him when it was already too late?

CHAPTER TWENTY

GABE APPEARED IN the entranceway and held the door open for Liz and Sam as they climbed the back porch steps. His eyes bored into hers. Suddenly, all she could think about was that night, not unlike this one, when she had been held under the moonlight in Gabe's arms. Only now her mind was filled with her grandfather's warnings about missed opportunities and lost years.

"Can I talk to you, Liz?"

"We were just going in to dinner." She looked at her grandfather, who gave her a slight nod. In light of everything he'd just revealed to her, she couldn't tell if he was giving her permission to have it out with Gabe once and for all, or if he believed she should yield to her emotions and see where they led her. Anticipation and fear crept over her like dew, causing her to shiver.

She hesitated on the top step.

"Five minutes, Liz? Please?"

Sam moved past Gabe. "I think I hear Emma calling me. Excuse me," he said, leaving Gabe and Liz alone.

Liz backed down the steps, not taking her eyes off Gabe. She wondered how much he knew about his mother and her grandfather, if anything. Liz had seen Gina's affection for Sam only a few moments ago in the gazebo. Even if Gina considered Sam to be just a friend, her grandfather clearly felt more than that for Gina.

Gabe moved boldly toward her with a purposeful expression that swept all thoughts of her grandfather and Gina from her mind.

"I understand there's a gazebo back here somewhere," he said, taking her arm. "I thought we could talk there."

"Aren't you angry with me?"

"I am. I was. Mostly, I'm frustrated, and that's what I want to talk to you about." He took her hand in his and then started kissing it. "I don't like fighting with anybody, and I especially don't like fighting with you."

She nodded. "I don't like it, either. I don't understand why I do that. I've never been one to pick fights, but with you I seem to do it so naturally."

They reached the gazebo and stepped onto

its wooden floor. Still holding her hand, Gabe pulled her closer.

"You've never been like this with anyone?" he asked.

"No," she said, dropping her eyes to his lips, remembering too easily what they had felt like pressed gently to hers.

"That's good," he said.

Liz blinked. "What? How can my anger toward you be a good thing?"

"It's just as I thought. You're falling in love with me." His grin was much too confident, and that *really* made Liz mad.

"I am not!" Even if it was true, she didn't want to admit it.

"Sure you are," he replied. "Think about it. I bring out your bad side because you've never been in love before and the idea that you could lose control like that terrifies you."

Gabe was hitting the bull's-eye, making Liz even more uncomfortable. She tried to retract her hand, but Gabe held on to it.

Then he put his arm around her, splaying his fingers across her lower back.

"It's okay if you fall in love with me, Liz, because I'm falling in love with you." Gabe wanted Liz to know that she was the most important person in his life. Land or no land.

"You are?"

"Uh-huh," he replied, his eyes brimming with sincerity. "I told you I wanted to be your friend and I truly do, but I also want more than that. I don't know yet how I can win your trust and respect, but I'm willing to push the limits for you. How can I stop you from feeling anxious every time you look at me?"

"I'm not anxious right now," she protested.

"You're shaking."

"It's just chilly out here." She tried to deny his observation, but it was true. It was his closeness and his daring that made her nervous.

He closed his arms tighter around her. "Then I'll keep you warm."

It would be so easy to cut the tether that held Liz's emotions in check and float away on this rushing tide of romantic promises. His eyes had always been deep, hypnotic pools—she lost her train of thought whenever she gazed into them. Reluctantly, she admitted to herself that when she'd shunned him, she'd ached to hear from him. Even his text messages held a mysterious power over her that she didn't fully understand. At times, she thought he was the enemy. The opposition. Yet when her dreams were haunted by remembered kisses

and echoes of his velvet voice, she would suc-
cumb to his charm.

Just as she was doing now.

She felt safe and protected in his arms. But
at the same time, a terror that started in the
pit of her stomach rose up like an uncoiling
cobra, ready to strike out and kill her chance
at happiness. Liz had never had to battle with
herself, but the more Gabe pressed her about
her feelings toward him, the more she realized
that loving him was going to require a great
deal of courage. She didn't want to be afraid,
but she was.

Suddenly, Gabe cradled her face in his hands.
"You're thinking too much, Liz. Don't..." He
pressed his lips softly against hers.

Liz's thoughts ceased instantly. Gabe's kiss
made her feel more alive than she ever had.
She closed her eyes and lost herself in the moment, wondering if anyone on earth had ever
felt this giddy, this dizzy, this euphoric. She
wasn't sure if she was in love, but she felt as if
she were physically falling.

Then she felt as if she was being lifted
up, and together she and Gabe were sailing
through the cosmos, the stars sliding and spinning past them.

His breath was warm on her cheek and he

smelled of vanilla and spice. She placed her hands over his. She could feel the blood surging through his wrists to his hands and in that instant, she knew deep in her heart that what he was saying was true.

Gabe is in love with me.

He wasn't playing with her affections and he wasn't fabricating stories and scenarios to wrest her land from her. He was genuine. He was sincere.

When he pulled away, she felt the oddest sense of abandonment, as if she'd been truly cared for and now she was adrift again. Ever since their first kiss, she'd tried to convince herself that a second one would probably be disappointing. She'd been bowled over the first time because it had been just that—the first and it had rocked her world.

But surely such explosions of tenderness could not continue. Undoubtedly, the newness would eventually wear off. Then she remembered her father's journals. For some people, the thrill, anticipation and love grew deeper and more intense year after year.

For some people, love was everlasting.

She hadn't wanted that second kiss to end. She had wanted it to go on forever.

Gabe tipped her chin up. "Don't look so sad. I have a lot of those to give you."

"What are you talking about?"

"You were pouting," he said, kissing the tip of her nose.

"I was?"

He nodded and then pulled her into a hug, resting her head against his shoulder. "You do that a lot. I always know where I stand with you because your thoughts are written all over your face."

Liz sighed, thinking how lovely it was to be in Gabe's strong arms. "I'm that readable, huh?"

"You are." He chuckled. "But then, so am I."

"Who told you that?"

"Mother. She tells me everything."

Everything? Liz wasn't so sure. When the time was right, she would bring up the subject of Sam and Gina. But tonight, Liz was learning more about herself than she'd learned in the past twenty-seven years. And the bulk of it she was discovering while standing in the circle of Gabe's arms.

"Still cold?" Gabe asked.

"Not anymore." She wrapped her arms tightly around his back.

"I thought I'd find you out here!" Angelo's

voice boomed from the dark shadows, causing both Gabe and Liz to jump.

"Dad! You scared us to death!"

"Good!" Angelo growled and gestured at them with his wineglass. "I leave you alone for two minutes and you go sneaking into the bushes."

"Sneaking?" Liz stepped out of Gabe's embrace.

Gabe instantly reached for her hand and held it firmly. Liz got the distinct impression he was not only protecting her, but also seeking an anchor for himself.

"You didn't actually come out here to find me, did you, Dad?" Gabe asked through clenched teeth.

"I did." Angelo moved out of the shadow of the giant blue spruce and into the moonlight.

"I'm not a kid anymore," Gabe said, gripping Liz's hand a bit more tightly. She squeezed his hand back supportively.

"You're acting like one." Angelo took another step, and this time he wobbled to the left, tripping on a raised stepping stone "I thought we had this out weeks ago. Apparently—" he raised his glass in Liz's direction "—you lied to me."

Liz's eyes tracked from Angelo to Gabe.

"What does he mean? Were you two talking about me?"

Gabe whispered, "I'll tell you later." He glared at his father. "You and I have nothing more to say to each other about Liz or about any other aspect of my life. You got that?"

"We're not through by a long shot, young man," Angelo retorted, taking two long strides toward Liz and Gabe. He stumbled on a broken brick in the pathway. He tried to break his fall with his hands, and he landed on the wineglass, cutting his palm.

Angelo shouted in rage and pain.

Gabe rushed down from the gazebo and helped his father back to his feet. He turned to Liz. "Go inside and get my mother and Nate. No, getting Nate would break up the party. Get Rafe. Yeah, Rafe can take Dad to the emergency room."

"I'm not going to the hospital!" Angelo pulled a handkerchief from his pocket and wrapped it around his bleeding hand. "It's just a little cut."

Liz looked at the wound. Though it wasn't large, it was bleeding badly. "But the blood…"

Angelo cut her off. "It's from the warfarin."

Gabe's eyes widened. "What warfarin?"

Liz saw the warning look in Angelo's eyes and spun around. "I'll get Gina and Rafe."

Liz raced into the kitchen, where Gina was talking with Mrs. Beabots about her recipe for the beef marinade.

"Mrs. Barzonni, could you come outside, please? Mr. Barzonni fell and cut his hand. Gabe said I should get Rafe because he's bleeding pretty badly."

"Oh, dear!" Mrs. Beabots exclaimed. "What can I do to help?"

"Nothing," Gina answered, patting Mrs. Beabots's arm. "Angelo is just out of sorts and stumbled on the path. He'll live." Gina carefully placed her dinner plate next to the sink and went into the living room. When she returned she was followed by Nate, Rafe and Mica, like an elegant queen leading her princes to court. As they all marched to the gazebo, none of them spoke. They appeared to be calm, in control and unflappable. How often had this kind of thing happened in the Barzonni family?

"Gabriel," Gina said as they approached. "Talk to me."

"Dad stumbled on the path. He was holding a wineglass and when he fell, the glass cut his hand."

"Nate," Gina said, not taking her steely eyes off Angelo, who suddenly seemed quite mollified. Angelo stuck out his hand while Nate unwrapped the handkerchief.

Nate inspected the cut. "It won't need stitches. Just clean it up, use an antibiotic cream and put a butterfly bandage on it." Nate wrapped the handkerchief back around the wound. He patted his father's shoulder. "Go home and get some rest. Doctor's orders."

Gina turned to Rafe and Mica. "Your father has had too much to drink. You boys drive him home. I'll follow in Gabe's car. We'll stay till the party is over. There's been enough disruption for one night." Gina glared at Angelo with condemnation in her dark eyes.

"I'm not drunk," Angelo protested. "I just tripped."

Gina's gaze swung between Gabe and Liz. "Maybe not, but you were out here when you should have been having dinner with me and paying attention to the bride and groom, not to mention our hostess. Now go home and calm down."

"I'm fine, I tell you!" Angelo growled.

She stepped up to him until they were nose to nose. "You listen to me. This is Nate's party and I will not have you embarrassing me or the rest of this family. You go home. I'll make excuses for you." Then she looked at Rafe. "Take his blood pressure before he goes to bed and write it down."

"I can do it myself," Angelo said.

Gina put her hands on her hips. "But will you write down the real numbers or lie to me like you usually do?"

Rafe and Mica each took one of Angelo's arms and led him away from the gazebo.

"I apologize on my husband's behalf," Gina said to Liz.

Liz smiled softly and shook her head. "No need. I was just worried about the bleeding."

Gabe put his arm around Liz's waist, and the warmth of the gesture spread all the way to her heart. "How long has he been on warfarin, Mom?"

"A year. Nate's been watching his numbers like a hawk lately. He's supposed to avoid stress, but honestly, I think the man goes looking for things to make him angry." She sighed. "He's always been a hothead. Even when we were young. For years, he was too exhausted from the hard work on the farm to spend any energy on anger. But lately, he rages and rails at everything."

"What do you think it is, Mrs. Barzonni?" Liz asked, glancing at Gabe.

"Nate getting married."

"What?" Gabe's jaw dropped open.

Gina shrugged. "He's losing control of his sons. Nate is the first to marry and he won't be the last."

"But Nate hasn't been around Indian Lake for eleven years. I would think Mr. Barzonni would be happy to have him back in town. Nate and Maddie will be living here in their cottage. He can see them all the time."

"My husband is a complicated man," Gina said, a resigned smile on her face. "All men are." She placed her hand tenderly on Gabe's cheek. "That's what makes them so fascinating, I suppose."

"Fascinating and famished," Gabe said. "How about we join the party?"

"Splendid idea," Gina said, taking her son's arm. "Then over dessert you both can tell me your story."

"What story is that, Mrs. Barzonni?" Liz asked, taking Gabe's other arm.

"The one about how the two of you fell in love."

CHAPTER TWENTY-ONE

GABE WAS PENSIVE as he drove his Porsche down the highway out of Indian Lake toward their expansive farm. The moon was full and high in the sky with only a few clouds scudding across its face. Gina stared out the passenger's window at the acres of harvested summer cornstalks and the fields of ripening pumpkins and squash.

"Late summer has always been my favorite season," she said. "It's not quite autumn yet, but the days are still warm and long without the blazing summer heat. And all the crops are ripe and full."

"For me, late summer always means my back is going to be sore from all that harvesting," Gabe grumbled.

Gina pushed on his shoulder playfully. "Oh, you boys. Always complaining. I remember late summers when there wasn't enough left to eat."

"You mean back in Sicily, before you moved here?"

She smoothed the folds of her full skirt. "Yes. It was a difficult life for me when I was young, as it was for your father. I want you to remember that and try not to be so hard on him."

"Hard on him?" He guffawed. "He's the one making *my* life difficult. Not the other way around."

Gina paused thoughtfully. "I suppose I should tell you the truth about your father and our family."

"The truth?"

"Yes," she said. "I don't know if every family has secrets, but I'm going to guess that a great many do."

"This isn't about something Dad did back in Sicily, is it? I mean, Rafe and I always figured maybe he killed somebody back there and that was why he came to America."

"You boys watch too many mob movies." Gina laughed. "It was nothing like that, though he had to take every odd job he could from the age of seven or eight. By the time he was fifteen, he was already saving every dime he could to book passage to New York. He worked his way over to the States on a freighter to save even more money. When he got to New York he worked as a busboy, a waiter, a truck driver. Any position he could find. He told me he always wanted to be a farmer. He hated city life, which for him meant living on the streets and scrounging for food and clothing. He heard about the drought in Illinois and Indiana at that time. Farms were being sold for next to nothing. So one night, he got on a train and left New York."

Gabe jerked his chin up. "He stowed away?"

"On a freight train, yes."

"So the trip out here was free. That was thrifty of him. But what about you? When did you fall in love with Dad?"

"I never fell in love with your father."

Gabe coughed and choked on his words. "Come again?"

"I knew him when he delivered vegetables. My father owned a small restaurant. Just spaghetti and other pasta, basically, but we made an excellent gravy. I still have my mother's recipe."

"Which we all love," Gabe interjected.

Gina smiled. "Thank you, dear. Anyway, I was only fourteen, waiting tables and cleaning up alongside my five older sisters. They were always flirting with the American sailors who came to town on furlough. They all dreamed of sailing across the ocean with a handsome American and I guess their dreams became my dream. When I met Angelo, he was young and focused on his goal to live in the United States. I would give him free scraps from the kitchen and he would share his dreams with me. One day, he told me he had saved enough money to leave Sicily, and that if I waited for him to make his fortune in America, he would send for me so I could join him. We sat at the back table in my father's restaurant and shook hands on the deal. I promised to wait till Angelo sent for me and then we would be married and live in America together."

"That's…pretty incredible," Gabe said as he slowly absorbed what his mother was telling him. "But you were just kids. How could you honestly think he would stand up to his end of the bargain?"

"I had faith. I prayed about my future every night. I was only fourteen when we made our pact. Angelo was nineteen, I believe. Do you know he doesn't know his real age? It's always bothered him that he was an orphan, born in the streets. I think that's why he loves his land so much. The dirt is his ancestry. His literal roots. But that is only part of my story."

"There's more?"

"Yes. So much more." She inhaled deeply.

Gabe glanced at his mother, and in the light from the illuminated dashboard he could see tears in her eyes. He reached for her hand. "If this is too difficult, Mom, we don't need to do this now."

"Yes, we do. I've held the truth back far too long and now I see what is happening with you…and Liz. She's a wonderful girl, Gabriel. Do you think she loves you back?"

Gabe swallowed hard. His mother had just asked the one question that could sink a dagger into his heart. He didn't know the answer, and he was afraid to find out. "I don't know," he said. "There are times when I believe I can convince her to love me, but it doesn't work like that, does it?"

"No, it doesn't. Love just *is*. We can't pick who or how or when. Oh, I know the psychologists have all kinds of books filled with theories about relationships—that's what they call love now, relationships. That's so silly to me. To take the romance out of love. It's just so un-Italian."

"Well said, Mother." Gabe chuckled. "Then I think I have fallen in love."

"You're not sure?"

He raked his hand through his hair. "I know I've never felt like this before. I want to be with her all the time, and when I'm with her, it's not enough. I swear I could talk to her all day and night about wine, but then we get into these arguments—she thinks I have some kind of ulterior motive. Like I'm a crook. I don't know where she gets these ideas—"

"I do," Gina interrupted.

Gabe nearly swerved the car. He gripped the steering wheel tightly. "What? How can you possibly say that?"

"That's the other part of my story."

"Believe me, I'm listening."

"When I came to Indian Lake, I was still in my twenties. I had this idea in my head that if I waited half a year to get married—half a year to get settled in America—then the decisions I made about my future would be smarter."

"Okay…"

"Angelo had acquired most of the farms around his by that time, and he was working full speed. He'd hired some farmhands and they were very busy. I took a room in town. I joined my church and a few of the ladies' groups that appealed to me. I went to the library nearly every day and to the movies on the weekends."

"You did this alone, while Dad was on the farm?"

"Not exactly. I met someone who was very nice to me and a lot of fun to talk to. We laughed so much. I hadn't known what it was like to laugh that much. He introduced me to all of his friends. That's when I met Mrs. Beabots and Helen Knowland and others."

"And this man's name was…"

"Sam Crenshaw," Gina admitted.

Gabe pursed his lips and then slammed his palm over his mouth. "This isn't for real."

"We didn't have an affair, if that's what you're thinking," Gina added quickly. "But I did fall in love with him."

"You did?"

"And it wasn't until tonight that I found out he'd also fallen in love with me."

"Oh boy." Gabe exhaled.

"When I met him, Sam's wife, Aileen, had recently died, and I was afraid I was just a substitute for her. I didn't dare let him know my true feelings. But I can tell you, I counted the hours until I knew I would see Sam again. I knew Sam thought he was too old for me. He was forty-three then. But I knew I wasn't in love with your father."

"I'm afraid to ask. Does Dad know about any of this?"

Gina hung her head. "Yes. He's been horridly jealous for years. He caught Sam and I coming out of the Roxy Theater one night. We were laughing about something in the movie, having a wonderful time as we always did, and Angelo was sitting in his truck across the street. He stormed up to Sam and punched him. I broke that fight up, but Angelo knew all kinds of ways to hurt a person. He'd lived on the streets in Sicily. He'd seen a lot, even if he hadn't ever hurt anyone himself. To protect Sam, I broke it off and married Angelo. You boys were my life and I know I've spoiled you all in too many ways, but I didn't care. I still don't. I believe you can't give a child too much love."

"You are, and always were, the best mom ever," Gabe said.

"Thank you, dear. I want you to know I was always true to your father. He's jealous and controlling, but I never gave him cause to doubt my loyalty to him. It's because Angelo knows I fell in love with Sam all those years ago that he wants to control your connection with Liz. He believes if he allows her into the family, I'll be thrown into Sam's arms, and maybe the next time he won't be able to stop it."

Gabe looked at his mother's sad face. "Maybe he's right to worry."

"Maybe."

"The one thing I know about my father is that he's been a tyrant all his life. He thinks he can control everything—even the weather. But none of us can control anything, especially not another person's feelings."

"Although I believed and felt that Sam had feelings for me back then, he never came out and said it. Sam told me tonight he'd fallen in love with me back then, and when I told him I'd felt the same, we both realized we'd lost thirty-five years. I'm not going to leave your father. I believe in my commitment and I take my marriage vows seriously. I made the wrong choice back then. I didn't speak up when I had the opportunity to do so. I didn't believe enough in my own feelings to act on them. I chose the path of duty."

"And you're going to do it again. Choose your duty."

"I am. I owe your father that much. I could never give him my love, but I can give him my promise."

Gabe exhaled. "You're an amazing woman,

Mother. I don't know if I could ever be that strong. I don't know if I'd even want to."

"I hope this helps you to understand this underlying feud, as I guess you might call it, between Angelo and Sam. It's been going on for thirty-five years."

"And it will probably continue for another thirty."

"So, if you and Liz do work things out, you need to understand your father's motivations. I'm sorry, Gabe. I really am." She reached over and touched his worried face.

"One more thing...I want to talk a little more about duty."

"What about it?"

"Liz feels obligated to carry out her father's dream of making her vineyard the best in the nation. She's put her entire life on hold trying to make that happen. She's gambled everything she's got on it. Her vineyard and her grandfather are everything to her. I get the feeling that her sense of duty is just as ingrained as yours. And according to you, nothing will shake a woman out of that kind of commitment. Not even true love."

Gabe felt his heart sink. That kind of duty was what bound Liz—and kept her away from him. Hopelessness clung to his heart.

Gina looked away from Gabe to the darkening highway as they drove through the night. "Unfortunately, Gabriel, you're right. Not even true love can shake a woman free."

CHAPTER TWENTY-TWO

THE INDIAN LAKE Sunflower Festival was held the third weekend in September of every year. Kids, grannies, moms and dads competed with one another all summer long to nurse the sixteen-foot Sunzilla sunflowers and the spectacular Titan with its twenty-four-inch-wide face and lush golden petals. Then the entrants had to muster up the nerve to cut down their prizes for the competition and haul them in trucks and cars to the cordoned-off, three-block area of Maple and Main Streets. There, judges awarded prizes for the tallest flower, the flower with the widest and most colorful face, and even for the flower with the most petals. As the years had passed the growers had become more knowledgeable about their hybrids. In order to accommodate everything from midsize Chocolate Cherry sunflowers to Moulin Rouge sunflowers, with their dark burgundy petals, the festival had increased the number of categories. Now there were blue ribbons for dozens of achievements.

The past few weeks had meant backbreaking work for all the farmers in the area as they had finished the bulk of the harvesting. It was time for a bit of fun, and the sunflower festival was just that.

For Liz, the festival was an opportunity to advertise the winery. Just yesterday she'd gone to Hawkins Printers and picked up her newly designed brochures and flyers. At the festival, local merchants, artists and vendors rented tents and booths in which to sell their wares. Due to local laws, Liz couldn't sell her wine at the booth, but she could pass out brochures, direct buyers to their tasting room north of town and, most important, take orders.

Sam had been looking forward to the festival for a month. It was one of the highlights of his summer, he always said. This year, Louisa would be experiencing the festival for the first time. Liz was filled with more anticipation than ever before.

This was also the first year Liz had tried her hand at growing sunflowers. Louisa had encouraged her in the spring, claiming that not only were they her favorite flower, but that back in southern France it was nearly a patriotic duty to grow them, since they reminded natives and tourists of van Gogh's and Gauguin's paintings. Louisa had her favorites—Lemon Queen and Van Gogh, of course—but Liz preferred the Early Russian type. So they'd planted all three.

With the nutritional aid of Liz's organic compost, the sunflowers had grown tall, colorful and resplendent. Birds had fed on the fatty seeds and bees had flocked to the wide seed pods. Liz agreed completely that the sunflower garden had been an excellent addition to the vineyard.

Though Louisa was excited about the contest at the sunflower festival, Liz believed it was only charitable to tell Louisa the truth.

"I don't want you to get your hopes up, Louisa," Liz said. She filled a crockery vase with Early Russian and a smattering of Moulin Rouge sunflowers to display in their tasting room. "Everyone in town knows Bella Mattuchi will win the grand prize. Her sunflowers are truly the best. I don't know what she does to cultivate such prizewinners, but it works out year after year."

Louisa clamped her fist onto her hip. "It's the slope where she grows them. There's not a single branch to block the sun."

"We have plenty of sun," Liz argued.

"It's not the same. Her land is like my garden in France. *Magnifique!*" Louisa replied glumly as she touched the petals of a Hopi Black Dye sunflower. "We have more variety, *n'est-ce pas?*"

"We do. And your Kong hybrids are over fourteen feet tall. Even if we don't win the grand prize, we'll win something. I just know it."

Liz was sharply aware that Gabe had not texted, called or emailed her since the night of the shower. She didn't like it. She wasn't certain if he was avoiding her, if he was simply too busy with the harvest or if there was something else. Had he taken his father's commands to heart? She found that hard to believe, yet the silence was killing her.

The realization that she was falling in love with him had put a new perspective on everything. He occupied more of her thoughts than the worries about the missing check, the tax payments or the necessity for strong sales in the tasting room. Suddenly, the hours passed agonizingly slowly as she waited to hear from him. Although she'd tried to convince herself that everything between them was fine, she needed to talk to him. Hear his voice. See him, face-to-face. Liz had never been the one to initiate anything between the two of them, but perhaps the time had come for her to step up.

She dug in her pocket and pulled out her cell phone and sent Gabe a text.

Are you going to the Sunflower Festival? I was hoping to see you.

There. That should get his attention. Quickly, she put the phone back and breathed.

Not two minutes later, Liz's cell phone buzzed in her jeans pocket. She pulled it out and saw that Gabe had replied. She could feel a very big smile on her face.

"I bet I know who that is." Louisa grinned playfully and then sashayed away.

Liz read the text and frowned.

No.

Now Liz knew something had happened after the shower. She'd just told Gabe where she was going and she practically broadcasted that she wanted to see him. It had been a week since the party and whatever it was, she'd just been relegated to second on his list because of it. She felt her spirits dissipate. She didn't know what the problem was, but she wanted

Gabe back to the way they were. Her fingers flew over the phone keyboard.

Why not? I guarantee the smoked ribs will be the best ever this year. I'll treat.

The pause was long enough for Liz's hopes to wither.

Then her phone buzzed and she read his reply.

Is this a bribe? Or out-and-out wooing?

Liz's relief spread across her face in a bright smile. He was back to his humorous banter. Though she sensed that something was holding him back or even away from her, somehow, she'd said the right thing at the right time. She was amazed, as calm spread through her, how tense she'd become over his response.

Definitely wooing. Will I see you?

My mother wants to enter her sunflowers in the contest. I've just volunteered to bring her to town. I'm guessing Sam will be with you?

Liz was in the middle of writing back when her phone rang. It was Gabe.

"Hi," she said. "I just got your text."

"I decided to call."

"I'm glad. I haven't heard from you since the party and I wondered, well, if you were okay."

"I've been busy. Harvest. Contracts," he said in a faraway tone that led her to believe someone had just walked through the room...and that Gabe didn't want that person to know she was on the other end of the phone. Or that he really had been avoiding her. But why? After a long pause, he spoke in a rush. "I'll be bringing Mom to town for the competition. Where will you be?"

Liz flushed. Ever since she'd discovered the truth about Sam and Gina, she'd felt closer to Gabe. She believed him that he'd been at her parents' funeral. It all made sense. Many things made sense to her now that had not before.

She understood Gabe and his desires to leave his father's business and build a life of his own in a way she hadn't before. Angelo's jealousy and his need to protect—even keep captive— all that was his, including his wife and sons, must have created a stifling atmosphere for Gabe and his brothers. It was no wonder Nate had run away the first chance he'd gotten—and stayed away. Liz also understood Gabe's unswerving sense of duty to his mother, and even to his father. He wanted to help keep the family business profitable and, eventually, expand it.

Gabe had won Liz's admiration.

"I didn't tell you. We have a booth this year. We did so well with our booth at Sarah's carnival for St. Mark's that Sam thought we should give this festival a try."

"Good thinking," Gabe said. "So what time?"

"In about an hour. We'll all be going, even Louisa. She's gathering our sunflowers."

He groaned in reply.

"What's wrong?"

"My mother has five entries this year. She's going to be brokenhearted if she doesn't win something. It's bad enough Bella Mattuchi wins all the time, but I bet your flowers are going to beat everyone's in town."

"Why do you say that?"

"Let me put it this way. Did you sing to them like you do your vines?" he asked, lowering his voice to a whisper that sent shivers down Liz's arms.

"I did," she admitted.

"Then we're toast."

ONCE IN TOWN, at the corner of Main and Maple, Liz and Aurelio hauled the tables to the little blue canvas tent. In the booth beside them, Maddie was setting up her cupcakes.

"Hi, Liz!" Maddie exclaimed as she placed a double-sized yellow frosted cupcake on the top of a four-tiered tower. She licked a smidge of frosting from her finger and threw her arms around Liz. "How are you? You look fantastic in that dress."

"Do I look too much like a sunflower myself? I found it in my mother's closet. I've been doing that a lot lately."

"Good for you! Recycle. Reuse. It's perfect on you."

"Is Nate here?" Liz asked, glancing around.

Maddie shook her head. "An emergency up at the reservation clinic. But after he's finished, he's coming here. He said he wouldn't miss the baby back rib contest."

Liz smiled broadly. "Grandpa says the men come for the smoked ribs and the women come to shop. And that even the losers in the rib contest are winners."

"Men," Maddie harrumphed as she opened another bakery box of her confections. "All they think about is their stomachs." Then she laughed heartily. "Thank goodness!"

Liz glanced over to the tent next to Maddie's and saw Isabelle Hawks's familiar sign. "Isabelle is here, too?"

"Yeah, she just went to her car to get more paintings. I hope she does well this year. She's getting so discouraged about her art. No gallery has stepped forward yet, and she's sent out over a hundred résumés and portfolios."

Liz inhaled deeply, knowing how hard Isabelle had worked on her art, and how discouraging those rejections must be. "I have to give her credit, though. She never stops. She just keeps at it. I don't think I'd be that resilient."

"Me neither." A patron walked up and asked for a half dozen cupcakes. "Talk to you later, Liz."

"Sure." Liz turned just in time to see Sam carrying a tote bag filled with the brochures, bottles of water, pens and all-important order forms. "I hope we have everything," he said.

Liz unfolded a canvas chair for him. "It's warmer than I thought it would be. Maybe I should have brought a fan. We could overheat in here."

Sam glanced at the front table, where Louisa was placing brochures in a plastic holder that would keep them from flying away. "There's a little breeze."

"Not much of one," Liz grumbled. "If it gets bad later, I'll have Aurelio go back home and bring the fan and an extension cord."

"Would you stop fussing?" Sam scolded.

Aurelio returned from the truck with a portable wooden display shelf he'd made for them. Liz draped the table at the back of the booth in dark purple cloth then placed a short easel with photos of the tasting room and vineyard on top. She arranged a display of empty wine bottles on the shelves, then wrapped an artificial grape vine garland around the top of the display and wove a crystal strand of lights into it.

The back of the booth looked festive and inviting.

Louisa considered the display. "If I don't win a prize for my sunflowers, we can put them in a vase next to the wine bottles."

"Omigosh! Your flowers," Liz said, her eyes widening. "We have to get them down to the judging stand right away!"

"Grandpa, you can take care of this till we get back, right?"

"Absolutely, *ma petite*!" He grinned proudly.

"Okay. I have my cell phone if you need me." Liz scooted out of the booth. "C'mon, Louisa. Let's get your flowers."

"Our flowers," Louisa corrected her.

The streets were filling up with tourists and townspeople, and as Liz and Louisa carried their sunflowers toward the judges' booth, they saw the other entrants arriving with their precious sunflowers, as well.

Talking to Calvin Craig, the head of the sunflower judges, was Gabe. He handed Calvin an entry form then turned around. His eyes fell on Liz immediately and his face lit up as if he'd just been awarded first prize himself.

"Liz!" He darted around Bella Mattuchi and Helen and Chloe Knowland, excusing himself as he made a beeline for her.

Helen didn't take her eyes off Gabe, even when he put his hands on Liz's shoulders and kissed her cheek.

"Gosh, you look fantastic," he gushed. "More beautiful than ever."

"Gabe, you just saw me last weekend."

"Really? I thought it was last year," he joked. He glanced at Louisa and the sunflowers she was carrying. "Hi, Louisa. How are you? Those look...really terrific, actually."

"Merci," she replied, shooting Liz a sly look.

"I just entered my mom's flowers, but yours are bigger and brighter—frankly, they look like winners." He smiled sheepishly. "Don't tell my mother I said that."

"I won't," Liz replied as they moved forward in line. "Where is your mother, anyway?"

"She went back to the car. She forgot her lipstick or something," Gabe answered. Then he leaned close to Liz's ear. "She's visiting Sam," he whispered.

"Oh, boy," Liz moaned. "Do you think that's wise?"

Gabe shrugged. "What could I do? I wasn't going to stop her. She can be very stubborn when she wants to be."

"I'll remember that."

Finally, it was Liz's turn to fill out her entry form and hand over their flowers. Louisa waited patiently as Liz answered the judges' questions, identified the flowers and tied tags to each stem.

The judges counted the petals, measured the width and height of the stalks and made notes immediately. It all seemed so perfunctory and cold.

Liz studied her blossoms. All summer, they'd vivified their house and tasting room, bringing her joy as she moved from room to room and saw their happy faces smiling out from vases and pitchers.

Liz, Gabe and Louisa walked away silently as they realized all their hard work and tender nurturing had just been measured, weighed and judged. It was over. The winners wouldn't be announced until sundown, but Liz felt as if a killing frost had just ended her summer.

As if he understood every thought in her head, Gabe reached down and took her hand. He squeezed her fingers reassuringly.

Louisa didn't miss the gesture. "I'm going back to the booth to help Sam. I'll see you later."

"I'll be there in a sec," Liz replied as Louisa sprinted down the street.

Gabe lifted Liz's hand to his lips and kissed it. "I hope you win," he said. "I think your sunflowers meant more to you than you'd imagined they would."

"Crazy, isn't it? I've never been that attached to my grapes, and I sing to them all the time."

"Ah, but flowers are different," he offered with a gentle smile.

"How's that?"

"Especially sunflowers, I think. They have faces, almost like people. The grapes are more like jewels—sparkling but inanimate rocks. You've loved these flowers, nurtured them. It makes sense that you're sad."

Gabe's efforts to dispel her dour mood after giving up her prized flowers to the judges showed not only that he was thoughtful, but that he cared about making her happy. As her thoughts about Gabe grew more affectionate, she began to squeeze his hand back.

"I'll grow them for us. In my little greenhouse."

"Tell me about your greenhouse," she said.

Gabe slowed his gait and placed his arm around Liz's shoulders. The gesture was so natural that Liz nearly didn't realize she'd slid her arm around his waist. Suddenly, they were walking the way she'd seen Maddie and Nate walk. Arm in arm, their steps so synchronized, so perfectly matched to the other that they walked as one. They walked as if they'd been walking together like this all their lives.

"Well, I made it myself. It's just a wood frame and clear plastic sheeting right now. I've got humidifiers and space heaters for the winter. I rigged up some misters for when it really gets dry. Mica helped me with timers, but the whole thing is pretty rudimentary. It's got a dirt floor, which is fine, since I'm always spilling a ton of compost and potting soil anyway. I made the tables myself. Some of the tables are actually raised boxes for seedlings. I built the trellis and arbors overhead for the grape vines I'll plant next summer. I've already tried my hand at orchids. I do okay with those. But if I could grow sunflowers for you in the winter…"

Crowds were pouring in from the side streets and the nearby church parking lots. Liz and Gabe found themselves in a sea of people moving from booth to booth, inspecting everything from self-published books to honey in the comb, quilts, hand-carved wind chimes and even albums by a local guitarist.

"Liz! Liz!"

She stopped in her tracks. "Someone's calling me."

"On your cell?" Gabe asked.

Liz took her cell phone out of her skirt pocket. "No, I thought I heard Louisa…"

"Liz!" Louisa yelled as she raced toward them.

"She looks—"

"Panic-stricken," Gabe interjected.

Louisa was out of breath by the time she reached them. "I tried to call, but my cell phone battery was too low. I'm sorry. It's Sam. He's sick. *Vite. Vite!*"

Liz shot away from Gabe and Louisa and charged through the crowd. She felt as if she was living inside one of those slow-motion dreams in which her legs were mired in tar and she couldn't move them quickly enough or lift her knees high enough to move the way she wanted to. Her grandfather was in trouble. He needed her and she was being impeded by gawking people trying to barter for half of a broiled chicken.

"Grandpa!" she shouted as she neared the booth. Aurelio's head popped up from behind the front table then disappeared again.

As she entered the tent, Liz saw Maddie struggling to perform CPR. Sam wasn't responding.

"Liz!" Maddie cried. "He just fell. Crumpled, really. I didn't know what to do."

"Grandpa!" Liz screamed, falling to her knees beside him. Sam's face was ghostly white and dotted with perspiration. He was motionless.

Gabe rushed into the tent behind her. "Liz, I'm here," he said. He picked Liz up by the elbows and turned her to face him. "Call 911. Now! Then call Nate."

Liz's mouth was dry. All she could do was nod, pull out her phone and pound the numbers.

"I need an ambulance," she said. "It's my grandpa. I think he's had a heart attack."

Gabe bent over Sam, felt his pulse and immediately started doing CPR.

As soon as she was off the phone, Liz stood over Gabe's shoulder, watching as he fought to save her beloved grandfather from the jaws of death.

Not since her parents died had Liz felt so tiny, so unimportant, so forgotten. She felt as if she were standing on the edge of the planet staring into infinite space, the unknown. She was filled with terror and desperation.

"Please, God. Let him save my grandpa."

GABE COUNTED OUT his compressions and then repeated them again. He had to keep Sam's heart pumping. Bring it back to life. And pray.

Maddie had done the best she could, but even a few minutes of performing CPR took a great deal of strength and endurance.

Gabe didn't care if it took all night. He would save Sam. He had to. Sam had been Liz's world since she was a child. He knew her well enough to know that without Sam, she would be lost. And if Sam didn't live, there was the chance that Liz might blame Gabe for not doing all he could have done to save him. If Sam died, Gabe could lose Liz forever.

Sam counted another one hundred compressions. "One thousand one. One thousand two. C'mon, Sam. You can do this."

Gabe tried to keep track of his count but thoughts of his mother invaded his mind. This was the man his mother had loved for more than half her life. This man was the answer to his mother's happiness. In these terrifying moments, Gabe understood more about his own life and his mother's than he ever had.

She had sacrificed her happiness because of her loyalty to Angelo. Even when she hadn't yet married Angelo, she'd already felt bound to her duty. Gabe's own sense of responsibility had started when he could barely talk. His brothers had been born, one after the other, and Gina had needed his help. The little jobs had become obligations. Then they had become duties, done out of loyalty to the family. He'd abandoned his dreams of moving to California because Nate had run away and his father had needed him. The farm had needed him.

But the only real loyalty he didn't despise or regret having was his loyalty to his mother. She had shared her heart, her secrets and her dreams with him alone.

Gina loved Sam. If he died, Gabe feared his mother would wither and perhaps die, as well.

Gabe was taking responsibility for Sam's

life, but at that moment, he was up to the challenge. He would face down death itself to save Sam and spare the two women who loved him.

CHAPTER TWENTY-THREE

THEY GATHERED OUTSIDE the doors to the ICU, huddled with their arms around each other. Despite the panic and dread settling into their bones, each tried to be supportive of the others. Gabe alternately held Liz and then his mother. Maddie hugged Liz when Gabe wasn't holding her, and Louisa held Mrs. Beabots's hand. The older woman had walked the seven blocks to the hospital after Maddie's phone call, carrying a cooler with her ginger, lemon and mint iced tea, plastic cups and a still-warm batch of cookies she'd been making for Timmy and Annie. Sarah had called Liz and said that she and Luke would come to the hospital as soon as Olivia arrived at her house to watch the kids.

Liz knew Sam was in good hands with Dr. Caldwell and Nate, but still, the minutes droned by like slowly moving summer flies. The only time she felt the world was even slightly intact was when Gabe had his arms around her, whispering words that her mind didn't register, but which soothed her heart. Gabe's loving intentions were suddenly apparent to all her friends. What astounded her was that none of them seemed surprised and none offered censure.

When Liz glanced at Mrs. Beabots, she saw only compassion and a gentle smile. Liz got the distinct impression the only person in her sphere who held doubts about Gabe's presence in her life was Liz herself.

"What's taking them so long?" Liz asked Gabe as she pulled out of his embrace. "I don't like it."

"I'm sure it won't be much longer. Nate knows we're all out here." He glanced at the closed door to the ICU warily, as if he wasn't all that confident about what he was saying.

Liz looked over at Gina, whose eyes were still glued to the door. She nervously picked off her nail polish. "Your mother looks more worried than I feel. And that seems impossible," Liz whispered. "If this takes any longer, maybe you should take her to the cafeteria for a cup of coffee or something."

"There's no way she'll move an inch from that spot until she knows about Sam," Gabe said firmly.

"I just thought…"

At that moment the door whooshed open. Nate and Dr. Caldwell entered the corridor.

Nate took in each of their worried expressions. "Liz, Dr. Caldwell and I would like to speak to you privately." Nate gestured to an open area down the hallway.

"Sure," she said and followed the two men.

Dr. Caldwell spoke calmly as he explained to Liz that Sam had suffered a heart attack due to three severely blocked arteries. Sam was also experiencing congestive heart failure. A lack of oxygen being distributed to his circulatory system was causing his forgetfulness and early signs of dementia.

"Liz, your grandfather is going to need a triple bypass," Nate told her.

"Open-heart surgery? That's so drastic. You'd have to cut his sternum in half. Right?" Liz was shocked. Sam had always appeared to be so healthy. He could practically lift the ATV by himself. True, he'd been forgetting a few things, but all this sounded so dire. "And if he doesn't have the surgery?"

Dr. Caldwell rocked back on his heels and blew out a puff of air, inflating his cheeks. "I wouldn't recommend that at all."

Nate took Liz's hand. "Sam is strong constitutionally and there's no reason he shouldn't survive the operation, but he'll only deteriorate without it. I don't want to see him have a stroke or another heart attack. Or worse. Both Dr. Caldwell and I believe that if Gabe hadn't stepped in at the moment he did, Sam might not have made it."

"Gabe saved Sam's life," Liz said flatly. She'd known it from the instant Gabe took over and ordered her to call 911 as he'd laid his strong hands on Sam's chest. She had a great deal to thank Gabe for. He'd saved the most precious human being in her life. The thought that Sam could have died sent waves of terror through Liz so powerful, she feared losing her sanity in the undertow. She'd lost both her parents in a single day. She'd built the rest of her life around Sam, the vineyard and their mutual dream of carrying out her father's wishes.

Her heart swelled with an expanding warmth she'd never felt before. She wasn't sure if this was gratitude or something more, but she did know that for the rest of her life, she would be in Gabriel Barzonni's debt.

"Is he conscious?" she asked Nate.

"Yes. And we have spoken to him about his need for the operation, but he wants to talk to you. We're hoping you'll convince him the bypass is the right choice."

"And how soon do you think he should have it?" she asked.

"First thing in the morning. We've checked the schedule and can fit him in," Nate said. Dr. Caldwell nodded his assent.

Liz swallowed hard. The situation was more critical than she'd thought. She had naively guessed she would have a few nights to think about this, weigh their options and do some research, but Sam was obviously more ill than she'd imagined. He'd already suffered damage from the heart attack. She'd heard stories of people having multiple attacks, one right after the other in the hospital, until it was too late. She looked into Nate's somber and resolute eyes.

"Okay. I'll talk to him." She turned and Nate reached for her hand.

"I have to tell you, Liz. He's a stubborn old guy. He wouldn't listen to us at all. That's why we need your help. Without the surgery, well... no promises."

"You're right, Nate. But I will *not* let his intractable attitude be the cause of his death. I'll shoot him myself first!" She marched off.

As Liz came toward him, Gabe was surprised to see her earlier anxiety replaced with fierce determination. He had a fairly good idea of what Nate and Dr. Caldwell had been talking to Liz about. Gabe had pounded on Sam's chest for ten minutes until the paramedics had arrived. Not since he'd helped Rafe with a difficult birth of one of his foals had Gabe been a witness to that very fine line between life and death. Gabe had noticed the heavy clouds in Liz's eyes when she'd seen Sam lying on the ground and watched Maddie's valiant but ineffective CPR. Gabe had seen that same look on Liz's face when she was only six, standing over her parents' graves. Loss. Defeat. Emptiness. Hopelessness. If it took the rest of his life and all of his energy, talent and strength of will, he would move heaven and earth to make sure Liz never had to go through tormented times without him by her side.

"I'm here to help," Gabe told her.

She peered longingly into his face, her cornflower-blue eyes filled with gratitude and...something else. Was it love?

"You already have, Gabe. They said you saved his life. If it weren't for you, Sam would have died. You were wonderful. How can I thank you?"

He put his hands on her shoulders and let them slide down her arms. Never before had his urge to kiss her been this strong. But the corridor was filled with all their friends and his mother, staring at them, waiting for the verdict. Now wasn't the time. "I'll think of something later. What do you need? What's going on?"

"He has to have bypass surgery. Nate wants me to talk to him about it."

Gabe glanced worriedly at his mother.

"What is it?" Liz asked.

"Nate can convince the devil to reform. He only calls in the troops when the battle isn't going well."

"Oh, I gathered that. Sam can be so stubborn, but I'm not willing to let him risk having a stroke or another heart attack just so he can get his way."

"Want me to come with you?"

She tilted her head. "Sam claimed he hated the Barzonnis. One is about to be his surgeon and one"—she glanced at Gina—"apparently still loves him. Except I don't think Sam knows that."

"Let's do it, then," he said and pushed open the door for Liz.

"Hi, Grandpa," Liz said as cheerily as she could.

Sam's bed was surrounded with monitors. Various screens beeped and blipped with different colored lights, informing the medical staff of his second-to-second cardiac condition.

"Hi," Sam groaned as Liz and Gabe entered the brightly lit room. Sam lifted his hand to adjust the oxygen cannula in his nose. "Seems I can't get away from the Barzonnis no matter what I do," he said, looking at Gabe. "Your brother wants to whack me open."

Liz pursed her lips. "Yes. He does. He's going to save your life, Grandpa. You need this operation."

Sam closed his eyes slowly and rolled his head from side to side, crinkling the plastic covering on his pillow.

Oh, how she hated hospitals. The very air smelled like death. In their halls, she felt claustrophobic. If she had her way, she would wrench Sam out of this place and take him back to their life-giving hills and let him lie among the vines. Nature could heal him, couldn't it? Was he so far gone that only this barbaric surgery could keep him on the earth? She needed him to stay on this earth—she couldn't be alone without someone to love her. Without someone she could love back.

"They can fix you, Grandpa," she said. "Nate is a very good surgeon."

"He's a pup."

Gabe moved to Sam's right side, placed his hand on the headboard and leaned down so Sam could see his face clearly. "Do you remember falling in the booth today, Sam?"

"No. But the back of my head hurts. Actually, I feel like I've been run over by a truck."

"I'll bet," Gabe said. "Well, you did fall, and Louisa ran to find us right after. When we got there, I performed CPR on you—"

"He saved your life, Grandpa!" Liz clasped Sam's hand between both of hers.

"My brother is one of the best heart surgeons in the Midwest and I would trust him with my life," Gabe said. "With anybody's life. If you don't have this surgery, you could very well have another heart attack or stroke. You could die."

"I don't care," Sam said very quietly as a tear slid out of the corner of his eye.

Liz gasped. "How can you say that? You have so much to live for. This year is going to be our finest one yet! You said so yourself. And the cabs you bottled two years ago are just about ready."

"Everything looks different to me now, *ma petite*," Sam said. "I see the world—my life—differently than I did just this morning."

"I don't understand," Liz replied, taking his hand and kissing it.

The door opened and Gina slowly moved into the room to drop off a sunflower. She never took her eyes off Sam. She didn't smile or say a single word.

Sam's gaze never left Gina. A flicker of a smile illuminated his face as he remained still and silent.

The tension in the room was palpable. Liz felt that Sam's and Gina's eyes were conversing in a soul language the two of them had developed over decades of being forced to remain apart—and alone. Gina's eyes welled with tears, making their sparkling, dark depths resemble a night sky. She didn't smile or give a single word of encouragement or advice.

She turned and left the room, closing the door quietly behind her.

Liz peered down at Sam. Before Gina had walked into the room, his skin had been ashen gray and there had been deep hollows in his cheeks. Now a pink flush was spreading from the top of his head to the tips of his toes. A slow smile was filling out his face and banishing the death mask he'd been wearing. Sam was transformed in front of Liz's eyes and if she hadn't seen it for herself, she wouldn't have believed it.

Sam lifted his eyes to Gabe. "Go tell your brother I'll let him practice his medicine on me."

Gabe's face lit like a burst of fireworks. "My pleasure!" Gabe enthusiastically grabbed Liz's face and placed a kiss on her cheek. "I'll be back."

Liz turned to Sam. "Do you mean it, Grandpa? You'll sign the papers for the surgery? No second thoughts?"

"None," he replied. "Second thoughts have gotten me nowhere in this life." He squeezed Liz's hand. "What was I thinking? I could never leave you, Lizzie. You've been my world since the day you were born. And that is never going to change."

"No, Grandpa. It's never going to change."

CHAPTER TWENTY-FOUR

THERE WAS NO such thing as textbook open-heart surgery, Liz discovered after pacing in the family waiting room for five hours. She consumed more coffee than she thought possible without creating a cardiac arrhythmia of her own, and though Maddie and Mrs. Beabots stayed with her, she was achingly aware of Gabe's absence.

In order to allow Gina to visit the hospital without raising Angelo's suspicions, Gabe concocted a plan to stay home and work with his father in the fields. Gina's story was that she was meeting Maddie to discuss wedding plans and then have lunch. Since Maddie was at the hospital and they ate lunch in the hospital cafeteria, they rationalized that their story was not a complete lie.

Three hours into the surgery, one of the nurses came out and explained to Liz that they had found three more clogged arteries that required stents, and the doctors were going to repair as much as they could while Sam's chest was open.

Liz had been told that fixing a heart was much like fixing an automobile engine. The MRIs and ultrasounds only told half the story. It wasn't until the surgeons were "under the hood" that the real assessments could be made.

Finally, after more than five hours, Nate appeared in the waiting room and told them Sam's prognosis would be good once he got through the next twenty-four hours.

Relieved, Liz hugged Maddie, Mrs. Beabots and Gina. "He's going to be fine," she said, tears filling her eyes. Her emotions slowly subdued in her chest, as if she were a balloon that was deflating.

"What a blessing," Mrs. Beabots said, her hands shaking. "We'll have to have a special party once Sam is up and around!"

"That's a splendid idea," Gina concurred. "I will be most happy to help."

Mrs. Beabots eyed her carefully and then pulled her aside. "You'll have to dim those love-lights I see in your eyes," she said quietly. "Your husband can't ignore them forever."

Gina smiled softly, laugh lines appearing around her lovely eyes. "Maybe I will. Maybe

I won't." She picked up her purse. "I'll give Gabe the good news, Liz."

"Thanks." Liz turned to Nate. "Can I see him now?"

"He's in recovery, but we'll bring him down to his room soon. You can wait for him there."

Gina kissed Nate on the cheek. "I'll see you two later," she said and walked out of the waiting room.

They all said their goodbyes and left Liz standing in the waiting room alone. She couldn't help but think how fortunate she was to have such good friends. They all looked out for each other, and they would all have a lot to celebrate once Sam was home.

As a nurse walked out from the corridor that led to the surgery area, Liz heard a voice from a speaker down the hallway. "Code blue. Paging Dr. Barzonni. Code blue."

Liz's blood turned to ice. For the second time in two days, death had come to take her grandfather away.

IT WAS ENDLESS DAYS of walking between the worlds for Liz as Sam's heart refused to quiet down. His pulse raced to over one hundred and eighty-eight beats a minute. The doctors were so afraid any exertion could cause another heart attack that they would not allow him to feed himself or get out of bed, nor would they allow anyone to bathe him.

Liz learned the names of all kinds of medicines she hadn't known existed. Digoxin. Warfarin. Beta-blockers. Atorvastatin. Clopidogrel. They were all meant to save his life, but Sam insisted he didn't need any of them, only a glass of his good merlot.

She spoon-fed him yogurt, applesauce and pudding and applied cool washcloths to his forehead. She held a disposable cup with a straw to his lips. She watched the clock with supercilious anticipation and paced the room when the nurses were seconds late with his next medication. She asked a hundred questions and then asked them again.

Gabe came to visit every night, though it was late and he looked exhausted from spending long days on the farm. By the time he arrived, Liz was wrung out from feeling stress, seeing visitors and trying to pretend she wasn't terrified.

Gabe was quick to notice the dark smudges under her eyes and the flicker of panic that crossed her face each time Sam rolled in the bed or laughed at one of Gabe's jokes, which sent the pulse monitor soaring and the nurses running in with another injection of digoxin.

"His heart just won't settle," Liz explained as she stood with Gabe just outside his room.

She didn't respond when Gabe brushed her cheek with a kiss or even when he put his arm around her. Gabe realized he was suddenly not part of her universe. He supposed that was the way it should be. They were in a life-and-death crisis. At any minute, she could lose the person she loved most, but he couldn't help the fact that he felt slighted and vastly unnecessary to her.

"You have to trust that the doctors know what they're doing," Gabe tried to reassure her.

Still staring into the room, where a nurse was taking a new EKG, she said, "They found that Sam has had an arrhythmia for years. He never told anyone he had an irregular heartbeat."

"What about when he went for checkups?"

She sniffed back a tear. "He's so stubborn, you know. Always thinking he's capable of running the vineyard—"

"Don't tell me," Gabe interrupted. "He didn't go to the doctor."

"Never. Sam is—was—the healthiest man I've ever known. Oh, he had his eyes checked and he never missed an appointment with the dentist. But a doctor?" She shook her head. "I don't think he's ever had a physical."

Just then the nurse finished and rolled the EKG cart out of the room. "I'll be back in a few hours."

"How'd it look?" Liz asked anxiously.

The nurse gave her the kind of patronizing smile Liz had come to despise. The entire staff had been performing this don't-tell-the-family-the-truth act so that if anything happened to Sam, Liz wouldn't sue.

"The report gets sent to the doctor immediately. He'll be happy to give you the results."

"I know that," Liz replied. "I was just hoping to find out something before morning."

The nurse smiled vapidly once again and whisked her cart away.

Gabe frowned at the woman's retreating back as he followed Liz into the room again. Liz went right to Sam and grasped his hand.

"Can I get you anything, Grandpa?"

Sam opened his eyes, as he had dozed off during the EKG. "You still here, Barzonni?"

"Yes, sir."

"Why don't you make yourself useful and run over to the ice cream shop and bring me back a chocolate shake?"

Liz's eyes bulged with horror. "Grandpa! You can't have a milk shake! Who knows how your heart would react to the cold and the cholesterol."

Sam sighed. "What I really want is a glass of my cabernet. Special vintage. I keep the bottles secreted away in the cellar." He tried to wink at Gabe but failed. He winced with pain instead.

"Grandpa, what can I do?" Liz fumbled with a washcloth as she tried to wipe Sam's forehead.

Suddenly, the heart monitor started beeping. Sam's pulse rose to one hundred sixty, and then jumped to one hundred eighty-eight.

Liz pressed the nurse's call button, but because there was no instant response, she shoved it into Gabe's hand. "Don't let up!"

With tears in her eyes and panic in her voice, she raced from the room. She shouted down the hall, "Come quick. Digoxin! He needs digoxin!"

The monitor was blaring by the time Liz came racing back to the room with a nurse who was carrying the lifesaving injection.

Gabe stood back and allowed the nurse to perform her duty. Two more nurses entered the room and surrounded Sam's bed.

Sam's eyes were closed. He'd turned a ghastly

gray. "Don't die, Sam," Gabe whispered. "Don't die."

It took nearly twenty minutes for Sam's condition to stabilize. The doctor and nurses confirmed that this had been one of his worst episodes. They questioned Liz twice about what had brought on this reaction.

She shot Gabe a look both times, and he knew he would never be sure if her expression was accusatory or simply questioning. But Sam had been joking with Gabe and talking about his wine. Was Liz blaming him for Sam's condition?

Gabe wondered if Sam thought he was dying. And if he did, what were the things he valued most in his life? Sam had spoken of his precious vintage of cabernet sauvignon and the fact that he had saved the bottles in a secret place. But who was he saving them for? Liz? Or had Sam been thinking of Gina?

Was Sam thinking about how he could change the future? Did he feel he had missed all his chances, or that he would have done things differently if he were well? He was flat on his back in a hospital bed, hooked up to a half-dozen machines. Sam's will might have been as strong as that of an ox, but his body was useless.

The one thing Gabe knew for certain was that he never wanted to see even a glimmer of accusation in Liz's eyes. She was obviously distraught, and only minutes ago, Sam had been on the brink of death. Sam had survived, for the moment. But what about next time? Gabe had wanted to cheer Sam up, but their conversation had had the opposite effect. Gabe had been well-meaning. But the truth was that his presence alone reminded Sam of Gina. Clearly, that was not a good thing.

It would have been judicious for Gabe to stay away from Liz until this crisis was over, but the idea of not seeing her caused his breath to hitch in his lungs. Every day, he worked till his muscles ached, knowing that in the evening he would see Liz. Talk to her. See her smile. Even hold her in his arms.

Gabe understood there were times in life when one's own needs and wants had to be disregarded in favor of doing the right thing for a loved one. That's what Liz was doing.

She continued to talk only to Sam. She seemed to be unaware that Gabe was still in the room. She put a clean pillowcase on the pillow and helped Sam to get comfortable. She gave Sam a neck rub and gently massaged his temples, humming an old song Gabe recognized—

one that his mother sang often. Something about loving for "sentimental reasons."

"I think I'll go," Gabe said quietly.

Liz lifted her head and nodded, but she didn't say anything.

He got the impression that she was almost glad to have him leave. Maybe she was.

"Thanks for visiting," Liz said and went back to humming her song and massaging Sam's temples.

Sam lifted his hand a few inches off the bed to say goodbye, which appeared to be an enormous effort for the sick man.

Gabe walked out of the hospital and looked up at the stars in the clear, dark night sky. The chill in the air told Gabe the last of the warm summer days on the vineyard hill were over.

Gabe realized he loved Liz to the deepest recesses of his heart. Only one woman would ever hold his life in her hands the way she did. But he knew he had to back off so she could care for Sam.

Her grandfather needed her now. There was no question about that. She was the only family Sam had, and it was right that their days be consumed with each other. But after that?

Even if Sam survived, which Gabe prayed he would, would Liz ever want more for herself than the life she'd always known on the vineyard? Especially now that she'd almost lost it?

Gabe knew this wasn't the time to press Liz for a commitment of any kind. Yet Sam's illness had revealed to Gabe just how much he wanted Liz in his life. He wanted everything. He wanted marriage. He wanted to have kids and work side by side with Liz forever.

It was a dream. A good dream.

But was it achievable?

After leaving Liz tonight, he believed the real truth had just come out from the shadows. Liz's commitment was to Sam. Not Gabe.

Gabe had never felt so hopeless in all his life.

LIZ ASKED LOUISA to bring her fresh clothes every day. She showered and changed each morning in Sam's hospital room, and she received reports on the vineyard from both Louisa and Aurelio each evening. She continued to place orders for the tasting room, since her business contacts were stored on her phone, and Louisa brought her laptop in so she could stay on top of the accounting.

Each day, Liz hoped she'd be able to take Sam home, but his "numbers" crept toward normal at such a slow pace, Liz was reminded of the kind of patience she needed when waiting for wine to ferment.

By the eighth day in the hospital, Sam had gotten bored. On the ninth, he was angry. On the tenth, he was resigned. And then they told him he could go home.

Gabe had stopped coming to the hospital at night, though he'd texted her that he was overwhelmed with work, as they were bringing in the last of the harvest.

When the doctor informed Liz and Sam that he was finally well enough to go home, the first person Liz wanted to share her joy with was Gabe. She called him while the nurses removed Sam's IV and readied him for the trip home.

The call went straight to voice mail. "Hi, Gabe. It's me. I wanted you to be the first to know that Sam is going home! Can you believe it? He's finally out of the woods. Oh, the nurse wants me. I gotta go!"

ONCE THEY WERE HOME, Liz set up an inflatable bed in the living room until Sam was strong enough to climb the stairs to his bedroom.

Liz set up a blood pressure cuff attached to a digital readout monitor and placed a three-ring binder that contained a food log, medicine log and exercise schedule on a small collapsible table next to Sam's recliner. She plugged in a space heater that would keep Sam's area of the living room toasty for him and gathered for him a stack of winter throws and blankets.

For the first few days, Liz's attention was pulled in a dozen directions, and she realized how much her absence had nearly brought the harvesting and winemaking to a halt. Though Louisa and Aurelio were competent, they still expected her to make decisions.

She'd put everything on hold for Sam.

Including Gabe.

The revelation was stunning. Gabe had come to mean a great deal to her, and she'd looked forward to the sound of his velvety voice on the phone, and even better, his surprise visits.

But she hadn't seen Gabe for six days. Not since the night she'd almost lost Sam—again.

And he hasn't returned my call, she thought as she walked to the kitchen to get a glass of water for Sam. This was a hugely important day for her, and she'd wanted to share it with him. Honestly, she'd hoped Gabe would offer to come to town and help her take Sam home. But he hadn't called.

She felt a pang in her heart and she realized she missed him—tremendously. She had him to thank, just as much as the doctors, for saving Sam's life. She knew she needed to express her gratitude properly, though she couldn't think anything to do that would be in keeping with the magnitude of his actions.

She mixed aloe vera juice with the water and stirred it. She knew Sam wouldn't like the moldy, tinny taste of the juice, but Liz believed what the woman at the health food store had told her—that aloe vera healed human organs faster than any pharmaceutical drug. Liz was willing to try anything to speed up Sam's recovery.

She glanced out the kitchen window at the falling autumn leaves. Winter wouldn't be far behind.

The winter months would be perfect for Sam's recovery, because the vineyard wouldn't be as demanding as it was in the spring and summer. They would have time to make their goals for the following year and adjust their schedules to fit around Sam's new limitations. Liz knew her grandfather would never be physically able to handle the workload he once had. He would have to cut back, but through a bit of trial and error, they would find their balance.

Balance was precisely what Liz needed in her own life. Since the day she'd caught Gabe on their land, swiping a vial of her soil, she'd been off-kilter. Gabe made her feel as if she were spinning at a dizzying speed. He'd shown her that a canopy of stars was the only ball-room they needed, that his dreams were every bit as expansive and visionary as hers. He wanted the same things she did out of life, and of all the people she knew, he was the one who understood the loyalty she had toward Sam—because he demonstrated the same steadfast-ness toward his mother. What had happened? Had Gabe realized he was still chained to the Barzonni farm? Had he given up on his dream for himself and his own vineyard? She hadn't heard another word from him about buying her land.

Of course, she'd been overwhelmed with her grandfather's care in the past few weeks, but still, she had a nagging impression that some-thing irreparable had occurred between them.

Her heart felt like lead. She had come to love Gabe, but something had happened while she wasn't paying attention.

And now he was gone.

LIZ DECIDED TO USE Gabe's own tactics against him. When she spoke on the phone with Mad-die on Saturday afternoon, she learned that

Nate and Gabe were at the local feed store getting supplies for the farm.

"They're there right now?"

"Yes," Maddie replied.

"I have to go." Liz hung up and dashed out of the house, grabbing the truck keys on her way out.

The Indian Lake Farm and Feed Store was only two miles from Liz's vineyard. When she pulled into the parking lot, she saw Nate's SUV close to the front door. She took out her phone to text Gabe.

Where are you?

Please answer me this time, Gabe. Please.

She crossed her fingers. Two minutes passed. Then three.

Liz decided that if he didn't answer, she'd go in after him. Right as she decided that, she got a text from him.

At the feed store.

She took a deep breath. This was it.

I'm in the parking lot.

He texted back.

I'm coming out.

Gabe was wearing faded blue jeans, work boots and a cotton blue-and-white-striped shirt with the sleeves rolled up to reveal the chiseled muscles in his forearms. He had a huge sack of seed slung over his shoulder, and he walked toward her with long, purposeful strides.

The look in his eyes was so electric and loving she felt her heart rip to shreds on the spot. But he wasn't smiling, and her concern morphed into worry. She'd never wanted to run to anyone as much as she wanted to run to Gabe at that moment. She just wasn't sure what kind of reception she'd receive.

"Hi, Liz. I'm surprised to see you. Nate's here for the sale on riding lawn mowers. What about you?" He pressed the remote to pop the SUV's back end open. He dropped the bag of feed then walked toward her.

He took his time, as if debating what to say to her. His expression was solemn, and he wasn't rushing to scoop her up and spin her around. He came to stand in front of her precisely at arm's length so as not to invade her space. Ironically, he wasn't putting pressure on her at the one time when she would have welcomed his intrusion.

The air between them was like an invisible steel wall.

The hair on the back of Liz's neck prickled, and she felt as if a killing frost had spread across her whole body. Then she saw his transfixed expression.

"You didn't answer my call," Liz said. "I wanted to tell you—"

"That Sam is home," he finished for her. "That's great, Liz. I'm really happy for you both." He smiled, but it was forced, and she could see a trace of sadness around the downturned edges of his mouth.

"That's not what I was going to say."

"Then what was it?"

"That I missed you, Gabe," she replied honestly. She hadn't realized how true that was until this moment. Yet he seemed more distant than ever.

"Is that so?"

"I was hoping you could come out to see us. I could make a special dinner. And I promise a very good wine." She attempted to smile at her own joke, but it dropped quickly off her face when she saw the icy flecks in his eyes.

GABE GLANCED BACK at the store and shoved his hands in his pockets. Since the day he'd walked out of Sam's hospital room, he'd realized exactly what needed to be done, and what was best for him and Liz. He'd been trying to back away from Liz ever since his mother had revealed her past to him, as well. "So, why did you want to see me?"

She brightened, but only a bit. "Because I— well, I thought it over. I need your help, Gabe."

"My help?" He nearly spat the word back. He felt a frigid flow of ice shoot through his veins. When he'd seen her text message, Gabe realized, he'd been hoping for something to change in their relationship. In the back of his mind, he'd conjured visions of Liz rushing up to him and telling him that she loved him. He understood now that that was a fantasy. "Go on."

"I want to sell my land to you," she said all in a rush.

At first he thought he hadn't heard her right. "What? What would make you change your mind so suddenly?"

"It's not sudden," she countered.

"Yeah, it is. I'm betting that because Sam got sick and you've been hit with some expensive medical bills on top of the back taxes and everything else, things look pretty grim."

"They do," she confessed as she looked at his offended expression. She rushed on to explain. "I thought you'd be happy. Maybe even excited to know I'd finally come around."

"Oh, you did, did you?"

WHAT WAS THE MATTER with him? Liz was handing Gabe his dream wrapped up with a bow, but he looked as if she'd just spit in his eye. She'd never expected ingratitude. In fact, she'd expected a lot of reactions—all positive, even joyous—amid visions of Gabe throwing his arms around her. Kissing her. Definitely kissing her.

She stared at him. "You're not happy with my offer?"

He pushed his breath out through his nostrils. "You need my money, is that what you're saying, Liz?"

"Well, I wouldn't say it like that—"

"I would," he replied. "I'll make you a deal."

Liz teetered slightly, feeling her confidence wane. She'd faltered somewhere, somehow, but she didn't know what she'd done to repel him.

"I don't want your land, Liz."

"What?"

She felt the blood drain from her face.

"I can't take your father's dream away from

you. I've been fighting his ghost since I met you. I know you love him very much, and you want him to be proud of you. It kills you to see that expanse of earth just sitting dormant every year. But if I bought it, you'd grow to despise me, Liz. I'd be working his dream and you'd always feel you failed. I couldn't take that. So, no, Liz. I won't buy your land."

"It wouldn't be like that…" Her voice trailed off as the reality of his words settled in.

He continued. "I'll loan you the money you need to get through. No interest. Just friend to friend. But you keep the land."

Gabe held his breath. If she took the deal, it would be a sure sign all she'd needed from him was his money, nothing else. But the vineyard would go on and she and Sam would be financially secure; Gabe would always know he'd been the one to buoy her up when she'd needed it. That's what friends did for friends. Yet if she didn't take the deal, he believed her pride would keep her out of his arms, as well.

"But that would be like charity and that's not right, either," Liz answered.

For a moment, Gabe considered the wisdom of his next move. He stared down at the concrete and contemplated getting into Nate's

SUV and driving away. But that was too cowardly. "Liz, you're one of the most special people I've ever met. What you're doing for Sam is exemplary. Truly. He's very lucky to have you. It's the right thing for you to do."

"What is?"

"Spend your life caring for him," he said bluntly.

"He took care of me. Now it's my turn." She hesitated, her eyes searching. Then revelation broke across her features. "Is this why you didn't call me? You think I should be with Sam and not you?"

"Listen to me," he said fiercely, his gaze sincere. "I know you. If anything happened to Sam, if he died when you and I were someplace else, you would never forgive yourself."

"And you think I would blame you?" she pressed.

Gabe's mouth went dry. He couldn't get the vision of her face in the hospital out of his mind. It haunted him constantly. This was the truth behind all his fears. "Wouldn't you?"

She rolled her eyes and folded her arms across her chest. "So, you've got me all figured out, do you?"

"Yes, I think so. You are ferociously loyal

to Sam, and to your dad's dream. Frankly, I admire that about you. You'd do anything for Sam because you love him."

"That's true. But I wouldn't blame you if something happened. You just saved his life, Gabe."

"I know what I'm talking about. You'd come to hate me. We'd grow apart and I would lose you. It happens to people all the time," he replied.

"Not to me, it doesn't," she said. "You know what, Gabe? I get it. You don't have to come up with a bunch of reasons why you don't want to see me. I'll do it for you. I'm out of here. You're off the hook. No guilt. No worries." She yanked her truck keys out of her pocket and started toward her truck.

"Liz."

"I was a fool to think I was someone special to you. So there you go, add me to your list. Thank goodness I didn't really fall in love with you."

"Liz," he said and grabbed her arm to pull her back to him.

They were nose to nose, angry breath on each other's cheeks. His eyes blazed into hers. Her eyes dropped to his lips.

"Tell me you love me, Liz."

AT THAT MOMENT, Liz realized she was so deeply in love with Gabe, she'd never get over it. This wasn't just attraction or even a crush. It was love. He was everything she'd dreamed a man could be for her. He was more than just tender and affectionate—he was smart and courageous. And he'd put her above himself and his family. He'd defied his father for her. He'd shown her repeatedly, in just about every way imaginable, that he cared for her. He'd never said the words to her and he certainly had never brought up marriage. But she'd thought about what it would be like to be with Gabe forever. Her daydreams of him occupied a vast territory in her mind and heart.

"Liz," his eyes plumbed hers.

"I do…"

"But all the rest of it—what I said about Sam holding you back. I can feel it."

Tears welled in her eyes until they spilled onto her cheeks. "I can't believe I'm saying this. I want you so badly, but at the same time, I do owe Sam. He's taken care of me all my life. I owe my father to build his dream."

"And you think I'd get in the way."

"You have dreams of your own. Important ones."

"I just tossed all my dreams on the table for you, Liz."

Suddenly, every bit of reasoning in her head disappeared. She saw no color. No thoughts. No words. Everything was black, as if panic had erased all her brain cells. She was done for. She didn't know how she could continue, but she had to.

She hated that Gabe knew her better than anyone, including Sam. What if Sam died and she *did* blame Gabe for it? What if she were the cause of bitterness and anger between them? She would never forgive herself for not letting him go. He had a chance to find a girl who was unencumbered by responsibilities, as she was. She brought so much baggage along with her that even she wondered where the real Liz was beneath it all.

She had to do the brave thing and let him go. But as he stood there, his blue eyes piercing her with so much hope and love, she didn't think she could do it.

She was terrified of loving him any more than she already did. What would it be like in five years, or ten? And what if she lost him then, to an accident, or worse, to her own faults?

She could barely bring herself to pronounce her next lie. "It's my duty."

Gabe winced and his mother's words cut through him like a saber, quickly and cleanly. *Duty.* Liz would always belong to her father's world. To Sam. Just as his mother had committed herself to a loveless life with his father. *Duty.*

"I understand completely. Well," he said, releasing her, "you take care, Liz."

His arms fell and did not linger, as Liz thought they might. He seemed relieved to walk away from her.

She climbed back into her truck and watched Gabe through her rearview mirror as he walked into the feed store. His image wavered, as if he were floating through the cosmos or underwater. She wiped the tears from her cheeks with the palm of her hand and then depressed the clutch and struggled, as she always did, to put the truck into Reverse.

Slowly, without grinding the old gears, she backed out of the parking space. She braked and then put the truck into first gear. She drove away from the feed store, wondering if Gabe had seen her leave. Or had he dismissed her from his life before she'd even shown up today?

Liz burst into sobs before she reached the

traffic light at the highway. Her lungs heaved with sorrow and pain. She'd never felt worse in her life. When the light turned green, she turned right and headed back north toward the vineyard.

But for the first time, Liz felt as if she weren't going home.

Home, she realized, was behind her—at a feed store, dressed in a pair of faded jeans. And for the rest of her life, she knew she would never experience a deeper hollow than the one she was experiencing now, driving away from Gabe.

CHAPTER TWENTY-FIVE

GABE SAT ON an unpadded chaise next to the swimming pool, watching the surface of the water fill with falling golden leaves. He'd felt numb ever since he'd seen Liz at the feed store. He was stunned that she wouldn't tell him she loved him. Gabe had bet his heart on the fact that Liz was the love of his life. He wasn't one to wax wistful, and he didn't consider himself to be a romantic man. But the vision of a stoic little girl at her parents' funeral had haunted him all his life, and when he had met that girl again on the very vineyard he could only dream of owning, he'd fallen in love with her faster than he'd thought possible. She wore her heart on her fingertips, and everything and everyone she touched was blessed by her magic. Gabe felt grateful just to have known her. In his soul, he felt that if the universe had ever made two people who were perfectly suited for one another, it was him and Liz.

But something was holding her back from him and all the love he had to give her.

His stomach was in knots and he felt as if he was walking in a fog.

After hours of contemplation, Gabe was certain fear was imprisoning Liz, and he didn't have a clue how to help her escape it.

Since their last words to each other, he'd walked through his days like a zombie. He barely ate or slept. He was suspended in a time warp of hopelessness. He had no plans for the future, and without Liz he didn't give a whit about the present.

The cold autumn air cut through his windbreaker, but he didn't feel a thing. A large maple leaf got caught in the skimmer and made a loud, obscene noise for a long moment before moving away from its oblivion and scooting to the side of the pool.

"Gabe. What are you doing out here?" Gina asked, pulling a huge black wool sweater on. She hugged herself and looked down at Gabe.

"Thinking."

She glanced up at the dark storm clouds that were rolling across the western sky. When she sat down on the chaise next to his, her ebony eyes shone with bottomless love and compassion. These were the eyes Gabe had always cherished. He was glad he'd loved her completely all his life. Maybe it made up for his father's lack of love and gratitude. A woman like his mother deserved so much more. Suddenly, he felt tremendous pity for her.

She placed her hand on his folded ones. "Hmm. Thinking. Again. Seems to me you've been doing a lot of that these past few days."

"Yeah," he said, staring back at the emotionless pool water.

She leaned over and placed her hands on his cheeks, turning his face toward hers. "Stop it."

"Stop what?"

"Grieving over Liz. Acting like you buried her. Trying to forget her."

"That's exactly what I'm doing."

"I'm telling you to stop," she replied with a catch in her voice. A tear filled her eye and fell quickly down her cheek. "I can't bear it, Gabe, watching you destroy your life when it's not necessary."

He started to get up, and she pressed his shoulder down with more strength than he'd imagined her to have. "You sit down right now and you listen to me. I'm your mother."

He shook his head. "It's over, Mother. I should have seen it coming. I really do love her. And I've realized that when you love someone completely, you give them the world, isn't that right?"

"Yes, that's true."

"Well, Liz's world is her vineyard, which was her father's world before her. It means everything to her. She's built her entire life's plans on it and I want her to have it.

Gina peered at him. "You know I like Liz. I could grow to love her like the daughter I never had. But she's wrong. You're both incredibly wrong." Gina wiped away a new round of tears. "I've done everything wrong myself, so I should know. I've taught you to be loyal to your father and the farm, and that was wrong. I stayed with your father out of duty. And what did it get me? A life without romantic love. I'll go to my grave never having experienced that. I won't let that happen to you, Gabe. You've found the real thing. Don't let it slip away."

"But I've tried, Mom."

Gina guffawed. "Believe me. You have done no such thing. You get very close, and then your duty pulls you back. You fight with Liz and then you retreat to the farm. You venture out to her and then you come back here, taking care of your father and worrying about me. I hate that I'm going to say this, because no mother ever loved a son as much as I love you.

But you have to leave us, Gabe. Don't put me first or even second in your thoughts. It's time for you to break away. We'll be fine. Rafe and Mica will step up to fill your shoes. There'll be an adjustment period, sure, but they're very competent."

"What about you, Mother?"

"We have a special bond, Gabe. Very few mothers and sons have experienced our kind of love and friendship. I'll be fine. You go to Liz. She's worth it."

Gabe reached out to his mother and hugged her.

The tears in Gina's eyes fell in a torrent, and he felt his heart swell to proportions he hadn't known possible.

"I just don't know how, Mom. These past few days without her, I've come to realize that all those dreams I had for myself don't mean a thing anymore. I'd give it all up for her. I don't care if I ever make a bottle of wine or if my name is on a label. If she needs money, and believe me they do, I'd just give it to her. No strings attached."

"You would do that for her?" Gina asked.

"I even tried to do just that, and she turned me down," he said resolutely.

"Gabe." She stood up. "If you'd offered the

right thing to Liz, you wouldn't be sitting here. Come with me."

"Where are we going?"

"To find the seal to your fate." She smiled.

CHAPTER TWENTY-SIX

LIZ HAD SPENT the day delivering her annual autumn gifts of homegrown Cinderella pumpkins, white pumpkins, butternut squash, acorn squash and Northern Spy apples to Sarah, Mrs. Beabots, Maddie, Isabelle, Olivia, Cate Sullivan and of course the Mattuchis. Liz had festooned the tasting room with raffia garlands, corn shocks and grape vines. She decorated the garlands with sunflowers she'd dried outdoors, hollowed-out gourds, clusters of mini Indian corn she'd bought in town and bright orange, gold, bronze and chocolate-brown ribbons. Liz's autumn decorations were always an attraction for tourists, and every year, she had Chicago residents asking to buy her creations. Naturally, she sold them.

It had been nearly a month since Sam's operation, and he'd been diligent about going for a walk every day. The first week he was home, he barely made it from the front porch to the tasting room, even with Liz's help. Now he was talking about walking to the top of Matt's hill to look out on Lake Michigan once again. Liz had put an end to that idea quickly.

"What if it's too much, too soon? What if you wind up in the hospital again? You have to be sensible."

"Sensible? I want to live, Lizzie. That's what I discovered in the hospital."

"I agree. And I am absolutely going to make that happen."

"You call this living? You hanging on my every breath? Getting me my heart pillow every time I sneeze?"

"The doctors all said sneezing is dangerous. So is coughing. You have metal wires holding your sternum together. Don't forget that."

"Yes. And half the men my age have hip replacements. So don't talk to me about foreign parts."

Liz sighed and glanced out the tasting room window. It was a picture-perfect autumn day. Gold, yellow and purple chrysanthemums bloomed in giant mounds around the front porch and down the walk to the tasting room. They would last all the way till Christmas if the snow held off.

"Okay," she said. "So you're bored. It's

nearly Halloween and we haven't gone for a ride to look at the decorations in town."

"Or to Enzo's for some baked ravioli and salad…"

"I can make ravioli," she countered.

"Not as well as they can." He looked down at the paper napkin on the table. "I bet Gina makes a good one," he whispered. He must not have known Liz could hear him.

"Grandpa. You thinking about her?"

His head shot up and his eyes locked on hers. "No more than you're thinking about Gabriel."

She lifted her chin haughtily. "I told you. It didn't work out."

"Really?" Sam guffawed and then rose from his chair. "Lizzie. I had a heart attack, not a lobotomy. I'm going up to the house."

Liz went to her office, shut the door and watched Sam from the window. His gait was quick and steady. He was healing rather well, she realized. Liz knew he'd asked Aurelio to go buy him a set of small barbells at the sporting goods store. He started last week with two pounds. But the minute the doctor told him he could lift ten pounds, Sam had pushed himself to lift those heavier weights. It was as if Sam couldn't wait to be super fit again. Was he doing all this because of Gina? Liz wasn't sure, but she had her suspicions.

Liz knew she was naturally paranoid, and that it was a terrible way to live, always lacking faith. She knew she was the way she was because she'd been traumatized by her parents' deaths. And nearly losing Sam had thrown her completely off her axis yet again. She hadn't known how to react. How to make decisions.

And she'd made a very bad one.

To make matters worse, she hadn't the first idea how to rectify it. She couldn't go to Gabe and say, "Oops, I messed up. I want you back."

His first reaction would be, "Oh, yeah? For how long? A month? A day? Then what?"

Admittedly, Liz was scared to death of love.

Her fear had brought her to this empty, agonizing moment of clarity, when she finally understood that she'd been clinging to her father's dream for so many years she hadn't sorted out what *she* wanted from life.

For years, she'd believed her father's desires were hers. She had turned him into an icon, a philosopher, rather than honoring him simply as a man and as her father. A father who had loved her and whom she had loved back.

Gabe had shown her that.

Gabe had made her see that her own life was waiting right in front of her.

But what had she done? She'd walked away. Gabe had begged her to tell him she loved him, but she'd been so stubborn, so arrogantly glued to her past, that she had pushed Gabe away.

Today, she'd walked through the yellowing grape vines and watched the golden leaves turning to autumn dust. Their energy would go back to the earth and be reborn in the spring.

But what about her?

She'd been singing to her vines for years. But she'd never had the beautiful opportunity to sing to her own child. She'd never once considered what it would be like to take the risk of giving her heart and dreams to someone other than her dead parents.

What a fool she'd been.

She should have known from that first dance with Gabe that for the rest of her life, no other arms were going to hold her as his had. And no one would understand her and all her flaws as well as he did. Till the end of her life, she wanted to spend every moment with Gabe.

Euphoria filled Liz's heart and she felt like jumping into the air. Her life had just taken a new turn, and though it looked like an ordinary day to anyone else, it was monumental for her.

She ran her fingers through her hair. *Think, Liz. You have to make this happen. You can do this.* She spotted the new stack of personal stationery she'd just ordered for her holiday notes.

A letter! Not a text or a phone call or an email, but a good, old-fashioned letter. That's what she should do. Write Gabe a personal note of apology and explanation.

Eerily, every word and emotion that had been bottled up in her heart flowed out of her so quickly, her pen flew across the paper. At times she cried and at others she laughed at the memories she and Gabe had already made. With each word, she felt hope bloom inside her. Suddenly, everything in her world felt right, joyful and...possible.

She would mail her letter today so Gabe would get it the very next day. She couldn't wait. She folded the letter and put it in the envelope then tugged on the desk drawer where she kept her stamps.

The drawer was stuck. She yanked on it, but it only moved slightly. She yanked again, and this time she heard a scraping sound, as if something were caught in the back of the drawer.

"What in the world?" Liz tried to slip her hand inside, but the opening was too small.

Using both hands, she pulled on the drawer again. It budged a little, but she heard a ripping sound.

Liz groaned and knelt on the floor in order to investigate the problem from underneath.

Caught between one of the wooden slats and the bottom of the drawer was a long legal envelope. Liz eased it out and got back up in her chair.

Out of the envelope, Liz pulled a cashier's check made out to the Indian Lake County treasurer.

Her mouth fell open. Her heart pounded and her blood raced through her body. She jumped out of her chair. "It was here all along!" Liz danced around the office, and when she stopped spinning, her eyes fell back to her desk, to the snapshot of her father smiling up at her.

Chills covered her body, and in that split second, Liz believed her father had guided her to the money.

With this check, she no longer needed money from the bank or from Gabe to shore up their finances and pay the taxes, and even Sam's medical bills wouldn't be such a burden. She didn't need help from anyone. She had exactly what she needed.

"But what I want…" She looked down at the letter she'd written to Gabe. "What I really want…"

Smiling, she went to the desk drawer, opened it easily, took out a stamp and placed it on the envelope. "He's all I really want, Dad."

Just then, she heard a car pull up outside. Louisa was in the riddling room tending to her newly bottled chardonnays. Liz had been left alone to take care of the tourists, though there had been none this morning.

She heard a car door slam, then the crunch of shoes—boot heels?—on the gravel. She waited for the tasting room door to open. But it didn't.

That's odd.

She walked to the door and looked out into the parking lot, spotting a single car. A newly polished black Porsche.

Sucking in her breath, she stood stock-still. Her heart was banging so hard in her chest, she thought she was the one having the heart attack. "Gabe?"

No. It couldn't be. He was here?

She dashed outside to see.

Gabe was walking toward the farmhouse, dressed in a pair of black slacks, a white shirt under a black cashmere V-neck sweater and black Italian loafers.

No question. The man knew how to dress.

And she loved it. Now that she knew Gabe and Gina better, there was no doubt that Gabe had learned his fashion sense from his mother. Odd as it seemed, it was yet another trait that endeared Gabe to her. He was just as close to the parent he loved dearly as she was to Sam.

She glanced at his hands and noticed he was carrying a bouquet of roses with aluminum foil wrapped around the stems.

Liz guessed he'd clipped them from Gina's rose garden.

Her heart leaped in her chest. She closed the tasting room door behind her and headed quickly toward the farmhouse.

"Hi, Gabe," she said nervously. She had a thousand things in her heart she wanted to tell him, but she didn't know where or how to begin.

Oddly, he didn't look back at her, but kept walking.

Anxiety whittled away at her confidence. She wasn't sure of her next move. He must have driven all the way from the farm. He'd cleaned up his car and he'd brought flowers. What was he doing here? Her hopes lifted inside her. "Are those for me?"

He stopped dead in his tracks and Liz nearly

collided with him. For a split second she thought she saw merriment in his Mediterranean-blue eyes. In a flash, it was gone, replaced with determination. "These? They're for Sam."

"Sam. Of course." Liz felt as if her insides had turned to lead. It made sense. Gabe had saved Sam's life. They would want to visit and talk. But still, she felt wonderful just being this close to Gabe. She wanted to take his hand and rush up to her father's hill with him and tell him all about her revelations and the miraculous recovery of the cashier's check. Most important of all, she wanted to tell him that she loved him. He *had* to know she loved him.

Gabe answered quickly. "My mother picked them."

"Right," Liz said glumly, lowering her eyes to the roses.

Gabe continued toward the house. He took the front steps two at a time and rapped on the screen door. "Sam, it's me. Gabe."

Maria appeared instantly, which surprised Liz, who had never seen the woman go to the door until the third or fourth knock.

Her suspicions were instantly aroused. Something was off.

"Welcome," Maria said, untying her apron from around her waist.

Maria never took her apron off unless it was the end of her workday or a special visitor had arrived. Was Gabe a special visitor?

"These are for Sam." Gabe handed her the flowers.

"I'll put them in a vase with water," Maria said.

"Excellent," Gabe replied, stepping into the house.

"Barzonni? Is that you?" Sam shouted with all his old vigor.

"Thank you for seeing me, sir," Gabe replied as he entered the living room. Sam shut off the television and caught Liz's eye as she followed Gabe in.

"What's going on?" Liz shot a skeptical look at her grandfather, who ignored it completely.

"As I was saying on the telephone, sir," Gabe started.

Closing her eyes and shaking her head, Liz threw her hands in the air. "Wait a minute. You've been talking with my grandfather?"

"Yes, Liz. Besides requesting this visit, I wanted advice about something that only he could give me."

"But why?"

Gabe clucked his tongue. "There's that word again, Liz."

Glaring at him, she clamped her hand on her hip. "I find it gets me answers, Gabriel Barzonni. Which brings me to another 'why.' Why are you here, Gabe? What do you want?" she probed.

"I want to hear what *you* want, Liz."

She'd known since this morning, but now she was more certain than ever. All she had to do was tell him the truth.

Liz pulled the envelope out of the back pocket of her jeans and held it up. "I put it all in here. I want you, Gabe. I think I've been in love with you since our first dance. I want you to have your dreams, too. I've come to realize that by refusing to live my life, I was pushing everyone out of it. That's not what my parents wanted for me. They wanted me to be happy. And I know I won't be happy if I'm not with you."

Gabe slipped his hands around Liz's waist. "Do you really mean that, Liz?"

She nodded.

"Good, because I was running out of ways to win you over. I only had one trick left."

Gabe's eyes blazed such a deep blue, Liz felt as if she'd found everything in the universe in them.

For the first time in her life, Liz was not

afraid. And she'd never felt so free. She let her heart fill to capacity. She had found a love she could believe in.

Her eyes met his on a magical, ethereal plane where only those who understood true intimacy were allowed to venture. Here, they gave their hearts unconditionally. Here, there were no scores to keep, no faults to find, no blame to cast. In life and death, love prevailed. It was this plane of existence that true lovers understood as no others did. It was not a concept, but an actual state of being.

"More tricks?"

"Uh, huh," he answered, winking at Sam. Taking Liz's hand, Gabe led her into the hallway for privacy.

"What are you doing?"

Gabe smiled mischievously. "Darling, will you marry me?" he breathed and pulled her close to his chest. "I promise to do everything I can to make you happy."

"This is the only place I want to be," she said earnestly, snuggling her face into the crook of his neck. And then she kissed him. Softly and with all the love in her heart.

She'd never experienced such happiness as she did now in Gabe's arms. Reluctantly, she pulled away. "We have to tell Sam!"

She pulled on Gabe's arm as they went around the corner to the living room. "Gabe just asked me to marry him, Grandpa. And I said yes."

"It's about time." Sam grinned widely, looking at Liz's left hand. "But did you forget something, Barzonni?"

Gabe blinked then he dropped to one knee. "I almost forgot," he said, reaching into his pants pocket. "I got you something. I didn't want to be like my brother Nate. Proposing to the love of his life without a ring." He held up a square-cut amethyst surrounded by diamonds. "I wanted it to remind you of your most beloved grape. Always abundant. Always flowing with life."

"Oh, Gabe," she said, kneeling and placing her hands on both sides of his face. "Yes. Of course I'll marry you. The ring is beautiful!" Tears flowed from her eyes. "It's perfect for us."

"It was my mother's. It's her gift to us."

Gabe put the ring on Liz's left hand and when she looked at it, glittering bright with promise, she threw her arms around Gabe's neck.

"I love you!"

"Liz." He started to kiss her, but she had such a grip on his neck that he lost his balance and they toppled over onto the floor just as Maria came into the room with the vase of roses.

Horrified, Maria glared at Sam, who was laughing. "They look like they're trying to crush the grapes!" she huffed.

Sam was laughing so hard he had to grab the heart-shaped pillow the nurses had given him to hold next to his chest when he sneezed, coughed or laughed too much. "I don't think winemaking is on their minds right now."

Gabe held Liz's face in his hands, glanced at Sam and then back at Liz. "We could do that, you know. Merge our talents."

"And we'll live here at the vineyard?" Liz asked.

"Looks to me like there's plenty of room upstairs." He touched her nose. "I'll do whatever you want."

"Merging," she said thoughtfully and snuggled closer to him. "It sounds wonderful."

Gabe smiled up at Maria. "So, there you have it, Maria. We'll all be making lots of Crenshaw wines." Then he kissed Liz softly and smiled with that impish grin she adored. "Maybe we'll make some other things, too."

Gabe kissed her again, and though Liz felt dizzy, for the first time, he had not unbalanced her. She had found her bearings. She knew in her heart every year for them would be a fine one.

* * * * *

The next
SHORES OF INDIAN LAKE *story*
is coming soon!

LARGER-PRINT BOOKS!

GET 2 FREE
LARGER-PRINT NOVELS
PLUS 2 FREE
MYSTERY GIFTS

Love Inspired

Larger-print novels are now available...